# FORTUNE & GLORY

# A TREASURE HUNTER'S HANDBOOK

WRITTEN BY DAVID MCINTEE

ILLUSTRATIONS BY HAUKE KOCK

First published in Great Britain in 2016 by Osprey Publishing,
PO Box 883, Oxford, OX1 9PL, UK
PO Box 3985, New York, NY 10185-3985, USA
E-mail: info@ospreypublishing.com

Osprey Publishing is part of the BLOOMSBURY PUBLISHING LTD.

© 2016 Osprey Publishing Ltd.

A CIP catalogue record for this book is available from the British Library

Print ISBN: 978 1 4728 0784 7
PDF e-book ISBN: 978 1 4728 0785 4
EPUB e-book ISBN: 978 1 4728 0786 1

Typeset in Berling and Adventure
Maps by Bounford
Originated by PDQ Media, Bungay, UK
Printed in China through Worldprint Ltd.

16 17 18 19 20   10 9 8 7 6 5 4 3 2 1

www.ospreypublishing.com

Osprey Publishing is supporting the Woodland Trust, the UK's leading
woodland conservation charity, by funding the dedication of trees.

# CONTENTS

# *Introduction: Why Search for Lost Treasure?*

Think of lost treasures or treasure hunting, and you tend to think of Blackbeard digging holes on golden beaches, grizzled adventurers fighting Nazis for possession of ancient relics, or even a lycra catsuit clad debutante swapping finishing school for parkour in lost cities.

Tales of lost treasures and buried loot from years gone by have always been a staple of adventure stories, mythology and popular history. In books, movies, games and the daydreams of millions of people, the prospect of unearthing a chest full of historic gold and jewels is one to excite absolutely anyone.

Most people simply enjoy the tales as escapist entertainment, but history is filled with genuine treasures, and people who created, lost and found them. People also go searching for those, adventuring in real life as well as in fiction.

Perhaps you'll be inspired to join them, after considering a basic question. It seems like a no-brainer: *Why search for treasure?*

The most obvious motive for taking up shovel and map and going off in search of treasure is the simple fact that it *is* treasure. Gold coins, jewellery, precious stones … Find a good hoard and you'd be able to live the life of luxury, and never work an hour at a boring day job again. Money may not buy happiness, or wisdom, but it certainly can help make living in the material world a damn sight easier. Picking up a pile of gold or silver that's been left in the ground for years sounds like a great way to get rich with minimal effort.

Of course, the truth is not so simple. In fact, most people who have hunted or do hunt treasure find that it's actually more difficult than 'real' work. Worse still, treasure hunting properly, on a professional and industrial basis, is a very expensive business. Perhaps surprisingly, though, getting rich quick isn't the only motive that has driven individuals off in search of buried treasure, legendary historical artefacts and lost cities.

It's the historical side that interests some; to find something that no-one has seen or touched for perhaps centuries, and bring it back to public view. You could find glory without fortune: if someone found a buried empty chest proven to have belonged to, say, Blackbeard, the kudos of having found something so historically significant could still win book deals and a lucrative career on the lecture circuit.

The puzzle element intrigues others. Finding lost treasures isn't just about digging holes in the ground, or travelling to far-flung and exotic locales. There's a lot of putting the intellect to use, trying to figure out what happened to things. There is the mental challenge of pitting one's wits against the people who hid the treasures, or against the natural world that conceals them – and, of course, against rival seekers. There is bound to be a great thrill in out-thinking the deviousness with which some Obergruppenführer stashed his truckloads of Reichsbank gold and looted art. On a treasure site, you have to think, plan, negotiate with authorities and put a lot of brainpower into figuring out how to safely get at the treasure – especially since ancient artefacts are likely to be fragile, and you definitely don't want to destroy them in the process of digging them up (unless your name is Schliemann, in which case that's pretty much your *modus operandi*). Anyway, the fact is an awful lot of people like a brain-bending puzzle in real life, and not just in videogames.

There is the physical challenge as well. For some, the need to scuba dive in search of sunken galleons, or climb mountains, or trek across deserts, is exciting enough to make even the most fruitless search worthwhile.

Others are bitten simply by the straight-out lust for adventure, and the potential treasure at the end of the rainbow is merely an excuse to indulge in it. While a war correspondent during the Boer War, Winston Churchill wrote that 'there is nothing so exhilarating as to be shot at without result'. It wouldn't be much of a surprise if he was packing a shovel and a map showing buried Afrikaner gold when he said it.

# A Brief History of Treasure Hunting

People have hunted treasure for as long as the concept of material value has existed, although presumably they started off hunting it in the sense that a predator tracks its prey, as bandits hunting down the owners of said treasure in order to rob them. As people still do today.

Hunting for *lost* treasure is an only slightly more recent phenomenon, insofar as there needed to be a recognized past in which said treasure could actually have *been* lost. The Ancient Egyptians liked to loot the tombs of their ancestors, but this isn't necessarily treasure hunting in the sense that we know it, as they did so much sooner after the loot had been hidden and, as the saying goes, they knew where the bodies (and their bling) were buried. So that was just looting rather than treasure hunting.

The Greeks included treasure hunting in their myths and histories, so the concept of treasure being lost by previous generations, which can be found by adventurers, had taken hold in society. Greek heroes occasionally found themselves stumbling across valuables left behind by the gods, and had to learn the hard way that they should be responsible about what they did with it.

This is a natural product of the end of habitations. When a town, village, or temple has fallen into disuse and been forgotten, the next people who rediscover it would often attribute it to those – ancestors, gods, or supernatural creatures – who must have been wealthy, and who might have left something behind. If that sounds daft, just remember that, for example, Ancient Egypt lasted so long that even the Ancient Egyptians forgot who had built the Pyramids.

The Romans also conducted many treasure-grabbing missions of the conquer and rob variety, but the concept of stumbling across lost treasure was so established that they introduced the first treasure trove laws: defining buried treasure as 'an ancient deposit of money, of which no memory exists, and no present owner'. If someone found treasure on their own land, or on sacred ground, they could keep it. Otherwise the finder and the landowner – which could well be the Emperor – got half each.

Under the feudal system in Europe, things got complicated. In Britain, Edward the Confessor had the common law define treasure trove in the 11th century as a hoard of valuables consisting of over 50 per cent gold or silver, which been deliberately hidden. The original owner could turn up and claim it, otherwise it belonged to the landowner or the Crown. If the loot was *not* deliberately hidden, but simply lost, or buried as grave goods, then it belonged to either the finder, the landowner, or a combination thereof, depending on local laws.

## YE SEEK THE GRAIL?

Intentional treasure hunting as a genre archetype came to the fore in medieval times, when writers such as Wolfram von Eschenbach and Chrétien de Troyes gave the legendary King Arthur and his knights their most famous task: searching for the Holy Grail.

This was really the first time that searching for a lost valuable was viewed as a formal discipline, which could be learned and aspired to. It was seen as a votive act rather than a simple profession, however, akin to a pilgrimage or crusade, done in service of faith and God, to find the true Christian elements within the searcher himself. That was the official line, but should a knight happen to come across some gold or jewellery, then that was a bonus worth having.

Scholars then also began to take an interest in searching for artefacts that would prove evidence for biblical events. At first this meant relics of the Apostles and Saints, and fragments of the true cross – things that, again, would bring the seeker and/or his audience closer to godliness – but over time this expanded into the realms of other elements, to prove the existence and settle the facts about individuals and events from the Bible.

Although this is how archaeology began, and although it has over the past century or two altered to become more about seeking the historical facts regardless of their relationship (or lack thereof) to Scripture, there are still those who are motivated by this. For the most part, though, they are only really encountered now in the search for Noah's Ark.

Things changed, in Europe at least, around the time of the Renaissance, especially in Britain. Treasure hunting as a trade – rather than an opportunistic bonus mission objective for explorers or military units abroad – really got going in the Tudor and Elizabethan eras.

Because this was the time of exploring the New World and defeating the Spanish Armada, commentators tended to spin the reign of Elizabeth I as a prosperous golden age, and later novelists and Hollywood moviemakers have been more than happy to continue this impression. The great European powers of the time were busy following the Roman model of looting new civilizations found in South America, but these were not treasure hunting expeditions. They were pillaging and piracy expeditions, taking other people's possessions.

In Elizabeth's England, however, things were rather different. Expensive wars with France, Spain and Holland had depleted the treasury, and there were a series of bad harvests and famines throughout the first half of the 16th century. The practical upshot of this is that the Elizabethan era was actually filled with desperate poverty, leading to three courses of action taken by segments of the population: mounting expeditions to the New World in search of riches, or at least Spanish ships which had already found riches; an interest in the subject of alchemy, in the hope of turning lesser metals into more valuable ones; and digging for buried treasure, which was called hill-digging, because people viewed so many low hills as potential old burial mounds from which treasure might be dug up.

Before there was a bank on every high street, when people lived on the land and had neither the wherewithal nor the inclination to buy fancy strongboxes with stout locks, the most secure way of looking after valuables and coins was to bury them. The dissolution of the monasteries, and the view of the church as being corrupt beforehand, meant people assumed that the Church's dodgy funds might still be buried in the vicinity of churches, abbeys, monasteries, etc. (having been put there to keep it out of the hands of Henry VIII). So, hill-digging became a national industry.

Everywhere had its legend of clerical gold hidden from Henry VIII, or from the Vikings, or by Robin Hood or King Arthur … The tales of previous centuries had begun to inspire both beliefs about past events, and searches for their treasures.

As the age of exploration continued into the 17th and 18th centuries, it became clear that there were many places which were no longer occupied, but that previous communities had been lost to time.

The desire to learn and understand about the past became bound with the desire to plunder, while the recognition grew that taking people's current possessions was robbery. So explorers and adventurers began to search for those past treasures that couldn't be said to belong to any contemporary individual or society. They began to plunder the past of its art and valuables.

In Victorian times, antiquarian scholars began to take most of the interest, as anyone who's familiar with the ghost stories of M. R. James could tell you (his characters often come a cropper when meddling with ancient relics in old churches, or hunting for buried treasures, like lost crowns of East Anglia).

Throughout these eras, the treasure hunting action was mainly confined to individuals, and either scholarly or religious organizations. After World War II, however, many more people became beachcombers, due firstly to the spread of military surplus mine detectors, and then in the 1960s and 1970s, the adaptation of that technology to make outright civilian metal detectors, which were marketed with the image of finding pieces of eight or Spanish doubloons on the beach.

The post-war era also introduced a whole new type of treasure hunting: professional, 'commercial' treasure-hunting companies. It's true that people had always tried to commercialize things by selling maps and information (usually fake, or at least useless) to treasure hunters, and sometimes museums had commissioned adventurers to source exhibits, but now this took on a whole new identity.

With appropriate vehicles and equipment available, companies could conduct recovery operations for valuable goods from the past. Most of these companies today are, or at least started off as, subdivisions from, maritime salvage companies. They simply diversified into locating historic wrecks as well as conducting recovery operations at contemporary wreck sites.

Although there have been many discoveries by maritime companies, which could – and do – fill plenty of books on their own, these are not going to be the focus here. If you're looking to take part in that kind of treasure hunting business, then you need only go to the relevant company website and check out their vacancies page, and apply for a job there.

This book is aimed at the individual landlubbers who fancy themselves standing right where the treasure is going to be dug up in front of them. It is for the individual, willing to trek through hostile country, pore over dusty manuscripts, have punch-ups in seedy bars and plant a shovel in the right spot in the ground.

# LITERARY TREASURES

Treasure stories have been around as long as treasure. The mythologists of Classical Greece often had their heroes stumble across treasures, but the Romans, such as Virgil (himself often said to have helped and hindered in searches for buried chests), wrote about people seeking buried treasure deliberately, sometimes seeking supernatural aid, and usually forcing their servants and slaves to do the hard work.

Tales of pirates and robbers either hiding or distributing wealth remained popular for centuries, but usually with a focus on what the characters were like. As a genre of entertainment and inspiration, however, the definitive story that launched the genre is the 1881 magazine serial *The Mutiny of the Hispaniola* by Captain George North – or, as it's better known from its non-pseudonymous publication as a collected novel in 1883, *Treasure Island*, by Robert Louis Stevenson.

H. Rider Haggard's novels *King Solomon's Mines* and *She* followed later in the decade, and, between them, the idea of adventurous explorers swashbuckling their way around the world in search of historic loot became established in the public consciousness.

This was then reinforced in the visual media by the adventures of Tintin (most of whose stories involve lost treasures) and Indiana Jones, and the videogames about Lara Croft and Nathan Drake.

# X Never Marks the Spot. Usually

There is – or ought to be – a big difference between how archaeology and treasure hunting work. This is because the two things have somewhat different motives: archaeologists are looking to uncover, preserve and study historical artefacts in a way that keeps them in their original contexts as much as possible, while treasure hunters are looking to get the value of the artefacts.

This means that archaeologists are more likely to want to uncover material slowly, often leaving it in situ for study, and have a vested interest in co-operating with the authorities in order to get the use of facilities and local help. Treasure hunters are more about getting the artefact out and prettied-up so that it will fetch the best price. Except when they don't, because often it's scientists, archaeologists and governments who will be the customers.

In books, movies and videogames, we're used to seeing characters who are cast or coded as archaeologists actually behaving like treasure hunters – or indeed like soldiers, cops, explorers and bar-room brawlers.

Indiana Jones is the perfect example: officially an archaeologist, but goes around grabbing artefacts, fighting, bribing officials, dodging ancient booby traps, trying not to get bitten by wild animals and so on. Other fictional archaeologists and treasure hunters are similarly portrayed: Lara Croft, Nathan Drake, Benjamin Gates.

In real life, things are rather different for both treasure hunters and archaeologists. Research is king, and most work is actually done in libraries, archives and, nowadays, on the Internet. An unsung hero of searching since World War II has been aerial photography, as photos from high altitude show changes to the landscape that are not discernable at ground level. Even sub-surface differences show in high-altitude photos that don't show at ground level. Subsequently, satellite imagery has proved even more useful, and not just among professionals and academics – amateurs using Google Earth images have discovered over a hundred previously lost pyramids in Egypt.

Surprisingly, fictional characters rarely use metal detectors, ground penetrating radar, or any form of field equipment. This is doubly unusual since, although these types of equipment do have limitations, they have been used very successfully over the years to discover both historical sites and hoards in a variety of countries.

Archaeology in the field tends to involve uncovering the layers above the desired history, whether those layers be of soil, concrete, plaster, paint, wood, or anything else. Everything is measured, photographed and described – and this is good practice for treasure hunters too; partly because a lot of your customers for recovered treasure would be archaeologists and museums, who will want that sort of detail, and partly because you can prove *you* found it, rather than having nicked it from elsewhere.

Activities common to both reality and fiction would be bribery (and associated forgery of documentation and permission), artefact smuggling, and dodging the various treasure trove laws and taxes around the world.

# TOOLED UP

If movies and videogames have taught us anything, it's that adventurers in search of historic lost treasures in the wilderness ought to be carrying weapons to defend themselves.

Of the most famous fictional treasure hunters, Indiana Jones uses a revolver as his primary weapon in *Raiders of the Lost Ark* (it's a .45 calibre Smith & Wesson Model 1917 Hand Ejector in the studio and jungle scenes, and a British Mk II variant chambered for .455 Webley ammo in the Cairo scenes), and a Browning Hi-Power semi-auto pistol as his backup.

Indy then switches first to a Colt Police .38 in *Temple of Doom*, and a .455 calibre Webley WG in *The Last Crusade* and *Kingdom of the Crystal Skull*. The point to take note of here is that he always, even though automatic and semi-auto pistols are widely available, prefers a revolver as his primary weapon. This probably isn't just him being old-fashioned, but has solid practical reasons. Though having less ammo capacity, revolvers have fewer moving parts, and so are less susceptible to problems arising from humidity or sand in the mechanism. They also do not jam.

Laws on the possession of guns vary widely across the world, but most countries require some sort of licence and competency check, and almost none – Pakistan is the sole exception – allow non-resident foreigners to own guns. The wisest course, therefore, is to simply ensure that you have a licensed armed local if you absolutely need someone with a gun.

It is unlikely that you'll actually need firearms, but not impossible. There are some parts of the world in which you're likely to run into armed groups of people, but in such situations the golden rule is: never carry a weapon you are unwilling or unable to use correctly. The chances are that the local guerrillas are a lot better at using guns than you are, so it's wiser to leave the protection to professionals.

It can be advisable to carry weapons for protection against dangerous wildlife, however. In general, a regular hunting rifle will be adequate protection against larger animals such as bears or cougars. A .44 calibre or larger handgun will be effective against alligators at close range, but a rifle is recommended, along with distance. If your concerns are about smaller creatures, such as snakes, then any .22 calibre weapon should see you safe.

If you absolutely must carry a handgun out in the wild, the best option is to follow Indiana Jones's lead and use a revolver, as these are far more reliable. In the unlikely event that you do find yourself having to pick up a gun in an area of conflict in which actual people are shooting at you, grab whatever the most common local weapon is (and, let's face it, that's going to be a Chinese Type 56 copy of the AK-47, the most common gun in the world), since at least you'll be able to re-stock on ammo from fallen bodies.

Did X ever really mark the spot? Dr Henry Jones Jr tells us 'never, ever' in his classroom, but Indiana Jones on a trip to Venice says yes.

In truth, there doubtless have been some individuals who, distrusting banks, or having no access to them, have buried their personal valuables and made a note with an X on it to remind them where they put it. Groups and societies would not.

The problem with any treasure map is that somebody else might see it, steal it, or copy it, see the X you've made, and go and dig it up. You don't want this, if you've buried your life's earnings. That means that if you have two brain cells to rub together, you don't just draw a simple map with an X.

You either damn well remember where your loot is, and leave no paper trail for rivals, or you make your aide de memoire in a different form: perhaps in code or cipher, with no obvious locative markings on any attached map. And obvious gibberish codes and ciphers are themselves a bad idea because they automatically invite people to try to decode them.

What sort of people bury treasure anyway? Just about anybody from the dawn of time onwards, who either distrusted or had no easy access to banks, or lived in a remote area and didn't want burglars finding their goodies in the house. Burying valuables is, after all, one of the simplest tasks possible, requiring only the ability to find a cave or dig a hole, and for most of history, everybody had access to a pick or shovel.

# YOU KNOW WHAT A CAREFUL GUY I AM

The type of clothing you'll require will of course depend upon the environments in which you find yourself. If you're going to be looking for Nazi gold above the Alpine snowline, then obviously thick warm winter gear is going to be a good idea. Conversely, if you're exploring the Valley of the Kings in search of the lost tomb of Herihor, you'll want to be protected against the literally blistering desert heat.

That much is obvious, but what about clothes suitable for the travelling treasure hunter, who might require clothing that will fit in a variety of different climates and environments?

Leather jackets are always a good choice. They keep you cool in hot climates, and warm in cold ones. Also, depending on the type of jacket, may provide a degree of protection from cuts, scrapes and falls.

Lycra is often seen on female treasure hunters in popular media. In popular culture, this type of clothing is given to these female characters largely because, being form-fitting, it's generally considered to be sexy. However, it's not actually that bad an idea in certain circumstances, and not just for women. It is supportive of joints and muscles, while at the same time the form-fitting nature of it means it grants a certain amount of insulation. It can also be compressive, and this is helpful at high altitudes or in case of cuts. It is also therefore most suitable for use to make improvised tourniquets and compression bandages.

Hats are generally a good idea in both hot and cold climates. In the cold, most body heat is lost through the head, so a hat will insulate you and keep you a little warmer. In sunnier climes, a hat will protect the scalp from sunburn and generally insulate the head and brain. The brim will also shade against the sun. What sort of hat to wear is really a matter of individual choice and aesthetic preference, though one should always be careful with wide-brimmed hats that they don't get blown off by high winds.

Footwear: While perusing libraries and archives and the like, you can feel free to wear whatever is most comfortable, but, out in the field, you'll want to be sure to have a pair of stout boots, regardless of the environment – with Wellingtons or gumboots as an option for muddy and marshy ground (and you'd be amazed how dig sites always manage to become muddy and marshy, unless they're in the middle of a desert).

Stout boots are the best option because they will protect you against threats in the underbrush, sharp objects in ruins and the bites of hostile creatures – in particular, some venomous snakes have very powerful jaws, which you will want to be as protected from as you can get.

You won't need to carry picks and shovels and the like around the world with you – these things can be picked up on location. You won't even usually need a whip or a gun, though these can be useful in certain parts of the world (though more for protection against hostile wildlife than hordes of Nazis). That said, there are some bits and pieces that it's always worth carrying, and top of the list is a good camera. Remember, you'll want to record your finds, and be able to prove where it was, and what the surrounding context was.

A good solid watch, satellite phone (rather than cellphone), first aid kit, GPS and bottled water are all fairly essential. There's also no excuse for being ignorant of local laws regarding who owns treasure finds, what permissions are needed, or taxes must be paid – everything is on the websites of governments around the world.

Make sure also to check what diseases and venomous creatures you're likely to encounter, and be sure to be vaccinated against the most common illnesses.

Treasure hunting can involve a lot of exertion, and you'll want to keep yourself in good condition to do it. Drinking plenty of bottled water while out and about is important – hydration is the single most vital factor in maintaining fitness for anything that may involve running, fighting, or just staying functional in the wide variety of exotic climates that treasure tends to get lost in.

Now that that's cleared up, let's board a plane that leaves a dotted line behind it and head for the treasures.

RG IV. MEER

OCEAN

(SÜDLICHES EISMEER)

80
10 0 10
20 20
30 30
40 40
50
60
70
Westliche Länge von Greenwich
80
80
90
100
110
120
130
140 140
150 150
160 160
170 170
180 Paris
R. T. FORSCHTES

SÜD POL

Anzeichen von hohem Land

en Südpol erreichte Breite (78°10')
Ross, Febr. 1842

senkrechte Eiswand, 150-200 F. hoch

1842

Viele Walfische

Beaufort I.
Franklin I.
600 F.
Offenes Meer

Packeis, Ross, März 1842

Coulman I.

# TREASURES

# OF AFRICA

# THE PHARAOHS' TREASURES

✖ THE PHARAOHS' TREASURES

## WHAT IS IT?

Ordinarily, we think of Ancient Egyptian rulers as each being entombed with their own personal treasure, but one hoard may include the treasures of more than one pharaoh.

If it exists, it will probably be found in the lost tomb of Herihor. This is thought to be an intact pharaonic tomb dating from around 1075 BC, somewhere in the hills near the ancient capital of Thebes. It is believed to contain not just the amount of gold, jewels and artefacts typical to a pharaonic burial, but also a hoard of treasures and grave goods smuggled out of the tombs of previous pharaohs, that were taken out of their tombs by Herihor during his lifetime.

The total haul, therefore, could contain not just an intact mummy and sarcophagi – at least one perhaps made of solid gold – but also the finest model soldiers, amulets, statuettes, drinking goblets, weapons, chests, a throne and perhaps even boats or chariots. These are all things that were found in Tutankhamen's tomb in 1922.

In short, Herihor's tomb could well contain the combined wealth of several generations of pharaohs, as well as many vital archaeological artefacts of inestimable value to historians.

## HOW MUCH IS IT WORTH TO YOU?

If Tutankhamen's tomb is anything to go by, a reasonable ballpark figure would come in anywhere between about $16 million and over a billon dollars, depending on who is willing to pay for it.

The total net value of the gold found in Tutankhamen's tomb, simply as the price for that weight of gold today, is over $2 million. Throw in the historical value and his golden death mask is worth $15 million alone. The collection as a whole, on show at the Museum Of Egyptian Antiquities in Cairo, is insured for a billion dollars. However you look at it, a new find of similar or greater magnitude would be worth many millions in either sterling or dollars.

## THE STORY

Everybody knows that the pharaohs of Ancient Egypt were entombed with all manner of fancy grave goods, from obvious treasures like gold and jewelry, to weapons, furniture, chariots, and even ships, which would be of huge historical value today. People also knew this back in the days of the pharaohs themselves, and bandits and thieves were breaking into tombs almost before the paint had dried on the hieroglyphs.

The priesthood conducted all of these pharaonic burials, but they also, in the 20th and 21st dynasties (425–330 BC), conducted a lot of reburials, largely because this was a period when they were getting especially annoyed at all the tomb-robbing. Previously interred rulers were therefore moved from their original tombs to ones in the Valley of the Kings, which were intended to be more secure against burglary.

While this was the best-known period of Egyptian reburials, it was not the first era for them. Seven hundred years before, a man called Herihor was a scribe, a general, and eventually became high priest during the reign of Rameses XI (around 1075 BC). Being high priest meant that Herihor was in charge of burials and, under his command, the priesthood engaged in a series of innovative reburials in the hope of hiding royal mummies from looters.

If he moved the mummies, it seems reasonable to expect he also would have moved their grave goods and treasures – as these were intended to serve the deceased in the afterlife – yet when tombs containing these relocated mummies have been found, the treasures have been conspicuously absent. This means that either the new tombs were looted, or the treasures were not put in with the new burials. If the latter was the case, then what actually happened to the treasure?

When Rameses XI died, Herihor took on the mantle and duties of pharaoh, even though there was also an 'official' pharaoh, Herihor's fellow general and high priest, Piankh. How much of this was a split in the empire, and how much was a co-rulership deal, is open to debate. The men certainly worked together both in the military and the priesthood, and one of them was the son-in-law of the other – though Egyptologists disagree on which way round that was.

Either way, Herihor, though officially still only high priest, ended up having his name in pharaonic cartouches in Upper Egypt, and seems to have ruled there, while Piankh ruled Lower Egypt.

## PREVIOUS SEARCHES IN FACT AND FICTION

There have simultaneously been lots of searches for Herihor's treasure and none. This is because, historically, there have tended to be searches for tombs generally, rather than for specific ones. Usually archaeologists would find a tomb first, and then figure out who it belonged to. Archaeology also has a continuing vested interest in searching for lost pharaonic tombs, in order to set dates in stone, fill in gaps in the written records of history, and study how people lived in the era.

In Herihor's case, there's also the matter of archaeological authorities not quite agreeing on whether he counts as a pharaoh or not. This matters when expeditions are seeking funding. That said, since 1999 a Polish team have been scraping together funding to make a dig at Deir el-Bahri, where they believe Herihor and his treasure are buried.

John Romer, one of the most famous Egyptologists, and a familiar face on TV history programmes in the UK, announced in an interview in *The Sunday Times* in March 2014 that he had found what he believed to be the tombs of Herihor, Piankh and Menkephere, but has since fallen silent about the matter. What we do know about Romer's claim is that it relates to the Wadi el-Gharbi, a few miles north-west of the Valleys of the Kings and Queens.

# TRICKS AND TRAPS

Something that both professional and amateur treasure hunters will be concerned with for different reasons is the danger of large lumps of stone and other hazardous materials bouncing off their heads. Every adventure movie, videogame and comic book involving treasure hunters and archaeological adventurers threatens our heroes and heroines with all manner of devious mechanical contrivances which mean that putting one foot in the wrong place will result in spears shooting across, giant boulders bouncing around, or razor-sharp pendulums swooping down to cut the unwary in half.

Some cultures did historically build traps into certain types of building, especially tombs. Tomb-robbing has always been a popular pastime wherever tombs and mortuary temples have been built for the rich and powerful, and of course the rich and powerful builders have always known that. Therefore they would build traps to dissuade robbers from nicking all those fancy treasures, whether they be burial goods or the royal treasury. Over time the buildings perhaps became lost and forgotten, before being rediscovered in more modern times, so some of these traps still may remain for unwary archaeologists and treasure hunters.

That said, what is the likelihood of a carefully constructed trap still being fully functional after centuries or even millennia?

Frankly, not much. Wood will have rotted, as will ropes, especially if they were made from vegetable and plant fibres. Oil and grease to keep things moving smoothly will have soaked away or dried up and metal will have rusted, if the mechanism has not been maintained.

That said, ancient tombs and vaults are still going to be dangerous places to mess with, for much simpler reasons. Over time, natural environmental wear will have taken its toll on buildings and mechanisms, making them more fragile. Subsidence, earthquakes, the crumbling of cement and the rotting of support beams will all have contributed to making such old structures very dangerous. So, for all that primitive mechanisms are not going to function after so long, you're still likely to risk having large rocks dropped on your head.

Traps are a little more plausible where the search for more modern treasures are concerned; hoards dating from World War II, for example, such as Nazi loot, may well still be rigged with explosives or the like. While munitions also decay over time, this again actually makes it more likely that they could go off without being deliberately triggered, simply by the vibrations from nearby activity.

It is always possible that you could encounter modern-day traps, set by looters or rival treasure hunters to guard a site they've found until they can come back with suitable gear to loot it. It's up to you whether you include legitimate security precautions such as barbed wire, cameras and burglar alarms as traps near treasures in private hands.

## THE TRUTH IS OUT THERE

There is some debate over Herihor, and whether he was really a pharaoh at all. His parents were probably Libyans, and Herihor himself was certainly first a scribe, and then an officer in the army throughout the reign of Rameses XI. As a general, he booted the Nubian viceroy, Pinehesy, out of Thebes. He became High Priest of Amun at Thebes, married one of Rameses's daughters, Nodjmet, and became vizier, the de facto prime minister under Rameses.

At this point, the powerbase of the pharaoh was weakening, and the empire was dividing once more into Upper and Lower Egypt. Herihor was married into the royal family already, and as both general, vizier and especially as high priest, had plenty of political power. In fact, at this point, the priesthood largely ran the Egyptian economy, as they owned 70 per cent of the land, 80 per cent of the industry, and 90 per cent of the ships.

Although Herihor assumed the title of Pharaoh at Thebes, Rameses XI was still ruling the rest of the empire, and so there became what's known as the *wehem mesut*, or Renaissance, of the Two Kingdoms, with the High Priest of Amun being Pharaoh of Upper Egypt at Thebes, and the official pharaohs being based at Tanis in Lower Egypt. (Yes, the Tanis from *Raiders of the Lost Ark*. It would be Shoshenk I, aka 'Shishak' in that movie, who would reunite the empire 140 years later.)

Since Herihor had managed to take on the powers and duties of the pharaoh himself, at least some of the time, and over half of the empire, there is a likelihood that he may have kept many burial treasures for his own interment. The possibility that he was entombed with not just his own funeral goods, but also those of others, makes his tomb a potential hoard the likes of which the world has never seen outside of movies and comic books.

## WHERE IS IT NOW?

The mummies Herihor relocated which have since been discovered have not been accompanied by their grave goods – even when those tombs have been proven not to have been broken into by looters. There are three possible reasons for this:

1) Their treasures were looted from their original tombs before reburial. In which case why would Herihor, or anyone else, rebury them with an intent of hiding them from looters? In any case, this is what John Romer believes was done at the Wadi el-Ghabri site. In which case there is no treasure to be found.

2) There was only a limited amount of treasure available for a big funeral at the time, and the priesthood simply used the same items each time, ceremonially burying them with the deceased before retrieving them for use in the next royal funeral. In this instance, it was probably buried with someone else.

3) Herihor and his priesthood kept it for themselves, in which case it may have ended up buried with him.

## THE OPPOSITION IN YOUR WAY

In fiction, especially movies, people seeking to uncover the treasures of the pharaohs are most likely to have to face reanimated or reincarnated ancient wizards and mummies, flesh-eating scarab beetles, homicidal jackals, cursed tombs and so on. Thankfully most of these are unlikely to be encountered in the real world, with the obvious exception of the cursed tombs part.

In this rational age, few people (hopefully) believe that supernatural death will come on swift wings to those who disturb tombs, especially when we know that that most famous of curses – laid upon Tutankhamen's tomb – was made up in 1926 by a rival journalist to the official newsman attached to Carter's expedition (and not by a sorcerous priest thousands of years ago). However, there *are* some dangers likely to be found in Egyptian tombs.

Firstly, the original builders did like to put in the occasional deep pit, and stone slabs set to fall. Such things can still be dangerous, as it's all too easy to fall into a pit without seeing it when blundering about in the pitch-dark tunnel leading to a tomb. The mechanisms for booby traps would have rotted or been seized up with sand, but this also means that roof supports and the like may also have rotted, and thus will be more likely to come down upon you like a ton of the proverbials.

Tombs have also been shown to be havens for a particular type of fungal bacterium. On a more obvious note, cool dark places like tombs are ideal havens for cold-blooded reptiles such as snakes, which can fit in through the tiniest gaps. There is good reason why Indiana Jones found a lot of cobras in the Well of Souls. You're more likely to encounter asps and vipers, but cobras are also possible. If you're near the Nile, crocodiles are also a danger. Your biggest fauna problem, though, will be insects such as mosquitoes, and the occasional deathstalker scorpion.

Egypt is also home to some sectarian tension, and tourist buses have been known to be attacked by Islamic extremists (most famously at the Temple of Hathor some years ago). The Egyptian tourist police are somewhat under-funded and sometimes short of good equipment, but their hearts are in the right place.

Terrorism is more of an issue in the south and east, but one human opponent is nationwide: the Antiquities Department of the government. You will not be allowed to just bring finds out of the country, especially if they are as historically significant as this would be.

# KING SOLOMON'S MINES

KING SOLOMON'S MINES

## WHAT IS IT?

A misnomer. Well, yes, the mines are supposed to be the source of the fabulous wealth ascribed to King Solomon in the Old Testament, however the Bible describes that wealth being brought to him by the Queen of Sheba, so, technically, they should really be called The Queen of Sheba's Mines.

The basic idea is that they are gold and gemstone mines from which this wealth was originally dug. They'd have to be mines, plural, because gold and gemstones form in different ways and under different pressures.

Such mines couldn't exist without a workforce and support network, however, so they must be accompanied by a settlement also. Traditionally, therefore, explorers and fortune hunters have been looking for a set of mine tunnels full of gold and gemstone veins next door to some kind of lost city, in an area under the influence of King Solomon and/or the Queen of Sheba. What could be simpler?

# HOW MUCH IS IT WORTH TO YOU?

That would depend on what deposits still remain in the mines. The Bible doesn't specify a regular amount, but Biblical scholars on average tell us that Solomon was given 450 talents of gold every three years. Different ancient cultures defined the measure of a 'talent' differently, but the ancient Israelites of Old Testament times had adopted the Babylonian talent, which was 67lb, or just over 30kg.

If there remained even one shipment's worth of gold at source, that would be 30,150lb – 15 tons – of gold. In today's values, that's a good half a billion dollars worth.

There'd be the value of any gemstones to add to that, plus assorted other trade goods, so it's not inconceivable to imagine one shipment's worth remaining in the mines to go way beyond that half a billion.

# THE STORY

According to the Biblical *Book of Kings*, Solomon was famed both for his wisdom and devotion to the God of the Israelites, building the legendary first temple to house the Ark of the Covenant and other sacred goods. He also had 700 wives and 300 concubines, which seems a bit tiring.

According to 1 *Kings* 10, the Queen of Sheba came to test him on his devotion 'with hard questions'. Aside from the exam paper, she brought 'camels that bore spices, and very much gold, and precious stones'. Solomon answered all her doubts and questions perfectly, and she was thoroughly impressed with his temple and his theological rulership, saying, 'It was a true report that I heard in mine own land of thy acts and of thy wisdom. Howbeit I believed not the words, until I came, and mine eyes had seen it: and, behold, the half was not told me: thy wisdom and prosperity exceedeth the fame which I heard. Happy are thy men, happy are these thy servants, which stand continually before thee, and that hear thy wisdom. Blessed be the LORD thy God, which delighted in thee, to set thee on the throne of Israel.'

At this point, she rewards Solomon with, according to Kings, 'one hundred and twenty talents of gold, and of spices very great store, and precious stones: there came no more such abundance of spices …

And the navy also of Hiram, that brought gold from Ophir, brought in from Ophir great plenty of almug trees, and precious stones.'

Solomon turned the wood from the almug trees into pillars in his temple, and also into musical instruments such as harps. He then rewarded her with 'all her desire', which is probably as salacious as it sounds, and she went home satisfied. We're then given Solomon's annual income: 'six hundred threescore and six talents of gold', and that 'once in three years came the navy of Tarshish, bringing gold, and silver, ivory, and apes, and peacocks.'

## PREVIOUS SEARCHES IN FACT AND FICTION

People have been searching for the source of Solomon and Sheba's wealth for a very long time. Mainly they sought Tarshish and Ophir, which were sometimes thought to be lost cities, and sometimes thought to be lost names for known cities.

In the 1st century AD, the Roman-Jewish historian Josephus wrote that Solomon's wealth had most likely come from India. Other European and Islamic writers in the first millennium thought that it came from Arabia, or that Solomon never existed.

There also came to be something of a split between those writers who believed that both Ophir and Tarshish were cities, and those who thought that Tarshish was the word for a type of ship, capable of longer journeys than the shallow-hulled boats that plied the Arabian and Red seas. The Bible mentions two navies belonging to Solomon: the navy of Tarshish, and the navy of Hiram, but nobody ever seemed to think the latter was a place.

Today, say 'King Solomon's Mines' and most people think of Africa. In 1488, a Portuguese explorer, Pêro da Covilhã, arrived in Sofala, Mozambique. Sofala had been a trading centre for gold for 500 years by this point, and was frequented by Somalis, Arabs and Persians. By 1502, Portuguese ships were visiting, having made an alliance with the local Sultan, Isuf.

Portuguese chronicler Thomé Lopes had come along, and learned from the Arab and Somali populace that the local tribes retained folktales of ships being sent to Solomon every three years bearing cargoes of gold. The Portuguese of the time were most familiar with the Bible in its Greek translation – in Greek Ophir is called Sophir – and, knowing that Sofala was at the centre of a gold trade anyway, decided that the names must simply be variations of the same word. So they started looking for where the gold was coming from, not just with an eye to getting a piece of the action, but to confirming that they'd found Ophir.

In 1531, Portuguese Captain Vincente Pagada had learned that 'among the gold mines of the inland plains, between the Limpopo and Zambezi rivers, there is a fortress built of stones of a marvellous size, and there appears to be no mortar joining them'. Putting two, in the form of gold mines, and two, in the form of a stone-built fortress, together, Pagada came up with five: this was the palace of the Queen of Sheba, and source of King Solomon's gold.

This tale got repeated over the years, becoming tied up with the tale of the mythical African Christian king, Prester John, but becoming best known through being mentioned by Milton in *Paradise Lost*.

The idea seeped out into wider adventures, and the name of Ophir was altered only slightly by Edgar Rice Burroughs for his Tarzan stories, when he wrote Opar into *The Return Of Tarzan* in 1913, in which the city is actually a lost colony of Atlantis.

Despite this familiarity, fewer people were interested in actually looking for the place than you'd think. This is partly because it was overgrown and in an otherwise inhospitable area, and partly, perhaps, because people didn't feel the need, since they assumed that this mystery had been solved. Also, treasure-seekers tended to focus on trying to locate where Solomon's treasure had *gone*, rather than on where it had come from. European interest in Africa had also come to concentrate on other things, such as slavery, ore, diamonds and colonial lands.

Pagada's stone fortress, therefore, went largely ignored until around 1852, when a German boy named Karl Mauch was given a largely blank map of Africa, and access to the writings of Pagada. These inspired him to become an explorer set on finding King Solomon's Mines. In fact he was pretty much the first person to think of it in those terms, though he didn't really use the phrase in his journals.

Mauch took 11 years to teach himself botany, geology, entomology, English, Arabic, Latin, and French. He worked out, walking 6 miles a day to prepare himself for an African expedition, and, in 1863, he sought sponsorship from August Petermann, the publisher of Germany's *Geographical Magazine*. Petermann refused, but promised to publish any reports Mauch sent in if he ever reached Africa. This he did in 1865, having worked his passage as a ship's deckhand from London to Durban.

Mauch may have prepared for 11 years, but his packing was lacking; he started walking with only a compass, penknife, writing gear, blanket, and pistol. He never carried enough food, and turned out to be totally rubbish at hunting. Multiple instances of heatstroke, exhaustion, and starvation later, the readers of *Geographical Magazine* had a whip-round and donated enough cash to keep him going for a further eight years. He also had the good fortune to run into Henry Hartley, a famous (at the time) English big-game hunter, who needed some help with a wounded elephant. Newly funded, and now with some teaching on how to catch dinner, Mauch made his first actual discovery in 1867.

In the Tati region of the border between what's now Botswana and Zimbabwe, he found some curious quartz pits, with old traces of gold in them, and realized they had been used for smelting gold. The very next day, he found a gold field, which the *Geographical Magazine* was happy to trumpet as 'Solomon's Ophir' in its report on the find. Mauch knew from Pagada's writings that there must be a fortress city nearby if this was really Ophir, and sourced local stories of just such a construction, matching Pagada's description, in the hill country between the Zambezi and Limpopo.

This phase of his search lasted another three years (despite his goal being only 40 miles inland from Sofala), during which time he was abducted and robbed by Matabele tribesmen, and fell victim to starvation again despite having learned how to get elephant meat, which you'd think would last a while.

On 5 September 1871, Mauch walked into the stone fortress we now call Great Zimbabwe. The ancient citadel fit Pagada's description perfectly, and he immediately jumped to the conclusion that the city could never have been built by black people for two reasons: he was a white guy living in the height of 19th century imperialism (which was busily whitewashing history at the best of times), or, the tribes living in the area openly admitted that the place had nothing to do with them, and that they had no idea who had built it.

Mauch decided that the Phoenicians had built the city, and the local tribes had no objection to this idea. He decided from his impression of the architectural style that it must have been built to replicate the design of Solomon's Temple, and constructed with imported iron tools. He found pieces of wooden beams that he was sure were Lebanese cedar, because it looked like the cedarwood in his pencil.

The locals also called Sofala 'Sophir', so Mauch was satisfied that he had found Ophir. The *Geographical Magazine* agreed, publishing to a very limited audience. Mauch returned home to Germany, afflicted with liver disease from his near-starvations.

The story wasn't over, however, as an English writer, H. Rider Haggard, had heard the tale from Hartley, and used Mauch's adventures as the source material for his novel *King Solomon's Mines*, which cast Mauch as the young man searching for his lost father, and Hartley as the much better-remembered fictional hunter, Allan Quatermain.

# CRACKING THE WHIP

If you're the kind of treasure hunter who teaches archaeology by day but wants to be a cross between a motorcycle rebel and cowboy while off duty, you may be tempted to consider taking along a bullwhip. After all, the media over the past 30 years or so has made it an iconic piece of treasure-hunting equipment.

Is it really so practical as to be worth packing for your expedition? Well, it depends what you expect to do with it, and what you expect to use it for. Are you going to use it as a weapon, to disarm or deface your enemies, or are you thinking more of using it as an aid to gymnastic dealing with obstacles and terrain? Or perhaps you want to reel in your date for the evening?

The bullwhip definitely has some use as a weapon. It takes some training and getting used to, but it absolutely will wrap itself around a wrist or forearm and allow you to pull a weapon or tool out of an enemy's hand. The other way to use a bullwhip as a weapon, of course, is to use it in such a way that the tail at the end will cut into the skin. This can be extremely dangerous, easily blinding or cutting the faces of others. That said, if your opponent has a gun, you are not going to kill them with a whip before they can shoot you.

The other main purpose for which you may want to use a bullwhip is to climb, or to swing across rivers or chasms where there is no bridge, by a convenient log or branch. Again, the whip will wrap around such an object if used correctly, and the friction will enable a grip. However, getting that grip to stay is a different matter. A grip that lasts just long enough to jerk on an arm may take the gun out of an enemy hand, but is less likely to last long enough for you to climb up the length of the whip, or to swing across a gap.

Basically, the best way to ensure that a whip will hold on to that branch long enough to cross an obstacle is to tie a knot in it, around the branch or object to which you're securing it. The material of a proper bullwhip is certainly strong enough to support an active person's bodyweight and shouldn't break. The problem is that in order to tie a knot around the supporting object, you'd have to have already climbed up or been otherwise suspended or supported, which is somewhat paradoxical. For this type of purpose, really you'd be better off bringing along a coil of strong modern rope and a small grappling hook, ideally with folding arms.

As for any other types of whipping, let's just say it's probably safer to bring your own than to trust someone else's: you don't know where it's been.

Unfortunately, Mauch hadn't actually found the Biblical Ophir. At the turn of the 20th century, archaeology underwent a reboot of sorts, changing from being the search for physical remnants of Biblical myths to being the scientific search for evidence of what had happened in the past. So, in 1905, an archaeologist named Randall MacIver confirmed that the city dated to around the 14th century, and had been built by Africans.

In 1929, an all-woman dig led by Gertrude Caton Thompson confirmed that it had been built by the Shona tribe around 1150, and was a cattle-raising and gold trading centre until being abandoned around 1450 – which would have been within living memory when the Portuguese showed up.

Sadly, it never occurred to Mauch that the reason the local people had no idea about the building of the city was because they themselves were newbies to the area, preceding him by only 40 years. Since the place had been abandoned for centuries, it's no surprise that they knew nothing about it. Mauch didn't live to see his discovery debunked, however. He had expected a university tenure when he returned to Germany, but it never materialized. Instead he ended up in a dead-end job, living in a one-room bed-sit hotel. In 1875, either asleep or drunk, he rolled out of the hotel window and died on the cobbles below, aged just 37.

This meant that the search was still on, but, thanks to Haggard's phenomenally successful novel, everybody now thought of this goal as King Solomon's Mines.

Individuals and expeditions searched Africa for years afterwards, in the hope of finding another similar lost city, with attached mines. However, the first discoveries of historical evidence linked to Solomon came not in Africa, but in Israel, in 1993.

It's not really surprising that this should be the case, since it's where he was king *of*, but this discovery had nothing to do with his mines; rather it was a statue of his father, the legendary King David, from the right period. Shortly thereafter, however, in neighbouring Jordan, copper mines from Solomon's era were also uncovered.

## THE TRUTH IS OUT THERE

Ophir, Tarshish and Sheba were originally mentioned in the Old

Testament as being people's names, but by the time of the stories about Solomon these names had become the names of places with which Solomon's land traded. Scholars suggest that these lands were perhaps founded by the people in question.

Ophir was certainly a place – in 1946 some pottery was excavated at Tell Qasile, now part of modern Tel Aviv, bearing the notation 'gold from Ophir for Beth-Horon', which at least indicated that gold was imported to Beth-Horon from Ophir. The pottery dates from the 8th century BC, which is the right time to be trading with the Israelite kingdom.

Sheba is now pretty much settled as having been in the Arabian Peninsula, in what is now the Yemen, at the bottom end of the Red Sea. Long story short, it was a Semitic kingdom more properly named Saba which existed from about 1200 BC until the 3rd century AD, at which point it fell apart in a civil war. None of the Saba cities, however, were fit with the requirements to be Ophir, because sandalwood did not grow there. The Queen of Sheba had to get sandalwood from elsewhere and transport it.

Copper mines from Solomon's time have been excavated in the Timna Valley in southern Israel. Thought to have begun as early as the 5th millennium BC, these were part of Edom in Old Testament times. From around 1000 BC and up until Roman times, these mines were worked by the Nabateans and Israelites.

The Nabatean mines would have presumably had to pay taxes to, or be licensed by, Solomon, even if he didn't actually own them. So in that sense these would kind of be King Solomon's Mines.

Being copper mines actually makes the Timna Valley mines more likely to have been watched over by a king such as Solomon, for two good reasons. Firstly, at the time, copper was the most valuable trade good, because this was, after all, the Bronze Age, and copper is one of the two ingredients in bronze (tin being the other, of course). So, a king controlling the copper trade could make himself wealthy. Secondly, weapons such as swords, axe heads and spearheads were all made from bronze as well, and the king's government would definitely be sure to be in charge of that supply.

Nevertheless, the mines at Timna are still not what treasure hunters are looking for.

# WHERE IS IT NOW?

H. Rider Haggard's legendary *King Solomon's Mines* are – or, more accurately, is – the walled city of Great Zimbabwe, abandoned since around the 1450s. It's now an UNESCO World Heritage Site, covering 600 hectares of Masvingo Province, in the hills of south-eastern Zimbabwe.

This, however, is certainly not the source of the wealth brought to King Solomon in those ancient texts, and nor is it Ophir. It's not what you're looking for.

That leaves the legendary source(s) of tons of Solomonic gold to find. Where is, or was, Ophir and/or Tarshish?

If you're standing in Great Zimbabwe, you need to turn around, and head to the nearest airport, because you are standing on the wrong continent. If you are standing in the excavations at Timna, sifting through the copper mines, you also need to get yourself to the airport because you are also standing on the wrong continent.

Despite the Portuguese having thought so, and it inspiring Haggard, Ophir was definitely not Great Zimbabwe, on account of that city not being built for another couple of thousand years after Solomon's time. It seems similarly unlikely that Sofala was Ophir either, since Sofala, even if it was sometimes called Sofir, was founded by Somali and Arabic merchants in the 8th century AD. That's far too late to have shipped gold to a king who lived in the 900s BC, at least without access to a TARDIS.

Where you place Ophir is really going to depend on two things. Firstly, what capabilities do you ascribe to shipping in Old Testament times? If shipping was purely coast-hugging, over relatively short distances, then logically you'll be looking at the Red Sea coast. On the African side are the coasts of Egypt, Sudan and Ethiopia, down to Djibouti. Ethiopia and Djibouti in particular are home to a people called the Afar, and you can see how that could be shifted by pronunciation into 'Ophir'.

Although the Queen of Sheba brings Solomon stuff from Ophir, nobody ever said Ophir was actually in Sheba – or Saba – itself, and the historical evidence increasingly suggests that it was not. So, the second thing upon which your placing of Ophir depends, is the question 'where can I find gold, gems, apes, peacock feathers and sandalwood together for export in Old Testament times?' As luck would have it, there's actually only one answer: Southern India and Sri Lanka, under the Dravidians.

The Dravidians were famed for their exports of gold, ivory, peacocks, peacock feathers and sandalwood. Not coincidentally, the Hebrew words for ivory, cotton and peacock – among others – all derive from, and are phonetically similar to, the Tamil words for the same things. Tamil, of course, being the Dravidian language. The Biblical wood Almug is almost certainly Red Sandalwood, native to Dravidian India.

Oh, and there's one last giveaway to the other end of that Saba trading route: the Coptic name for India is 'Sofir'.

Given that if you leave a Yemeni port on a southward heading and turn left, the first land you hit is India, it's easy to see even coastal ships from Saba making that journey. In addition, the Persians could simply carry stuff across the Arabian Peninsula by land anyway. 'Sofir', India, became the legendary Ophir.

Not everybody will ever agree on this, mind you, because over time, the stories have become so bound up with national identities in the region that a dozen countries all want to lay claim to the honour of being home to the Queen Of Sheba. That's before even getting into the assorted 'alternative archaeologists' who want to assume that Ophir was in America, Antarctica, Atlantis, or, indeed, on a different planet altogether.

Basically, though, the Islamic traditions seem to have the most accurate views on this, presumably because Islam was founded in the same area as Saba, not too long after. Everyone assumed Ophir was a city, and it isn't. It's a region.

If you want a specific place to go to, and call Ophir, the most central town to visit would be Kudiramalai in northern Sri Lanka, which neighbours the ancient Thiruketheeswaram Temple, though large stretches of the coast of southern India and north and west Sri Lanka would all qualify.

Though Sri Lanka was historically famous for gold (it was once called Rathnadveepa, or "island of gold"), there aren't currently any major mines there. The deposits of gold and gems are scattered as alluvial deposits, and panning in the rivers has been a more common type of gold rush there, especially around the Kelani River.

# THE OPPOSITION IN YOUR WAY

The main opposition in your search for King Solomon's Mines is your own perception: what you are looking for is not what you think you're looking for!

If you're hoping to acquire any gold, you'll have to learn to pan for it, and you'll find many local people doing likewise, and they may or may not be happy about you joining in. It would definitely be advisable to keep both an eye and an ear out to judge the lie of the land where local opinion on visiting prospectors is concerned.

Thankfully you won't have to deal with Thuggee cults a la *Temple of Doom*, but there have been more political conflicts in the region recently. In India there has long been strife between the Hindu, Sikh and Muslim populations, culminating most memorably in the Mumbai attacks a couple of years ago. This is much rarer in the coastal areas of the south, however. The Sri Lankan military fought a 30-year campaign against the Liberation Tigers of Tamil Eelam, better known as the Tamil Tigers, famed for assassinations, torture, rape and the like. This civil war effectively ended in 2009, however, with the fall of their northern strongholds and death of their leader. Sporadic murders still take place.

The most dangerous fauna in the region are snakes. Cobras are common through coastal India and Sri Lanka, as are various subspecies of viper. What you'll really want to watch for, however, are the Sri Lankan Kraits, striped nocturnal snakes which particularly like to come into houses, huts and tents, and have the deadliest venom on the island.

Monkeys and apes in both countries have a gift for theft, exceeding even the human pickpockets.

Dengue fever and malaria, both spread by mosquitoes, are still common as is yellow fever. Ticks are also common in the forests and ancient historic sites and can carry all manner of nasty infections.

RG IV. MEER

80

10 0 10

20 20

30 30

40 40

O C E A N

50

(SÜDLICHES EISMEER)

60

70

80

R.F O R S C H T E S

90

SÜD POL

100

110

120

130

140 140

150 150

160 160

170 170
180 80

Westliche Länge von Greenwich

180° 7' Paris

Anzeichen von hohem Land

en Südpol erreichte Breite 78°10'S Ross, Febr.1842

Senkrechte Eiswand 150-800 F. hoch

290

410

Beaufort I.

Franklin I.

600 F.

190

1842

Offenes Meer

Viele Walfische

Packeis, Ross, März 1842

Coulman

# TREASURES OF

# THE AMERICAS

# EL DORADO AND THE AZTEC GOLD

X EL DORADO AND THE AZTEC GOLD

Think of lost gold hoards in the Americas, and you probably think of El Dorado, and the fabulous lost city's stash of Aztec gold. These are actually two completely separate types of lost treasure, so let's take them individually.

# EL DORADO

## WHAT IS IT?

El Dorado was originally thought of as a lost city somewhere in South America, filled with gold hidden by the indigenous population to prevent it from being looted by the Spanish Conquistadores in the 16th century.

That said, it's now known even by the general public and in pop-culture that the name itself referred not to a city, but to a person. 'El Dorado' is Spanish for 'the golden one', a native chief who was painted in gold and engaged in a ritual that involved dumping lots of spare gold into water.

This has never stopped anyone from believing in the city filled with gold being hidden from the Conquistadores, for two reasons. Firstly, it seemed like common sense to the Spanish that if a nation had so much gold that they were happy to simply dump the spares, then there *must* be vast stockpiles of it somewhere – such as in a city's treasury. Secondly, and in more recent times, Machu Picchu was discovered at the end of the 19th century – a whole lost city perched on a cloud-shrouded mountaintop. Naturally, many people were and are more than happy to believe that, with so much of South America's mountainous and jungle terrain unexplored, there is plenty of room for other such undiscovered cities to remain hidden.

Even though the name El Dorado has long been known to refer to a man, the idea that he must have been the chief in charge of a city full of treasures yet to be found has persisted. Referring to the city in question by his nickname is simply a convenient shorthand.

Interestingly, this treasure isn't really specific to one location, or even one historical civilization, but is attributed to pretty much every Mesoamerican culture, of which there were plenty. It's said to be an Aztec city, or an Inca city, or an Olmec city, or…

## HOW MUCH IS IT WORTH TO YOU?

Billions. A city the size of Machu Picchu, with storerooms full of gold, would be worth a huge amount in the cash value of the gold alone, to the extent that the discovery would probably risk causing a crash in the market value of the stuff. Then there would be the historic and archaeological value, and possibly even a huge impact on local tourism, depending on the location.

## THE STORY

By 1535, both the Inca and Aztec empires had been thoroughly trashed by the Spanish Conquistadores who had followed

Christopher Columbus's expedition to the New World, so Gonzalo Fernández de Oviedo turned his attention to what is now Colombia.

Oviedo led an expedition into the jungle, following the course of the Río Magdalena inland from the coast. His explorations overall would last until 1548, but after a year, he encountered a group of natives carrying fine textiles. This tribe was called the Muisca, and Oviedo's men followed them home to a mountain village over 300 miles inland.

The Spanish found gold artworks such as figurines and models throughout the village, in even the poorest of huts. The Muisca were happy to simply give them these artefacts, showing no desire to hang on to them. They had even tossed some of these golden objects away into pits and bushes.

According to the *Chronicle of Juan Rodríguez Freyle*, Oviedo then witnessed a ritual in which, as part of his coronation, the Muisca chief was decorated in gold dust, and taken out on a raft into the middle of a lake, where he threw gold and emeralds into the water as an offering to the gods.

The Spanish came to the only conclusion they were capable of understanding: that if the Muisca are willing to throw so much gold away, or give it to the Oviedo without a second thought, it could only be because they had much more kept back for themselves, in some hidden location. Thus the legend of El Dorado, the city of gold, was born.

## PREVIOUS SEARCHES IN FACT AND FICTION

As soon as Renaissance Europeans discovered the Americas, they also noted that the natives had bling. They also discovered various spices and other resources. The Conquistadores were sent out to find not just gold and gems, but also cinnamon, as spices were a hugely valuable commodity.

Although we tend to think of the Conquistadores as exclusively Spanish, the first military explorers striking out towards the Andes were Germans led by Ambrosius Ehinger, whose bankers had been given concessions by the Spanish king, in July of 1529, a few years before the Spanish really got into it.

A couple of years later, the Spanish Governor of Paria (in Venezuala), Diego de Ordaz, set out to explore the course of the Orinoco River. He was willing to believe in hoards of gold somewhere, being a veteran of Hernán Cortés's search for Aztec gold in Mexico.

In 1531, Francisco Pizarro landed on the west coast of Peru with less than 200 men and 70 horses. He soon ran into the largest empire of the Andes, the Inca, and found that they had a lot of gold going spare. Pizarro quickly steamrollered the natives and got the local chief – King Atahualpa – to promise to fill a room with gold. In this case the room was his prison cell, and Atahualpa kept his word, filling it with six and a half tons of gold. Pizarro killed him anyway, started a war, and brought down the Inca Empire.

Pizarro's lieutenant, Sebastián de Belalcázar, coined the phrase 'El Dorado' as reference to a location in 1535. He was told by a Tacumga native about a Cundinamarca chief, who allegedly hid tons of riches in a valley of gold: *dorado*. Pizarro sent an expedition, and then various Conquistadores started heading east of Quito (in Ecuador) in search of this valley.

Enter the aforementioned Gonzalo Fernández de Oviedo, who actually discovered the avocado on his travels, before stumbling across the Colombian Muisca tribe.

The Muisca had lived in the northern part of Colombia since AD 1000, on the shores of what is now Lake Guatavita. There, the Muisca Chief anointed himself each morning so that he shone like gold before washing himself off in the lake, into which golden objects were discarded by the people. Oviedo, writing in his journal, called the chief 'El Dorado' – the golden man – and wished he could have the 'sweeping rights to El Dorado's rooms', because so much gold dust must have fallen there.

What the Europeans wondered was where did the gold come from? If they had so much of it that they were willing to throw it away, there must be a helluva lot stashed somewhere. Oviedo himself was offered gold by the Muisca everywhere he went, but he never found a central source.

Next up, another Gonzalo, Jiménez de Quesada, gave up his search for a route over the Andes, to look for Muisca gold instead. He found 1,700lb of gold – 50 million dollars in today's money –

and 2,000 emeralds in the settlement of Tunha in 1537. Tunha's chief, Satipa, promised to fill a room with gold in 20 days, but didn't. In return, Quesada tortured him for the location of his source of gold, but Satipa died without revealing it. Two other expeditions in 1537 had the same result, and this quickly became the standard pattern for European imperialists in South America.

Quesada and his brother Hernán spread the word that there were natives with gold to spare and that, by extension (and through Chinese whispers as the message spread), there was indeed a lost kingdom of gold somewhere in South America, from which the Golden Man, El Dorado, got his gold.

A hundred years later, the tale was standardized by Juan Rodríguez Freyle, who wrote of how the chief was covered in gold dust and threw treasures into Lake Guatavita as part of his coronation. Freyle was editing and interpreting the journals of those adventurers to fit in with what had already become the prevailing opinion. An opinion which had already been coloured by both what had happened with the Aztecs in Mexico at around the same time, and by a completely separate legend: that of Cibola, the Seven Cities of Gold.

This was a slight diversion from El Dorado, in which survivors of an expedition to Florida in 1539, who had been shipwrecked on Galveston Island in the Gulf of Mexico by a hurricane, had been told by locals about gold in Cibola, north of them. This led Francisco Vásquez de Coronado to take an army up as far as Kansas in search of the cities in 1540, before he eventually figured out that the whole thing had been a lie to get the Spanish lost in the Great Plains, where they couldn't do any more harm.

Lake Guatavita is a bowl-shaped crater lake, 10,000ft above sea level in Colombia. The first attempt to drain it was made in 1545 by Hernán Quesada (brother of Gonzalo Jiminez Quesada). His workforce simply used a bucket chain, and took three months to reduce the water level by 10ft. They did recover what in today's money would be about £60,000 worth of gold.

A generation later, in 1572, Antonio La Sepulveda was licensed to drain the lake and excavate part of the mountain. He had Muisca slaves strip the forest from the mountainside and build a channel through which he could drain the lake, which was then about 100ft deep. When the floodgates were opened in 1580, 70ft or so of the lake's depth poured away, revealing the glint of gold and emerald under the water. A few pieces of golden ornaments were recovered...

At which point the walls of the channel collapsed, killing hundreds of slaves, and re-filling the lake. The cut in the lakeshore where the channel had been built is still visible today, but Sepulveda never managed to rebuild it or drain the lake again. Nevertheless, people now knew that there was indeed treasure in the lake.

When Alexander von Humboldt surveyed the Guyana River, he decided that the lake part of the El Dorado story was a myth inspired by seasonal floods at the confluence of rivers – even though he had already pronounced upon the value of the actual genuine lake which really was the source of the myth.

At the end of the 19th century, The Company for the Exploitation of the Lagoon of Guatavita was founded as a shell company for Contractors Ltd of London. The company tunnelled under the centre of the lake, and managed to drain it until only a few feet of mud and silt remained. Since this was essentially deadly quicksand, the explorers had to wait until it dried a bit. It did, like cement or concrete. They only managed to chisel about £500 worth out to auction off at Sotheby's, which was a lot less than the expedition had cost. The pieces ended up at the British Museum, and the company went bust. Finally, an American group recovered about $20,000 worth of gold in the 1930s.

In 1965, the Colombian government put laws in place to protect the area and clamp down on private treasure-hunting expeditions. They also know that El Dorado is a famous legend that could be a big tourist draw, and so are keen to attract environmental tourists, which means you can buy package tours to visit the site.

After the fiasco caused by Sepulveda, the Europeans focused more on where the Muisca had sourced their gold, rather than where they dumped it. Because of the contemporary legend of the Seven Cities of Gold, and the promises of the Aztec Empire up in Mexico, they began to conflate this with the source of El Dorado's gold, and assumed there must be a city full of it somewhere. There was no sign of any large gold mines in the territory, and the geology just wasn't right for those elements.

In total, about 30 per cent of the Conquistador manpower that set out searching for El Dorado made it to the Muisca lands, which they thought were paradise compared to what they had endured on the journey. The Muisca continued to offer the Spaniards gold, and in total the Spanish took about 80 tons worth from Muisca, most of which was shipped home to Spain.

This wasn't the end of the search, however. In 1595 Sir Walter Raleigh got his hands on a map showing El Dorado as being located in Guyana, on the shores of another lake, Lake Parime. There was actually an existing city there, called Manoa, and Raleigh believed this to be El Dorado, which it wasn't.

Raleigh did find various pieces of gold along riverbanks, and returned to make another search, but all he got was his son killed by natives, and himself executed back home. In the 17th century, there were more expeditions, by monks, the Governor of San Thome del Agostura (who conducted several massacres while mapping Paraguay), and two men commissioned by Spanish governors, Nicholas Rodriguez and Antonio Santos.

The main search for El Dorado faded after this, for various reasons, but the name stuck in the minds of other explorers, such as Hiram Bingham, who did actually find a genuine lost city, in the form of Machu Picchu in 1911. El Dorado was also doubtless in the minds of both the British (Thomas Payne) and German (August Berns and J. M. von Hassel) explorers who had also found Machu Picchu in the 19th century (it was also conveniently marked on maps by 1874, so wasn't hard for Hiram).

Milton wrote about the search in *Paradise Lost* in 1667, while, in 1849, Edgar Allan Poe wrote a poem called *Eldorado*, about an old knight who spends his life searching for it. Poe's poem also references the Mountains of the Moon, which are in Africa, so it's ironic that Joseph Conrad's *Heart Of Darkness*, which is set in Africa, echoes the legend by having the protagonists being part of the Eldorado Exploring Expedition.

Voltaire's *Candide* has a sequence set in El Dorado, which he casts as a city built of material finer than gold and diamond, and this is then echoed in the *Dr Who* story *Death to the Daleks*, which implies that aliens built such cities. Of course modern 'reality' shows on what is increasingly inaccurately called The History Channel, such as *Ancient Aliens*, have tended to suggest the same thing about El Dorado and Cibola.

On a more historical note, Werner Herzog's *Aguirre, the Wrath of God* is about a Conquistador (played by Klaus Kinski) who leads his followers to disaster in a search for the lost city of gold, and making it almost finished off both director and star. A happier film version of the legend came along in the form of a Dreamworks animated film, *The Road to El Dorado*, though the movie owes more to Cortez's campaigns in Mexico than to the search for El Dorado in South America.

El Dorado has been mentioned in quite a few Clive Cussler novels, since his Dirk Pitt series always has some historical artefact or treasure to find, but the closest he has come to doing it as a main story is in 1994's *Inca Gold*, which concerns the search around the Chachapoya region of northern Peru for Inca treasures first stolen from the Spanish by Sir Francis Drake, and swept back inland during a tsunami. The spin-off novel *Serpent*, by Cussler and Paul Kemprecos, also deals with pre-Columbian artefacts in Mexico.

The most memorable version, to a certain generation at least, is probably the Franco-Japanese TV series *The Mysterious Cities of Gold*, which was a huge hit in the 1980s. This was about a group of kids and Conquistadores, who were searching for the Seven Cities of Gold, of which El Dorado was merely one, and who got caught up in strife between the cities, helped by the daughter of an Inca high priest. Unusually, not all the cities were in South America in the series, but were spread around the world. A sequel series aired in 2012/13.

To a certain extent, the *Indiana Jones* and *Tomb Raider* franchises could well be said to have been influenced by the myth of El Dorado. Both the beginning of *Raiders of the Lost Ark* and the latter part of *Kingdom of the Crystal Skull* involve treasures in lost South American settlements, while in the game *Indiana Jones Adventure World*, El Dorado is the objective.

The treacherous Satipo, played by Alfred Molina at the start of *Raiders of the Lost Ark*, may well be named for Satipa the Muisca chief.

*Tomb Raider: Underworld* also delves heavily into South American lost cities, and especially Cibola, in its guise as Xibalba. *The Journeyman Project 3* is another game set in El Dorado, and also links it to aliens, while *Uncharted: Drake's Fortune* is based on a search for El Dorado, and for Francis Drake's semi-pirate treasure.

## THE TRUTH IS OUT THERE

Although the Spanish never found a lost city full of gold, they did discover lots of other things, including avocados, and the Amazon River. The river was discovered by Pizarro's younger brother during his search for El Dorado in 1540. His 340 soldiers were attacked by a group of female warriors at a riverside, and so he named the river after the Amazons of Greek mythology.

A golden model raft found between Bogota and Guatavita in 1969 provided proof of the stories about the chief taking to the lake in a raft, and since it was itself buried, also provided proof that the Muisca did not view gold as something to be hoarded, the way Europeans did. They saw it as something to be offered to the gods; its value wasn't in its rarity, or as a commodity, but in its holy *colour*, the colour of sunlight. For them, it was all about the religious symbolism of the material. To this end, they would alloy it with other metals to get the right colour to sacrifice, so it was never worth as much as the Spanish would have thought anyway. For example, the model raft found in 1969 turned out to be only 63 per cent gold, 16 per cent silver, and 20 per cent copper, with the rest in impurities.

What the Muisca were really sacrificing was their time and effort, because this showed their faith and devotion. This is why they were happy to give it away.

The biggest irony of the Spanish obsession with finding the hoard belonging to the Muisca is that they were looking at things the wrong way round, and so walked right on past the source of the gold on pretty much every expedition.

The Muisca never mined gold. What they mined was salt, a vital commodity in such a humid region, and which could not be obtained from seawater, as their territory was 300 miles from the coast. Having a monopoly on this vital-to-life substance, they traded it with the people who lived along the Rio Magdalena for clothes and gold. The Muisca gold came from veins along the Rio Magdalena, and was panned and mined by the very people of whom the Spanish only wanted to know 'which way to the Muisca?'

In the end, the Spanish took around 80 tons of gold from the Muisca. Most of it was shipped home, but some was used in churches, such as Santa Clara Church in Bogota, which is covered in gold leaf made from Muisca gold. It could be seen as an offering to the Catholic god, just as it used to be to the Muisca gods. Ironically, in 1575, Friar Vincente Brigiara, a priest in a Muisca village, left in his will an instruction that the people of his village should be paid 100 gold pesos each, in restitution for abuses against them. Muisca artefacts were melted down, made into coins and paid back to their original owners.

## WHERE IS IT NOW?

Most of the treasure looted from South America was shipped back to Spain and entered into the economy there. Some was used in palaces and churches across Spanish and Portuguese-held South America, and much of it is still there. Likewise, given that the Muisca liked to sacrifice their gold artefacts both to Lake Guatavita and to burial, a lot of it is doubtless still hidden from history.

There are a few Muisca artefacts in the British Museum in London, but there's a lot more of it at the Museo del Oro del Banco de la República – usually just referred to as the Museo del Oro – in Bogota, Colombia. The museum is both an archaeological centre of conservation and a tourist attraction.

El Dorado never existed in the sense that popular culture believes. Yes, there were settlements with gold, and there were cities of various sizes – and some perhaps still to be found – but there was never a city devoted to storing imaginative levels of gold.

The real, original source of the Golden Man's wealth, however, is not a city. It's the Magdalena River itself. So, if you want to try your hand at acquiring some of the gold from El Dorado's supply and storehouse, you need to try panning or mining along the Rio Magdalena in Colombia. You can also visit Lake Guatavita, though excavating is forbidden.

## THE OPPOSITION IN YOUR WAY

Nowadays there are fewer treasure hunters making actual expeditions to South American mountaintops in search of El Dorado, thanks to wider knowledge of the truth. However, there are still many scientific and archaeological explorers looking for ruins and relics of past civilizations who will not be happy at your interfering with such places in search of fortune and glory.

Sadly, there are also looters. So many sites were looted in the 20th century that the gold they were dumping onto the market actually caused a crash in the world's gold market in the 1970s. Because these looters – often paramilitaries, rebels and drug gangs seeking capital – needed plain gold to dump on said market, they melted down their finds, destroying forever their value as historical pieces that might lead to further understanding.

Many parts of South America – and especially Colombia – have been afflicted with drug and kidnapping cartels. Colombia's Medellín and Cali cartels may have been the most famous drug cartels, but were far from the only ones. Those cartels were put out of business in the late 1990s (movies leave the general public thinking they're still current), and – contrary to popular belief – Colombia is no longer the world's biggest cocaine producer, but there are still many smaller yet equally vicious drug gangs around.

The largest producer of cocaine in the world for the illicit drug trade is now the other country you're most likely to be looking for a lost city in: Peru. As well as these notorious gangs, you run the risk of falling foul of rebel and guerrilla groups who've still been fighting the Cold War, and other older class wars. In Colombia, there is FARC, Fuerzas Armadas Revolucionarias de Colombia, or Revolutionary Forces of Colombia. FARC is probably the biggest revolutionary government-in-opposition group in South America, and raises most of its funds by 'taxing' the drug cartels, and, in more recent years, other local and international corporations. They have been heavily into kidnap for ransom and follow the pattern more common to African paramilitary armies of pressing children into their forces.

These days FARC's stronghold is mostly in south-eastern Colombia, with a lesser outpost in the north-west. Thankfully the Muisca region is in the north-east.

Peru has the Shining Path, a Maoist insurgent group notorious for attacks on both government and civilians, in the forms of kidnapping for ransom, enslavement of local farmers, rocket and bomb attacks on government forces and utilities companies, and so on. In recent years, their leaders have been captured or killed, and have acknowledged that the war is lost, but some individual cells continue to fight, while others have just gone outright into the cocaine business and become private cartels. They are now the world's largest producer of cocaine, and are based between Lima and Cusco, which unfortunately is right on the way to Machu Picchu.

There are also plenty of everyday criminal dangers in Colombia, particularly drugging by a natural Mickey Finn called burundanga (made from tree sap) in order to commit robberies, rapes, kidnappings, robbery by fake cops, and armed robbery.

That said, things have improved a lot in the past decade, largely due to an excellent and trustworthy military and Federal police. Unfortunately local cops are still less reliable, with bullying and soliciting of bribes commonplace, though this can be handy if you're flush with cash and want to hire some private security.

If, like Indiana Jones, you're worried about snakes, you should be aware that Colombia is home to 295 species of them, several venomous. The most common is the coral snake, which is the red, white and black-striped snake you most often see represented in movies – though the movie ones are usually harmless milk snakes standing in so as to be less dangerous to the cast and crew. Coral snakes aren't aggressive, but can be quite easily overlooked until stepped on – which is not a good idea to do barefoot or in sandals.

Colombia is also home to aggressive eyelash pit vipers, but their venom isn't generally fatal to healthy adults – just unpleasant enough to make you wish it was – and the Fer-de-Lance, which is aggressive and dangerous. And then there is the especially dangerous and aggressive bushmaster, the longest viper in the world. Fortunately it's also rare and nocturnal. Unfortunately they're also around in Peru.

Health-wise, it's recommended to be aware of and vaccinated against (if possible) malaria, rabies, dengue fever and yellow fever.

# AZTEC GOLD

## WHAT IS IT?

When people who think about 'Montezuma's gold', they usually think about the treasury of the Aztec capital, Tenochtitlan, evacuated from the city on the orders of the Emperor Moctezuma (as it would more accurately be spelled) when the Spanish Conquistadores led by Hernán Cortés turned up in 1520.

According to legend, the hoard consisted not only of gold, though that is what the Spaniards were mostly interested in, but also silver, gems and turquoise, which was used a lot in Aztec jewellery and art.

There is, however, another Montezuma's treasure, this dating only from the 19th century. In this case, it would be the product of a gold mine in Arizona, in the vicinity of a mountain nicknamed 'Montezuma's Head'. This would amount to a much smaller hoard than the legendary Aztec treasure, however.

# HOW MUCH IS IT WORTH TO YOU?

If it exists, the Aztec treasure would be worth billions of pounds, let alone dollars, as it consists of several tons of gold, plus other precious stones and metals. It's said to have been more than enough to fill a room, and it took thousands of slaves to carry it from Tenochtitlan to its eventual hiding place. It was estimated to have been worth $10 million in 1914, and one 1990s entrepreneur believed there to be 45,000lb of gold in the haul – which would be worth over £5 billion (about $8.5 billion) today.

The stolen output of the Montezuma's Head mine would be nothing like as much, but still not inconsiderable. It would have amounted to thousands of dollars of gold in the early 19th century and, by extension, millions today.

# THE STORY

There are 'Montezuma's Gold' legends throughout the US, mainly the south-west and desert states – New Mexico, Arizona, California, Nevada and Colorado – pretty much all the way along the Colorado River. Partly this was because many tribal leaders called themselves Montezuma, so all their goods got assumed to be *a* Montezuma's treasure. The other reason is because of an Apache revolt against Mexican gold miners.

During the Mexican–American War, a Mexican noble, Don Joaquin, enslaved some of the local Apache populace to dig for gold in a mine in the Sierra Estrella mountains in Arizona, to fund the Mexican war effort. In 1847, the US Army began making serious inroads into the Estrellas, and threatened the mine. Don Joaquin began having the mine's output hidden in a canyon at a hill called Montezuma's Head. The Apache saw their chance and launched a revolt. Caught between the Apache and the US Army, most of the Mexicans were killed, the rest fleeing south of the border. Legend has it that they left the gold behind.

Around 1880, a survivor returned with a map, intending to recover the gold, but the Apache were still in a bad mood with Mexicans, and he failed.

From 1895 onwards, local papers have occasionally published stories of people finding at least part of it, but these stories stopped before World War II, so most likely it was all recovered, if it existed. Certainly the US Army would have made sure to gather as much as possible when the Mexicans were routed in 1847.

None of which has anything to do with the Aztec emperor of 1520.

The Spanish under Hernán Cortés were at first welcomed by Moctezuma – albeit warily – because they fit the description in a prophecy about some gods who were supposed to visit from the heavens. In fact, Moctezuma had reportedly promised them the treasure, having already shown it to them as a symbol of his strength and power, describing it as 'all the treasures of the world'.

When the Spaniards came to the treasure vault to take possession, the loot was gone. Moctezuma and his people had twigged that the Spaniards weren't gods, and changed their minds about giving them their entire gold supply.

The Conquistadores then embarked on the usual torture-for-the-treasure-location spree that they did all across South America. Most Aztecs wouldn't talk, but eventually they managed to get hold of some chatterboxes willing to say that the gold had all been smuggled out, borne by slaves and guarded by elite warriors.

These Aztecs suggested that the treasure had been taken back to their tribal homeland, Aztlán, north of Tenochtitlan, to be hidden away from the reach of the Spanish forever, by being dumped in a lake.

## PREVIOUS SEARCHES IN FACT AND FICTION

Cortés started his search immediately, focusing on Mexican lakes. In fact, he was so convinced by the torture confessions that over the next couple of decades he searched 5,000 lakes, without success.

This mention of a lake later got confused with the search for El Dorado, and the whole matter of the Muisca treasures in Lake Guatavita in Colombia. So the search drifted south, becoming part of the search for El Dorado.

While prospecting for gold in Arizona in 1913, a guy named Freddy Crystal was hit on the head by a crowbar, and had what he called a 'Panorama', but we'd call a dream or hallucination.

He saw the evacuation of Moctezuma's treasure, carried by slaves, escorted by warriors. They brought it north to Utah, and hid it in a cave. When the vision faded, he was left with an image of an Aztec petroglyph showing the course of the Colorado River.

Freddy was so affected by this vision that he gave up prospecting to research the Aztecs. He found that their treasure was supposedly smuggled north to Aztlán, the original Aztec homeland, and sealed in a cave watched over by warriors selected to be eternal guardians. This seemed to match Freddy's vision, and he thought a petroglyph of a serpent on a red wall was a marker to the treasure's location. Freddy then searched the serpentine canyons of the Colorado River in Utah for months, before giving up.

Months later, he saw a newspaper story about a Mormon leader called Levi E. Young, who had taken a picture of a petroglyph near Kanab, in Johnson County, Utah. Freddy was sure it was the glyph from his vision.

So Freddy Crystal cycled to Kanab (which had, a year before, seen the introduction of the world's first democratically-elected all-female governing body, their town council) claiming that the Aztec Emperor Moctezuma's gold was buried nearby. To his amazement, the local Mormons weren't interested in imminent enrichment. The only person willing to put Freddy up while he searched was a rancher called Oscar Robison, in return for a stake in any treasure found, which Freddy had described as $10 million worth of gold bars, shields, plates and jewellery of emeralds and rubies.

Everybody else thought Freddy was a crazy freeloader, but in 1916 he found someone who recognized the petroglyph and knew where it had been: Johnson's Canyon. It had been dynamited a couple of years earlier to make room for a cattle shelter, and no longer existed.

Freddy then disappeared for several years, going to Mexico City (formerly the Aztec capital of Tenochtitlan), where he sneaked into the basement of a monastery that was being demolished and found Spanish colonial records referring to an Aztec captured with a map in the 1520s. The map was with the documents, and showed a marsh below a cliff, which was surrounded by seven mountains, one of which had a set of steps on it. Freddy reasoned these would lead to the walled-up cave entrance from his vision – and he also thought the mountains on the map resembled Johnson's Canyon near Kanab.

When he returned to Johnson's Canyon, Freddy found he had the interest of some of the younger cowboys – in particular Robison's 16-year-old son-in-law Alvin Judd, and his friend Cowhide Adams. On Thanksgiving of 1922, they found a spot on Sheep Mountain, which Freddy recognized as being the point of view shown on the map, where the mountains lined up with the drawing.

They climbed a stepped slope, at the top of which was an indentation in the rock face. They used pocket knives to expose limestone mortar sealing the cave. This must have been artificial, as the nearest natural limestone was two dozen miles away. A rock fell on Freddy's leg, but they discovered a short corridor containing a couple of statues (which have since disappeared) and a pair of sandals, with another false wall at the end.

Freddy was suddenly popular in Kanab when the trio announced their find. The whole town pulled together to help excavate, in return for shares in anything found, and decamped to a tent city in Johnson's Canyon. Only a few people remained to make things seem normal, so that outsiders – such as legal authorities, rivals and tax inspectors – wouldn't get wind of what was happening.

Behind the wall was a series of caves, all separated by constructed walls, and the occasional rock-fall booby trap, some of which had previously collapsed. Mule bones and at least one human skeleton were found, but no gold. Over the next two years, people gave up and drifted back to town. In 1924, the final cave was opened, and found to contain one Spanish helmet, one rotted moccasin, and that was it.

Freddy decided the caves were a temporary storage facility while a proper vault was prepared, and wanted to re-dig *under* the cave system. Unfortunately, this was where the earth from the excavation had been dumped, which would have made digging there even harder. The townsfolk were disillusioned and annoyed, and all went back to their normal lives.

Freddy Crystal himself disappeared. No-one knows whether he was murdered for his map, died from an accident or animal attack while searching on his own, or just climbed into a bottle somewhere and died in obscurity.

Only Alvin Judd kept the faith, and continued searching around the Johnson Canyon area for 30 years. He eventually inherited the farm from Robison, and his family inherited it from him.

In 1982, a group led by Raymond Dillman approached the Judd family, looking for petroglyphs of three animals with three circles, leading to a spiral glyph with a bullseye at the centre. The Judds showed them the glyphs were right there, and Dillman said this meant Montezuma's treasure was on their ranch.

Dillman had spent 16 years studying 'Peralta Stones': stones with glyphs, which had been found in Arizona during a road construction in the 1950s. Most folklorists and journalists had thought they might be a map to a mythical Lost Dutchman's Mine, but Dillman knew better. He was half-Latino and half-Apache, and was sure he had deciphered the markings as being a guide to 'Montezuma's treasure'. He wasn't specific about which Montezuma it referred to.

His translation had led him to Johnson County, and now he and Brent and Bruce Judd used a bulldozer to shift the spoil heap from the 1920s dig.

Eventually they found some burnt bones, and a clay pot containing 213 turquoise beads, below a rock with a channel worn in it. Dillman and the Judds immediately assumed this was an Aztec sacrificial stone, and that the slaves who had carried the treasure were killed on it. Below this were small caves, 8ft deep, 2 or 3ft wide, filled with sand, and covered with flat stones. Skeletons were buried in them, and showed signs of cannibalism.

The Judd family still believes this treasure is on their land. They also believe it is too dangerous to search for. Local Native American tribes have warned against searching (saying it's 'not time for it to be found').

Kanab native and millionaire Brandt Child, meanwhile, thought it was under a lake 6 miles north of Kanab, on Highway 89. He and his son Lon came to believe that 2–8,000 Aztec warriors (in 1991 he believed 2,000, but it had increased to 8,000 by 2001!) came north and dammed a river in order to create Three Lakes, a single 35ft-deep lake in Kane County, 10 miles from Johnson's Canyon.

This theory says the treasure is in a cave in the sandstone cliff, with the entrance now underwater.

The Childs brought in a friend who had diving experience, Tony Thurber, to explore a tunnel leading from the Three Lakes water under the cliff. Thurber got into difficulties with the underwater currents and refused to dive again. In 1989 Child then brought in a team of four from San Francisco, armed with sonar, metal detectors, communications and tether lines. Their air tanks and compressors kept failing, but in the end one diver ran out of safety line about 65ft into the tunnel, just as his metal detector registered something. He had also dreamed the night before that he swam into a cave where an Aztec warrior threw a spear at him.

A fortnight later, they tried again, having been promised half of any finds made. This time they brought longer safety lines and extra air tanks. When they got into the tunnel, according to Brandt in a 1991 interview with local paper *The Deseret News*, 'They saw figures and forms and they couldn't breathe. We could hear them screaming to pull them back out. All of the divers who tried to get in had the same experience.'

The Childs' next step was to drain the lake, but the US Fish and Wildlife Department vetoed the plan, as the lake is home to a rare and protected species: The Kanab Amber Snail. Lon Child believes this was a sacred species to the Aztecs, the Golden Snail, who put it there as a special sort of guardian. Killing one snail would mean a fine of $50,000.

Childs then tried to drill down from the top of the cliff, but the drill's operator was spooked by apparently seeing an Apache spear-carrier watching him. Nevertheless, after a test bore, the drill bit had some flakes of gold on it. A camera was sent down, and the operator claimed to see figures on screen, which may have been statues, and shadowy piles of who-knows-what. The camera operator then died of a heart attack that night, and his wife followed shortly after. The drill operator (the cameraman's brother) never came back for his equipment.

The Childs claimed to have been visited by a tribal elder who warned them that the treasure is intended for Native Americans, to unite the tribes when the time is right. Supposedly when he left, his footsteps in the dirt just faded away. Brandt Child retired from treasure hunting in 1996, and died in 2002, when his car hit a horse. Naturally some people think this treasure is cursed, and that only a 'Chosen One' will be able to find it, when the time is right.

Nevertheless, Lon Child and a documentary maker called Mike Wiest are trying to raise funds to send some ROVs (remotely operated underwater vehicles) into Three Lakes to seek out and film the caverns. Lon Child now estimates the treasure to be worth over $3 billion.

Aztec gold turns up a lot in fiction, most famously in the movie *Pirates of the Caribbean: Curse of the Black Pearl*, in which the gold is in the form of coins that have been cursed to make the finder an immortal zombie. It has also featured in movies such as the no-budget *Montezuma's Lost Gold* in 1978, and the comedy-horror *House II: The Second Story*.

Likewise, if you type 'Montezuma's treasure' into Amazon, you'll find a lot of pulp adventure stories and YA novels about characters adventuring in search of the treasure, usually in the south-western US. The first such example was probably *Montezuma's Gold Mines* by Fred Ober, in 1888. In this one, Montezuma and his gold are described as Mayan, which doesn't bode well. *The Lost Gold of the Montezumas* by William Stoddard – which was actually brought back into print just a couple of years ago – came out in 1897, and bonded the legend with the Battle of the Alamo.

Arguably the output of the gold mine in the 1998 movie The *Mask of Zorro* is influenced by the legend of the Montezuma's Head hoard.

## THE TRUTH IS OUT THERE

Cortés was told that Moctezuma had sent his treasures to be hidden in caves back in the Atzec homeland of Aztlàn, somewhere north of their capital, Tenochtitlan. With hindsight, and the reading of histories that Cortés ignored, we can actually now tell that Moctezuma's folks were telling the Spanish conqueror a fib on the level of claiming that storks delivered new babies.

There was a legend among the Aztecs, and six related tribes – all part of the Nahuatl culture overall – that said they originally lived in seven cave systems, called Chicomoztoc ('place of seven caves' – they weren't big on poetic licence for names). The Nahuatl then were dragged out and enslaved by the Azteca Chicomoztoca, the rulers of what would become the Aztec tribe, at Aztlán. The god Huitzilopochtli then led the Nahuatl slaves – including the lower caste Azteca – away in a flight from Aztlán. The god also insisted that this latter group hide by not calling themselves Azteca ('people from Aztlán') but 'Mexica Tenochta' instead. So far so good; they came from Aztlán, they could go back to hide stuff there, right?

Well, no. The flight from Aztlán was said to have happened centuries before Cortés's time, and so the Aztecs themselves – who were given their ancestors' name back by the Victorians, to separate them from modern Mexicans, to whom the Mexica (whom we now call Aztecs) had given their name – had actually forgotten where it was. Moctezuma did indeed send men to Aztlán, but not carrying treasure to hide there. He sent expeditions to search for it, and to try to find the place, because it was a lost legend even to him and his contemporaries. In fact he probably was hoping to find an ancient lost city full of loot, just as the Spanish were.

Nobody's quite sure where Aztlán actually was, though believers in Aztec treasure in Arizona like to think that it was in the vicinity of the Sunset Crater Volcano. They say 'The Aztec calendar's Year One is AD 1054 , and That was when Sunset Crater was widened in an eruption.' Unfortunately for that theory, the Nahuatl started immigrating into the central Valley of Mexico in the 6th century AD, and the Mexica Tenochta really only finished settling in 1248, so they were never driven out of anywhere as a result of one event. Also, it turns out that the Arizona volcano erupted in 1085, and the Aztecs had started their calendar from the sighting of the supernova that formed the Crab Nebula – an event also recorded by Arab and Chinese astronomers.

In the 1570s, a Spanish friar called Diego Durán made a study of Aztec records, and wrote about Moctezuma's assembly of warriors and wise men, who were sent to find Aztlán. He also left some illustrations showing that the expedition did find a location that matched the unique characteristics of Aztlán, including a humped mountain rising from a lake. Unfortunately, Durán was writing so soon after the conquest of Mexico that the country hadn't been mapped yet. This meant that he couldn't actually tell us where the Aztec illustration referred to.

The records all agreed, however, that Aztlán was '150 leagues from Tenochtitlan', which narrows things down a bit. Though we usually think of a league as 3 miles, a Mexican league was 'as far as a man can walk in an hour', which, accounting for terrain and load is more like a mile and a bit. The one humped mountain rising from a lake within such a range north of Tenochtitlan is Cerro Culiacán, a shield volcano on Lake Yuriria, in Guanajuato province. That's probably Aztlán, and there are no lost cities full of gold there either.

Aztec cosmology didn't have a protective golden snail either. The moon god did sometimes carry a snail shell on his back, but more often a seashell. That said, just to really throw a cat among the pigeons, the *Inca* did have golden snail protective amulets … Sadly it's Moctezuma who's said to have left a treasure, and not the legendary Inca, Manco Cápac.

The Kanab amber snail was only discovered at Three Lakes in 1991, which is ironic, as they had previously been rendered extinct at Kanab itself. There is another population of them at Vasey's Paradise in Colorado (which is part of Grand Canyon National Park.) Someone released a flock of snail-eating geese into the lake, but they were rounded up before much damage was done. The geese were sent to an animal sanctuary, but whoever put them there was never found – though it wouldn't take Sherlock Holmes to figure out a list of possible suspects.

Some of the caves and rooms found in Johnson's Canyon still exist, and can be visited, though the entrance is well hidden and almost impossible to spot unless you or a guide already knows where it is. Most of the caves have been backfilled and are inaccessible.

Although the Judds' discovery of pit burials showing signs of cannibalism, and at least one skeleton (nicknamed 'Smiley' when he was found in 1922), had raised hopes that these were proof of Aztec sacrifices, carbon dating has proved them to be Neolithic. They date from 2000 BC, which is 3,500 years before Cortés had his eye on Moctezuma's gold.

What of the cursed divers and drillers? Well, Thurman was certainly cautious and wise to not get involved with such vicious currents. The dive team have never come forward to say, 'Hey. We were scared off by Aztec ghosts.' We only have the Childs' word that anyone saw such things, which do make for a more fun story.

The drill-operator who died of a heart attack seems to be a conflation of two different stories, depending on whether you believe Brandt Child's son Lon (who says it was an operator they hired), or nephew Robert (who says it was just some other random prospector).

The Montezuma's Head Mine output is a different matter, although people have appended the Aztec gold legend to that as well. There are three different versions of the tale, with different names for the guy running the mine (Ortega, or two different men with the surname Campoy). In one version, a guy called Campoy found 3,000lb of gold, including 20 gold bars, and buried them in a cave while the US Army and the Apache were after him. He took a local elderly guide with him, then killed him so he couldn't talk, but himself died in his sleep. The second version casts the mine owner as Ortega, but is otherwise the same story, except that the murdered guide is a young boy. The third version has a Don Joaquim Campoy run the mine, and lead a mule train on a trail from Montezuma Peak to Montezuma's Head, then on to a box canyon at the southern end of the Sierra Estrellas. He then likewise died before returning for it when the heat cooled off.

Arizona has one of the world's highest densities of local buried treasure legends, from Aztec gold, to lost prospectors' strikes, to multiple Lost Dutchmen's Mines (a traditional American folktale). It's also got quite a high density of actual gold veins.

That said, some elements of the Montezuma's Head stories have some backing. For example, there were only three effective trails that could have been used to cross the Estrellas – the northern end's foothills, a pass below Circus Ridge, and the one mentioned in the story. More interestingly, there have been finds of buried silver in the area, particularly in the 1960s and 1970s, when treasure-hunting with metal detectors became fashionable.

Somebody certainly buried that silver between the 1840s and 1880s. Since Mexico is one of the two biggest silver producers in the world (Peru is the other), it's likely that there is a core of truth to them having hidden funds during the Mexican–American War, to keep it out of US hands. Since the folktales that grew out of it all talked about vast piles of gold, there's no record of how much silver was actually deposited, and therefore no way to know whether it was all found by the 1980s.

## WHERE IS IT NOW?

Moctezuma's treasure was found by the Conquistadores back in the day: In fact, it was simply handed over. Like other Mesoamerican nations, the Aztecs put a religious significance on gold, rather than a monetary value. When King Ferdinand of Spain needed it to fund the spreading by fire and sword of the word of God, and Cortés declared war on Moctezuma in 1518, Moctezuma turned over his treasury in 1519.

The Spanish, as usual, simply couldn't believe that someone would hand over all their gold, so assumed there must be more stashed away. Moctezuma's brother attacked and drew Cortés into a war, which convinced the Europeans that the Aztecs were defending loot. By 1521 the Spanish had won their war, but found no more treasure.

This was repeated all over South America, culminating in Pizarro's conquest of the Inca, who thought of gold as the tears of the sun.

About 20 per cent of Moctezuma's gold was shipped back to Spain. The rest was melted down and turned into coinage for the colonies and décor for churches. Cortés also managed to lose a fair amount of treasure when fighting his way out of Tenochtitlan in 1520. Tenochtitlan was an island city in a lake, and when Cortés's deputy started a massacre, the Aztecs rebelled and started knocking down causeways so the Spanish couldn't get away. As Cortés fled along one remaining causeway, his army lost a lot of treasure and most of their equipment.

Over time, the lake and marshes became drained and the treasures were found a little piece at a time as Mexico City rose on the site. Such finds still continue today during construction work. One of the biggest finds came in March 1981, when a construction worker found a piece of gold weighing around 4lb, and shaped to fit in a Conquistador's armour. It was valued at $32,000 in 1981, and now resides in the National Institute of Anthropology, in Mexico City.

European explorers had always overestimated how much gold the South American civilizations actually had. They always assumed that there would always be more to find, but that did not make it so in reality.

## THE OPPOSITION IN YOUR WAY

The actual physical structure of Mexico City is the biggest obstacle, after the fact that there pretty much isn't any treasure hidden by Moctezuma. The city's built on top of what used to be the Aztec capital, and on the site of the lake into which Cortés lost his loot while legging it from a war crime gone wrong. Somewhere under the city there may still be loot that fell into Lake Texcoco along with dying Conquistadores and their cannons in the summer of 1520, but there's no way to search for it without demolishing the city.

Since most of the finds over the past century or so have been made by construction workers, your best bet is pretty much to apply for a job with a construction company in Mexico City, and hope to stumble across something while digging up a road.

Although there has been, at least, silver lying around the area of Montezuma's Head in Arizona, none of it matched the description of the legends, so you will have to put aside your preconceptions about the gold, and keep an eye for hidden silver.

Silver ingots are pretty small compared to a mountain range, and so the odds on finding any are long – and lengthened by the fact that the treasure that has been found doesn't have a legend attached.

Arizona is also one of the hottest desert parts of the Southwest, easily reaching 115 degrees in the shade in summer, so proper clothing, sunblock and a good supply of bottled water is essential. Wildlife-wise, there is a good population of rattlesnakes, mainly in the form of the western rattlesnake.

Then there's the Arizona bark scorpion, a straw-coloured little

EL DORADO AND THE AZTEC GOLD

# WHY DID IT HAVE TO BE SNAKES?

There are venomous snakes, spiders and other assorted creepy-crawlies in various parts of the world, and of course they especially love to hang out in caves, tunnels, jungle ruins and basically the kinds of places where treasure hunters and archaeologists are most likely to be stomping around in search of ancient booty and artefacts. Most people tend to call these creatures poisonous, rather than the correct term of venomous, so let's first clean up the confusion over terms.

If a creature bites you, and you get sick or die, it was venomous. If *you* bite *it*, and you get sick or die, then it was poisonous. More technically, a venom requires to be injected directly into the bloodstream to take effect, and should not be effective when ingested, whereas a poison is secreted and is effective when ingested and/or touched.

There's no reason why a creature can't be both; the rhabdophis family of snakes, common to Southeast Asia, are the only type of snake to be both poisonous and venomous, but many insects are as well, though mostly only to each other.

The most venomous snake in the world is the Belcher's sea snake, found in the waters around Indonesia and Australia. One venomous bite is toxic enough to kill a thousand people. Fortunately, three quarters of the time they bite without injecting venom and are quite docile in disposition. Most of their victims, therefore, tend to be fishermen who get them tangled in nets. On land, thankfully the most dangerous snakes in the world are mostly found in Australia, and none of the treasures in this book will take you there. The exception is the Blue Krait, which also lives in the Philippines and other parts of Southeast Asia.

There isn't really a simple definitive way to identify a venomous snake in general terms – they don't all have coloured markings or an unusual type of fangs. That said, the important thing is to look out for the general type of snakes in the area. Cobras, found across Africa and Asia, have a distinctive hood that can flare open. Rattlesnakes, found in North and Central America, have the distinctive bone rings on their tails that make the famous rattling sound and often a black diamond pattern on their backs. Vipers, found worldwide, have a very triangular-shaped head (rattlesnakes are also a type of viper). So, overall, if you see a snake with either a hood or whose head is particularly triangular, be extra careful.

varmint never bigger than an inch and a half in length, but one of the most dangerous scorpions in the US, and the only one that the government considers a serious threat to life. These guys like to hang upside-down from branches/rocks/cave roofs ... Though most adults survive a sting, it is one of the most painful venoms around, and can take days for the pain to subside.

Mountain lions are a potential threat in the, well, mountains. These big cats can easily take down a human. Fortunately humans are not their usual choice of prey, but attacks do happen, in which case the cougar will go for a bite to the throat or neck. If one takes an interest in you, the best thing to do is make yourself look big and threatening – shout and throw things at it.

Another danger to watch for in either Arizona or Utah is the actual medieval Black Death, aka bubonic plague. It's carried by fleas on prairie dogs, rock squirrels and other cute little rodents across the Southwest. The disease kills the rodents so quickly you're unlikely to meet an infected live one, but if you camp near a nest – a prairie dogtown – you might be in flea-jumping distance. There are about a dozen human cases a year in the region. Luckily bubonic plague responds to modern medicine. They can carry rabies as well, so make sure your inoculations are up to date.

There were a lot of open mines in the 19th century around the Sierra Estrellas, and a lot of them still are, albeit empty. Be careful not to fall in. In Utah, the biggest problem is that there never was any Aztec treasure there.

Aside from the fifty-grand-a-pop snails at Three Lakes, the region is also home to a reasonable population of rattlesnakes – a subspecies called the Great Basin rattlesnake – and people have died from rattler bites while exploring the Johnson Canyon site.

The same snakes, and diseased rodents mentioned above, are also valid warnings for Utah.

# Captain Kidd and the Pirates' Treasure

✗ CAPTAIN KIDD AND THE PIRATES' TREASURE

## WHAT IS IT?

Iron-bound wooden sea chests, filled to the brim with gold and silver coins – doubloons, pieces of eight, and silver dollars – looted from ships and the early Spanish colonies in the Americas, or, in Kidd's case, the Indian Ocean, and buried for safekeeping either on the east coast of North America, or on Caribbean islands.

You've seen pirate movies, right?

## HOW MUCH IS IT WORTH TO YOU?

As far as the average haul plundered from merchant ships by gentlemen of fortune goes, probably nothing. Zip, nada, nowt, zero.

The thing most people don't take into consideration is the nature of what pirates took from the ships they raided. Despite what Hollywood shows us, the Caribbean and Atlantic have never been exclusively the territory of treasure ships ferrying gold and gems between noblemen's estates in Europe and the colonies.

The vast percentage of shipping has always carried what were the most valuable trading commodities and practical supplies of the day: sugar, molasses, tobacco, rum, weapons, tools, emigrants and slaves. Slaves would often be freed and invited to join the pirates, while other commodities would simply be sold.

None of these 'treasures', therefore, would suit being buried anyway, and certainly wouldn't be shiny collectibles if you dug them up after 300 years.

That said, there are exceptions to every rule, and one legendary pirate who actually did properly bury his treasure is Captain William Kidd. The East India Company estimated Kidd's total treasure to be worth £400,000 in 1701. That's about £6.576 billion in today's money. They were revising upwards for the sake of their insurance claims, mind you, as we know that what he actually buried was worth $4.2 million today.

Another exception is a legendary treasure buried by a non-legendary pirate: The Treasure of Lima, stolen by Captain William Thompson in 1820. This treasure consisted of 113 gold religious statues (at least one a life-sized Virgin Mary with child), 200 chests of jewels, 273 swords with jewelled hilts, 1,000 diamonds, some solid gold crowns, 150 chalices, and hundreds of gold and silver bars. It was valued at tens of millions of dollars in 1820, and is usually referenced today as being worth around $160 million.

## THE STORY

Typically, some gentlemen of fortune on the High Seas have attacked and looted ships bearing treasure from the Americas back to England or Spain, and then decided to lie low while the heat cooled off. So as not to be caught with the loot, they buried it on an island to keep it safe. Later, they would have gone back and collected it, but either were caught or killed in battle, and so the treasure remains buried.

Islands and towns up and down the east coast of North America, from the Caribbean to Nova Scotia, have a plethora of local legends about buried pirate treasure, usually attributed to either

Captain Kidd or Blackbeard, although pretty much every pirate has a buried treasure legend attached to their name somewhere.

The most famous pirate to have actually buried treasure was Scotsman William Kidd. In 1695, he returned from the Colonies (having married a rich widow in order to go into business, and that not having worked out well) and persuaded several government figures from the ruling Whig Party – including Lord Bellomont, Governor of Massachusetts Bay and New York – and even King William III to invest in a proposal for a Privateering and pirate-hunting expedition to the East Indies.

Kidd got a Letter of Marque, authorizing him to attack French ships, and set off in the *Adventure Galley*, a warship with a pirate crew. What could possibly go wrong?

Well, Kidd, for a start – being an arrogant bully who beat a sailor to death with an iron bucket for no real reason, Kidd soon turned pirate himself, and attacked and plundered British and Indian ships. This culminated in the capture of the *Quedagh Merchant*, a treasure ship of the Mughals of India.

The authorities of several countries were soon after him for his crimes, and so Kidd sailed the *Quedagh Merchant* back to his old Colonial haunts, but ran the ship aground (he really was a rubbish captain). He acquired a new ship, and ran up and down the coast burying portions of the *Quedagh* Merchant's treasure in Anguilla and Hispaniola, before returning to Long Island and burying more treasure on Gardiner's Island, and possibly elsewhere too.

Kidd was captured, but he tried to bribe various Colonial governors with different amounts of treasure from the stashes he had buried. He offered amounts of £30,000, £40,000 and – after his trial – even the location of £100,000 in treasure in return for a pardon. It didn't work He was taken back to London for trial, and found guilty of both piracy and the murder of the crewman he whacked over the head with a bucket.

Kidd was hanged at Admiralty Dock in London in 1701, and his body tarred and left in a gibbet. Since then, people have been searching for his buried loot all along the Long Island coast, as well as in the Caribbean.

There was another William who turned pirate, in 1820, William Thompson, captain of the *Mary Dear* (no relation to Hammond

Innes's fictional insurance-scam ship, the *Mary Deare*, which was more based on a theory about the *Mary Celeste*).

In 1820, the Spanish Viceroy of Lima was getting jittery about potential revolution in the city. He and the top clerics at the cathedral decided to evacuate the cathedral's treasures, and some of the treasury's holdings – totalling over $12 million at the time – to safe holdings in Mexico. To transport the loot, they hired British sea captain Thompson, apparently not worried by the previous 400 years' worth of British sailors plundering Spanish treasure from South America. They did, however, at least send six trained soldiers, and a number of priests to keep an eye on this valuable cargo. The *Mary Dear* set sail from the Peruvian port of Callao, northwards up the Pacific coast of South America.

Quicker than a ship's parrot could say 'pieces of eight', Thompson had the soldiers' and priests' throats cut, and their bodies thrown overboard. He then landed on Cocos Island – or the Isla del Coco to the Spanish – and buried the treasure from Lima. He and his crew agreed to return for it later, but the *Mary Dear* was soon fallen upon by the Spanish Navy, and the crew captured. Captain Thompson and his First Mate bargained with the treasure for their lives.

While the rest of their crew was executed, Thompson and his First Mate returned to Cocos Island with the Spaniards, to lead them to the treasure. However, as soon as they were ashore, they disappeared into the jungle and were never seen again.

## PREVIOUS SEARCHES IN FACT AND FICTION

People have been looking for Kidd's treasure for a long time – there was already a popular folk song about him, called *Captain Kidd's Farewell to the Sea*, within months of his execution; the song referring to him having hidden 200 bars of gold. Originally the searchers simply looked on Gardiner's Island, starting with Lord Bellomont, who would be in an awkward position himself if Kidd didn't hang. He needed the loot as evidence, and this led him to remind the island's owner, John Gardiner, of how letting Kidd use his land for loot-storage could be construed as conspiracy. This spurred Gardiner to point out exactly where Kidd's loot was.

This didn't stop local tongues wagging with the suggestion that Kidd had buried more treasure than Gardiner had handed over. First the tales said there was more treasure on the island, then expanded to other islands. Oak Island got roped in to the legend in the 19th century, and nowadays people are even searching for Kidd's haul in the Pacific Ocean.

This is probably because Captain Kidd was said to have docked at various anchorages before giving himself up to Bellomont. All of the anchorages were common locations for ships to stop off and debark landing parties and take on provisions. Aside from Gardiner's Island itself, there were stories of Kidd visiting Block Island, Charles Island, and the Thimble Islands (all in Long Island Sound); as well as Raritan Bay in New Jersey (which no longer exists); Clark's Island in Massachusetts (locally called Kidd's Island) and various sites along the Hudson Valley. Old coins have been found in these places, but since they were regular stopping points for ships in general, there's no reason to assume they came from any specific crew.

The most persistent stories centre on Block Island, where Kidd was given supplies by a Mrs Mercy Sands Raymond, whom the legends say was paid off by having her apron filled with gold and gems. She certainly came into money at some point, as, when her husband died, she and her family moved to northern Connecticut, and bought a large estate. Local legend referred to the family as 'enriched by the apron'.

By 1875, local papers were reporting digs on the western coast of an island called Grand Manan, in the Bay of Fundy, and these references call the scoured coastline 'Money Cove'.

Things started to get really interesting for fans of Kidd's treasure in the late 1920s/early 1930s, when brothers Guy and Hubert Palmer, who ran a pirate museum in Eastbourne, claimed to have found four parchment maps leading to Kidd's treasure, inside pieces of furniture which Victorian historians had ascribed to Kidd's ownership.

These were obviously cool items for a pirate museum to have, especially since they depicted a mystery island. Neither the Palmers nor anyone they showed the maps to were able to identify the island or location, but the brothers claimed to have had the maps certified by experts. The Palmers traced over them and photographed them, before the originals conveniently disappeared.

By the 1930s, pirate treasure adventure stories were big business, and a writer named Harold T. Wilkins visited the museum. He viewed the map copies, but wasn't allowed to take copies himself. Nevertheless he recalled a variety of details, and combined them to make his own 'Skeleton Island', for his 1935 book *Captain Kidd and His Skeleton Island*. In this book the map is accompanied by coded clues and ciphers to the identity of the island, and the location of the treasure on it.

This inspired a lot of treasure hunters to associate Wilkins's map with assorted real life islands. Gilbert Hedden associated it with Oak Island, for example. Wilkins confirmed that he had made up the map from a variety of inspirations, but this didn't stop searchers believing that Skeleton Island was – and is – a real place.

Paul Hawkins, for example, claims to have deciphered the book's clues and located Skeleton Island in the Indian Ocean. In

1983, two treasure hunters named Cork Graham and Richard Knight decided that Skeleton Island was the Vietnamese island of Phu Quoc, and that they should go and dig it up. Two Americans digging up parts of Vietnam at the height of the Cold War; what could possibly go wrong? They were caught, accused of espionage, jailed and eventually released after paying a massive fine.

From 1952 onward treasure hunters starting looking at the Japanese island of Takarajima – which translates as 'Treasure Island' – in Kagoshima's Tokara Archipelago. Local stories told of English sailors under Captain Kidd demanding supplies of food and cattle from the islanders. When the islanders refused, a couple of dozen pirates raided, looted, pillaged and supposedly buried some loot in a cave. Again, people have spent decades looking for this treasure.

So far, nobody has come up with any treasure from any of those places, but one thing associated with Kidd *has* been discovered. In 2007, archaeologists from Indiana University responded to the discovery by fishermen of a shipwreck 10ft underwater and 70ft from dry land off the beach of Catalina Island in the Dominican Republic. This was the *Quedagh Merchant*.

Cocos Island, where the Treasure of Lima was taken in the 19th century, has also been associated with Captain Kidd and, of course, it has been identified as Skeleton Island. Prior to the past few decades, however, people only went looking for the Treasure of Lima there.

One John Keating claimed to have been an associate of Captain William Thompson, and to have met him in 1844. Thompson revealed to Keating how he had teamed up with another pirate named Benito Bonito and buried their combined loot in a cave on Cocos Island before a British ship put an end to their piracy. Thompson then died, and Keating sailed to the island with a Captain Bogue. There, Keating claimed, they found 100lb of gold, but their crew mutinied and stranded them there. The pair then tried to escape in a small raft with what they could carry, but the raft capsized and Bogue drowned. A less friendly version of the story has Keating kill his partner, grab some gold and jewels from the hoard they found, and leave the corpse with the rest of the hoard. Either way, Keating then moved to Newfoundland and died there.

On his deathbed, Keating supposedly passed on his secret to both his wife, and a ship's quartermaster called Nicholas Fitzgerald. Fitzgerald was never able to put together the funds to get to Cocos, but he did write down what he had been told, and his document still exists at the Nautical and Travellers' Club in Sydney, Australia. His description reads, 'At two cable's lengths, south of the last watering-place, on three points. The cave is the one which is to be found under the second point. Christie, Ned and Anton have tried but none of the three has returned. Ned on his fourth dive found the entrance at 12 fathoms but did not emerge from his fifth dive. There are no octopuses but there are sharks. A path must be opened up to the cave from the west. I believe there has been a fall of rock at the entrance.'

Keating's widow, however, said that the treasure had been found in a bay with a small crescent-shaped beach, which wasn't visible from the sea because it had a natural breakwater of black tree roots on both sides. Over the years, searchers have equated this with both Chatham Bay on the north-east side of the island, and the Bay Of Hope on the east side.

There are a couple of sets of directions supposedly written by Thompson himself. One refers to Chatham Bay, adding: 'Once there follow the coast line of the bay till you find a creek, where, at high water mark, you go up the bed of a stream which flows inland. Now you step out 70 paces, west by south, and against the skyline you will see a gap in the hills. From any other point, the gap is invisible. Turn north, and walk to a stream. You will now see a rock with a smooth face, rising sheer like a cliff. At the height of a man's shoulder, above the ground, you will see a hole large enough for you to insert your thumb. Thrust in an iron bar, twist it round in the cavity, and behind you will find a door which opens on the treasure.' Another says, 'Disembark in the Bay of Hope between two islets, in water 5 fathoms deep. Walk 350 paces along the course of the stream then turn north-northeast for 850 yards, stake, setting sun stake draws the silhouette of an eagle with wings spread. At the extremity of sun and shadow, cave marked with a cross. There lies the treasure.'

With so many variants, searchers have long since jumped to the conclusion that the loot must have simply been partitioned into multiple stashes – usually thought to be four – either one in each northern bay, or all within a hundred-yard circle around a waterfall, depending on who you want to believe.

In 1845, an iron-bound chest was found in a cave overlooking Wafer Bay, containing Spanish coins of unknown vintage. Legend says that in the 1880s, soldiers found $80,000 in silver and $30,000 of English and French gold coins in a cave in Wafer Bay, which also contained 300 silver ingots, clothing, a binnacle compass and a burst brass cannon.

The soldiers were supposedly also ordered to blast out a cedar tree in Wafer Bay, and the blast collapsed a cave revealing a chest with $10,000 of gold and letters written by Evan Jones, shipmate of Benito Bonito's. None of these hauls have been tracked down, or made it to any museums, and it's highly likely that they're all just fictions.

In 1895, it was reported in a Costa Rican government survey that, 'There are signs of mineral wealth, and gold has been found. In 1793, there was a mysterious cryptic carving found on the island on one of the big boulders in Chatham Bay that various seamen observed upon landing there. It read: *Look Y. as you goe for ye S. Coco*, with four branched crosses. The carving had originally been badly executed and had letters much defaced.' The survey also found a stone marked with a sombrero symbol, which locals took to calling 'Bonito's hat'.

A German explorer and treasure hunter called August Gissler was so obsessed with finding the life-sized gold Madonna statue from the Lima treasure that he lived on the island as a sort of Robinson Crusoe crossed with Indiana Jones for 19 years, from 1889 to 1908. Like many a crazed prospector in old Westerns, Gissler dug a maze of tunnels, some of which still exist, based on two maps he had acquired, which both indicated the same location for the Lima treasure. He was also aware of the stories of Bonito's treasure being located on the island, and finding that too would be a good bonus.

Gissler's expedition was funded by financial investors in the Cocos Plantation Company, a tobacco-growing body who also invested in (or bribed officials in) Costa Rica itself. In 1897, the government rewarded him with permission to set up a German farming colony on the island, of which they named him governor.

Unfortunately the island doesn't have the best soil or climate for tobacco growing, and is too far from the mainland to be economically viable to transport goods back and forth, so within a decade all the colonists had gone. August and his wife eventually gave up too, moving to New York with the treasure he had found over nearly two decades of searching: a total haul of six gold coins.

In 1910, a pre-presidential Franklin D. Roosevelt went with a group of friends to explore Cocos Island. In the 1920s, racing driver and land and water speed record holder Sir Malcolm Campbell also visited. Ironically, one of the most famous screen pirates, Errol Flynn, tried his hand at searching for the treasure in real life in the late 1940s, some years after playing the titular *Captain Blood*, a pirate who duels a villainous Basil Rathbone on the beach where his crew is burying their treasure.

Despite all of the above, there has been treasure confirmed on Cocos Island: In 1931, a 2ft-tall gold Madonna was found and sold for $11,000, while eight years later, a gold bar was found in a stream near a waterfall and sold for £35,000. Sadly, there's no record of which haul these came from – pirates and others have been reported as burying treasure on the island since the days of Sir Francis Drake.

The Treasure of Lima hasn't spawned anything like as many novels and movies as Captain Kidd, but in a way it has been the inspiration for the genre as a whole.

It's a tropical island upon which pirate treasure has been buried, and so is probably the ur-tale for every movie about buried pirate treasure from *Captain Blood* and *The Crimson Pirate* through to the *Pirates of the Caribbean* franchise. The treasure being in a cave is probably best visually expressed by the location of the hoard of cursed Aztec gold in *Pirates of the Caribbean: Curse of the Black Pearl*.

Just to be really awkward, in 2014 an art installation project called *Treasure of Lima: A Buried Exhibition*, drew 40 artists from across the world to create artworks which were then buried in a chest, somewhere on Cocos Island. This rather intrusive meta art project will doubtless confuse and frustrate future treasure hunters.

The association between pirates and buried treasure was made, however, by one man, and he wasn't a pirate. This was the writer Robert Louis Stevenson, and it was his book, *Treasure Island*, that created the whole idea of pirates burying treasure on Caribbean islands.

Stevenson had been inspired to base his fictional pirate crew upon some of the real pirates who had operated on the American coast in previous decades (for example, Long John Silver's first mate, Israel Hands, was in reality Blackbeard's boatswain). *Treasure Island* was published in 1883, a good 170 years after the time of Blackbeard, and more than 180 years after Captain Kidd was hanged at Admiralty Dock. He had done his research, however, in the form of both his own travels, and reading the book *A General History of the Pyrates* by the pseudonymous 'Captain Charles Johnson'.

This book, first published in two volumes in 1724, gave a potted – and fictionalized – account of the adventures of various 17th century pirates, including Kidd, Blackbeard, Bartholomew Roberts and various others (some entirely fictional). Johnson's book introduced peg-legs, eyepatches and so on, but it was Stevenson who really hit it big by popularizing the idea of islands with buried treasure as the definitive pirate trope.

Having decided to write about an island, Stevenson was particularly inspired both by Kidd having buried treasure on Gardiner's Island, and by the more recent – really the last classic act of piracy – Thompson's theft of the treasure of Lima, and his flight to Cocos Island. This was within living memory in Stevenson's day.

More specifically, Kidd has appeared in various media, being played twice by Charles Laughton (once in the adventure biopic *Captain Kidd*, in which psychotic and manipulative pirate Kidd is sent to provide safe escort to England for the *Quedagh Merchant*, as unlikely as that seems, and once in *Abbott and Costello Meet Captain Kidd*!)

Kidd has also been a character in several anime and manga series, is a major point in Nelson DeMille's *Plum Island*, and is namechecked directly in both *Treasure Island* and *Peter Pan*. His buried treasure is the hoard uncovered in Edgar Allan Poe's story *The Gold Bug*.

It's no surprise that he's one of the nine other pirates opposing the player in the videogame *Sid Meier's Pirates*, which itself lent the *Pirates of the Caribbean* movies their nine pirate lords (though one could argue that's a *Lord of the Rings* reference too). *Assassin's Creed III* has a set of missions in which the player must find four maps left by Kidd, which eventually lead to recovering his most valued treasure. He's also referenced in *Assassin's Creed IV: Black Flag*, when real-life pirate Mary Read claims to be his son, called James.

## THE TRUTH IS OUT THERE

Arrr ... Think of buried treasure and you most likely also think of pirates in stripey shirts being led ashore in a longboat by a peg-legged, hook-handed captain in a tricorn hat and a frock coat – all of them draped in cutlasses and flintlock pistols, and probably singing about rum – to dig a hole in the sun-drenched golden sands ready for a large wooden chest full of gold coins and gemstones.

Pirates and buried treasure go together like bread and butter, fish and chips, rum and cola; as the song says, you can't have one without the other, right?

Wrong.

Pirate crews were surprisingly democratic and even-handed, and since the crews tended to be in the business for, yes, treasure – or at least better pay than the miserable pittance offered by navies of the era – everybody expected to get paid their fair share. There was a scale of payment for everyone in a ship's crew, and even standardized rates of compensation for injuries sustained in battle or during raids. These rates varied from crew to crew but were usually around six to eight hundred pieces of eight (or silver dollars, depending on the period) for losing a leg or arm, one hundred for losing a hand or an eye. On a less salutary note, slaves could make up part of the payment, one slave being the equivalent to a hundred pieces of eight.

The crew would be paid a base salary for the voyage, and then shares in the prize money from successful raids. This would be paid out by the purser, and the crew would generally spend their wages ashore in dens of iniquity. As you can imagine, therefore, any captain who told his crew on payday, 'I buried the loot three islands back,' would very quickly find himself demoted from Captain to what is known in esoteric maritime terminology as 'shark bait'.

Pirates would more generally store their loot in a locked room attached to the purser's office. This is not to say, however, that individual pirates never buried their share of the loot, like many other ordinary people did with their savings in those days, but this is a different matter than a whole crew stashing their entire takings in one hoard. An individual wouldn't necessarily need a map either, as it'd basically be buried wherever he called home.

There are a couple of exceptions, of course.

The first 'pirate' – though whether you call him that really depends on your view of Elizabethan politics and imperialism – to bury his treasure ashore was Sir Francis Drake, who had raided a Spanish mule train at Nombre de Dios in Panama, and grabbed sackloads of gold and silver. He immediately legged it to where he remembered parking the ship – which wasn't there. He buried the loot and left a detachment of men to guard it while he set off to find the ship. Don't bother going looking for that site, because Drake returned, with his ship, a mere six hours later. He had gone to the right beach, but the ship had moved away to avoid a Spanish patrol. He and his crew then dug up their treasure and left.

Captain William Kidd, as an experienced privateer from a decade earlier, was requested by Governor Lord Bellomont to hunt down assorted pirates and French ships. Refusal would have been seen as disloyal, and caused trouble, and Kidd was happy to go back to sea with such a job. He also had a few ideas about how to get himself a new ship out of the deal, and persuaded several lords to front 80 per cent or so of the expense in fitting out a pirate-hunting expedition. These included Bellomont, the Earl of Orford, the Baron of Romney, the Duke of Shrewsbury, Sir John Somers, and possibly – through proxies – King William III himself. The king signed a Letter of Marque, legally empowering Kidd to attack French ships, with the proviso that 10 per cent of any booty be kept for the Crown.

Kidd bought a new ship in London, the *Adventure Galley*, armed with 34 cannons, and with a crew of 150. The 'Galley' in the name was accurate, as she had oars for propulsion in calm seas, which were a key advantage as they enabled the ship to manoeuvre in battle regardless of the winds. Kidd personally selected the officers for competency and loyalty.

Kidd got off on the wrong foot with the Royal Navy almost immediately, failing to salute a navy ship at Greenwich. The Navy ship fired a shot across his bows, Kidd's crew mooned them, and the navy immediately press-ganged a third of them as punishment. Kidd then sailed for New York, capturing a French ship on the way, and recruited replacement sailors there, mostly known criminals.

By September of 1696, Kidd set out for the Cape of Good Hope, and a bad start. They stopped off on the Comoro Islands, where a third of the crew died of cholera. The *Adventure Galley* had turned out to be very leaky, and there was a marked absence of pirates anywhere in the vicinity of the supposedly pirate-stricken Madagascar. So Kidd headed to the Strait of Bab-el-Mandeb, at the southern end of the Red Sea, and a notorious haunt of pirates. Again, there were no pirates around.

Kidd then may have attacked a Mughal convoy escorted by the British East India Company, but nobody's quite sure. Sailors deserted while on shore leave, and those who stayed were openly mutinous. On 30 October 1697, a gunner called William Moore tried to insist that Kidd attack a nearby Dutch ship – which, being neither a pirate ship nor French, would have been an act of piracy (and would have annoyed the king, who was Dutch by birth). They got into an argument which ended with Kidd cracking Moore's skull with an iron bucket.

*Adventure Galley* then met a British convoy, whose commander intended to press 30 of Kidd's crew into service. Undermanned already, Kidd decided to leave the convoy under cover of darkness, but this act was seen by the navy as disloyal.

On 30 January 1698, Kidd captured the *Quedagh Merchant*, and her cargo of satins, muslins, gold, silver, spices and silk. The ship was Armenian, owned by the Mughals of India, and her captain was an Englishman named Wright, who had passes from the French East India Company. Kidd tried to make his crew return the ship to Wright, but they reminded him that they were commissioned to take French ships, and this one had French passes.

Kidd, therefore, kept the passes and the ship, which was renamed *Adventure Prize*, and sailed for Madagascar, where he sold her cargo for £7,000. Under pressure from the Armenians, Mughals, East India Company and their own captains, the Admiralty decided that Kidd was a pirate and ordered the navy to hunt him down.

On 1 April, Kidd actually found a pirate, Robert Culliford of the *Mocha Frigate*. At this point, Kidd either was simply friendly to a fellow pirate, or was wary of engaging a warship which he didn't know had only 20 crewmen, depending on who you want to believe. It's worth remembering, though, that Culliford had hijacked one of Kidd's ships a dozen years before. Most of Kidd's crew joined Culliford, leaving Kidd with only 13 men. He had *Adventure Galley* scuttled, and sailed *Adventure Prize* back to the Caribbean, where he discovered that Britain was really not happy with him.

On his way to negotiate with his backer, Lord Bellomont, Kidd buried treasure in a ravine in Cherry Tree Field, between Bostwick's Point and the manor house, on Gardiner's Island, in June 1699. The spot isn't hard to find, as a plaque marks it today. He had permission from John Gardiner to bury a sea chest, a box of gold intended for Lord Bellomont, and two boxes of silver. He also gave Mrs Gardiner a bolt of gold cloth, part of which still exists in the East Hampton Library, and a sack of sugar, which at the time was hugely valuable.

Kidd was extremely polite, according to Gardiner's testimony at Kidd's trial in Boston. Since Bellomont would be an accessory to piracy (and not just him, but the other lords and even the king!) if Kidd didn't hang, he reminded Gardiner of how letting Kidd use his land for loot-storage could be construed as conspiracy to commit piracy, and this had spurred Gardiner to turn over the items, which were impounded as evidence against Kidd. The impounded treasure consisted of gold dust, silver ingots, Spanish dollars, rubies, diamonds, candlesticks and porringers.

Not all of this made it to the trial: Bellomont kept a finder's fee, and even Gardiner gave one of the diamonds to his daughter.

Lured by a promise of clemency from Bellomont, Kidd was arrested, tried for both piracy and the murder of William Moore, and hanged in 1701. The French passes, which Kidd had given to Bellomont to prove that the *Quedagh Merchant* was a legitimate target, mysteriously disappeared before his trial and turned up 200 years later.

But what of the rest of the loot? There's never been any proof that he had any – his crew would have stuck around if he had. For all that people have searched various islands, nobody has turned up any treasure belonging to Kidd.

Searchers for Skeleton Island have always been on a hunt for nothing. Firstly, the Palmers' maps were fakes, as the earliest copies have them dated with the year 1668 – decades before Kidd's alleged piracy. That later copies now say 1699 implies that someone spotted the error in the maps' creation and corrected it.

Wilkins always said that the map in his book was a combination of what he remembered from a look at the Palmers' maps, and some features of Mahe, the largest island in the Seychelles. In fact, when Wilkins originally delivered his manuscript, the map of Skeleton Island had no markings on it. The coded clues were added overnight at the request of Wilkins's publisher, who thought they'd make it more treasure-map-ish.

The Japanese island of Takarajima is also out as far as Kidd is concerned – the story of the raid by a British ship is actually true, but it happened in August 1824, a century and a quarter after Kidd's execution.

The Treasure of Lima is one of the biggest hoards still missing, yet no search has found it. Various fake, or at least unreliable, documents exist in different museums to confuse the issue – some are about Benito Bonito, or other, earlier, pirates.

Benito Bonito's most famous exploits involved raiding a mule train at Acapulco, en route from Mexico City in 1819. Despite this, there's an Australian legend that he sealed his loot in a cave in Queenscliff, in Victoria, rather than on Cocos Island. Nobody has ever found anything there either, though.

Veins of natural gold, mixed in with quartz, were found in a survey of Cocos Island in 1933. Nowadays people are more interested in that gold.

## WHERE IS IT NOW?

Captain Kidd's treasure was returned to the local economy of the time. His plunder was sold and the proceeds that weren't spent in trying to clear his name were used in evidence against him.

The Treasure of Lima is still somewhere in the environs of Cocos Island, but given how many expeditions have failed to find any significant amounts of it, it may well be that the majority of it is now underwater, either due to landscape changes, or in a shipwreck.

## THE OPPOSITION IN YOUR WAY

The Costa Rican authorities want to discourage treasure hunting on Cocos Island, so permits do require the searchers to bring some other value, such as by conducting geological surveys, or environmental work, as well as hunting for treasure. The permissions also include conditions that if any part of a treasure hoard is actually discovered, the searchers must immediately cease operations and notify the authorities.

There are plenty of insect species on Cocos, but no predatory animals. In fact all the mammals on the island have been introduced by man, and are considered a threat to the original ecosystem: deer, goats, pigs, cats and rats.

There are indeed plenty of sharks around – notably whitetip reef sharks and hammerheads – and giant mantas, which can give a very nasty sting.

The biggest natural threat to visitors, however, is the mix of natural caves and man-made tunnels, which have turned parts of the island into Swiss cheese, and are in great danger of collapse.

Other than that, the main problem is the island's physical remoteness from the rest of the world.

# THE OAK ISLAND MONEY PIT

✖ THE OAK ISLAND MONEY PIT

## WHAT IS IT?

It's a shaft last excavated to a depth of over 180ft on Oak Island, an island covered in oak trees (hence the name), in Mahone Bay, Nova Scotia. It's only 200 yards off the shore of Lunenburg County, on the southern coast of the province, and is connected to the mainland by a causeway.

Nobody knows for sure what treasure is supposed to be buried down there, but lots of people are convinced that *something* valuable is buried there. Popular theories include pirate treasure (Blackbeard and Captain Kidd are popular suspects, as is Henry Avery), Templar treasure, evidence that Francis Bacon wrote Shakespeare's plays, Marie Antoinette's jewels, the Ark of the Covenant, Masonic regalia and many other things.

## HOW MUCH IS IT WORTH TO YOU?

Since nobody even knows what the treasure is, it's impossible to put a likely value on it.

## THE STORY

The pit was first discovered by a young man called Daniel McGinnis in 1795. He had seen lights on the island from shore, and the next day he found a round depression in a clearing at the southern side of the island, with block and tackle suspended from the trees over it.

It was clear that someone had been trying to move heavy objects in the clearing, so McGinnis and some friends – John Smith and Tony Vaughan – decided to dig into the depression. They found that there were already well-defined walls to the pit, on which they could see pickaxe marks. Only a couple of feet under the surface turf, they found some flagstones, covering an area about 13ft across. They removed the flagstones and kept digging, finding a floor of logs about 10ft down. They dug the logs up and kept going, only to find another log floor at 20ft down, and a third at 30ft. Winter interrupted their digging, but the next June, they came back and got another 15ft down before giving up for good.

The story had started to spread across Nova Scotia, and people came to the conclusion that someone had gone to a lot of trouble to put something in the pit – and that nobody went to that much trouble unless it was for something *really* valuable. A treasure hunt was born.

The hunt has long been hampered, however, by the flooding of the pit, which various excavators have attributed to a deliberate engineering project to prevent anything being brought up out of the shaft. Five tunnels run from the sea through Smith's Cove, with an elaborate series of gates and valves placed there by some unknown creator.

Over time, excavators have announced finding fragments of chests, coin-sized metallic pieces, and have even taken pictures of skeletons and chests.

# PREVIOUS SEARCHES IN FACT AND FICTION

John Smith, being the oldest of the three original treasure hunters, bought the land on which the pit lay. Then, in 1804, the Onslow Company from Truro in Nova Scotia, hundreds of miles away, came to use professional measures to recover the treasure. This company was composed of four men: Simeon Lynds (a cousin of Tony Vaughan), Robert and David Archibald, and a local sheriff, Thomas Harris. Ten feet down from McGinnis's last attempt, they found another log floor and a layer of charcoal. Logs and putty were found 10ft below that, and logs and coconut matting 10ft below *that*.

The company took all these finds to be good signs, as coconut matting was used at the time to protect ships' cargo. Finally, 30ft below the coconut matting, at a total of 90ft down, the quartet found a stone bearing an inscription in a simple symbolic substitution cipher. Supposedly the cipher translated as 'Forty feet below, two million pounds lie buried.'

Onslow redoubled their efforts and tunnelled for another 10ft, at which point the pit flooded with sea-water all the way back up to the 30ft level. Bailing the water out with buckets didn't work, and, since they didn't have the equipment to dig 60ft underwater, they paused. In the autumn, Onslow returned with a mechanical water pump which emptied the shaft, but broke down, so the pit flooded again. They tried again the next year, this time opening a new shaft 15ft south-east of the pit, to a point below the suspected water trap, intending to tunnel across. Unfortunately this shaft flooded when they reached a depth of 12ft.

The inhabitants of Truro launched another attempt in 1849. The aging Vaughan teamed up with Lynds's brother and several other men for a new expedition under the name The Truro Company. Either Onslow or nature had filled in the pit over the previous half century, as they had to dig again, rather than swim. When they reached 86ft, the pit flooded (while the workers were in church!), up to the 30ft mark.

It occurred to some bright spark to drill with a device called a pod auger, from a platform above the water. This way they could drill into the bottom of the pit without draining the water, and bring up samples of whatever was down there. They hit spruce at a depth of 98ft, under which was – in order – a foot of empty space, 2ft of what felt like metal fragments (and were said to be small links of gold chain, though other reports say whatever it was dropped out of the auger and was not recovered), 8in of oak, another 2ft of what felt like metal pieces, 4in of oak, a layer of spruce, and then enough clay to convince the company that there was nothing else below.

At the same time, one member of the team, James Pitblado, was said to have pocketed something from the auger. Pitblado then left the company and tried to get a separate licence to excavate the pit, but was only granted permission to dig elsewhere. Since this was useless to him, he soon disappeared.

They also tried digging in sideways from a different location, but with the same result: flooding. This alerted them to a new discovery on a part of the coastline called Smith's Cove: five tunnels, subsequently named the finger drains, along with coconut matting. They also noticed that the new flooding rose and fell with the tide, and thought that blocking these shafts would prevent the shafts from flooding. They were baffled when the water didn't recede after this, and gave up.

Next up were the Oak Island Association in 1861, who had terrible luck. Things seemed to be going well as they dug two shafts parallel to the original pit, down to 112ft, and tunnelled across. They flooded mere inches from the Money Pit. Worse, the steam-powered water pump failed, and the bottom of the pit collapsed into a presumed booby trap, taking much of the wooden shoring with it. Later, their boiler exploded, killing a worker. They ran out of funding, and willingness, in 1864.

In 1890, a one-and-a-half ounce copper coin was found. Inspired by this, Frederick Blair and S. C. Fraser formed the Oak Island Treasure Company in 1893, with the rights to everything discovered for three years. They couldn't afford a pump, were digging in the wrong shaft and only made it to 55ft before it flooded.

In 1895, the Attorney General said that, despite the lease agreement, any treasure acquired belonged to Queen Victoria. In 1896, the Oak Island Treasure Company got a water pump and tried again, but the pump failed, and when a worker being lifted out of the shaft fell in and was killed, the other workers decided the place was jinxed. They kept drilling, however, and hit solid iron at 153ft. A few inches to one side, the drill passed through wood, and what felt like pieces of loose metal, but only coconut matting, wood and pebbles came up in the auger – along with a piece of parchment bearing the letters 'vi', with no indication of what the rest of the word or message was.

In 1898, dye was poured into the pit in the hope that following the colouration in the water would reveal the flood tunnel exits. Surprisingly, not only did the dye appear from points all around the island, but did *not* appear from the finger drains in Smith's Cove. Nothing the company did, including blasting with dynamite, prevented flooding.

Future US President Franklin Delano Roosevelt got involved with the Old Gold Salvage and Wrecking Company's – a new name for the Oak Island Treasure Company – unsuccessful dig of 1909. He spent that summer in the area, remained fascinated

by the pit throughout his life, and wrote in a letter in 1939 that he hoped to return to the island to search again. The outbreak of World War II put paid to that plan, however.

Things took a more determined turn in 1928, when New York steelmaker and engineer Gilbert Hedden saw a newspaper article about the Money Pit and got intrigued by the engineering involved. Hedden researched all that he could and came to believe that the pit contained treasure buried by Captain Kidd, having decided that a map in the book *Captain Kidd and His Skeleton Island* referred to Oak Island. When his company was bought out in 1931, the money he made funded his investigations.

After years of research, Hedden bought the Money Pit site, and started his own dig in 1936. He used an electric turbine pump to remove the floodwater. In 1937 his men found old mining equipment, including unexploded dynamite at 65ft. One hundred and fourteen feet down one shaft, Hedden found a horizontal tunnel large enough for a man to walk along. In the end, however, even he ran out of money.

In the 1940s, Errol Flynn became interested in the legend and hoped to mount an expedition, but the rights were held at the time by a company owned by, believe it or not, John Wayne, who refused him permission.

In the 1950s, the Treasure Trove law in Canada set out that 10 per cent of any findings would belong to the government, but it would be a decade before there was another notable expedition. That expedition would spawn a local legend that the treasure would only be found after seven deaths.

Robert and Mildred Westall had run a Globe of Death motorbike stunt show since the 1930s, before settling down in Ontario with their sons and daughter. Robert soon heard of the Money Pit, and determined to find the treasure, which he believed was pirate loot. In 1959, the land was owned by William Chappell's son Mel, who agreed to let them dig in return for a half share of anything found. The Westalls moved to Oak Island, and lived there for five years, in cabins with no running water. On 17 August 1965, Westall was overcome by fumes and fell into a flooded shaft. His son Bobbie, and two other workers, Karl Graeser and Cyril Hilt, tried to help but shared his fate.

Geologist Robert Dunfield brought in bulldozers and modern cranes, and built a causeway to the mainland. He spread clay over Smith's Cove in a failed attempt to jam up any flood tunnels. His team dug a 140ft-deep, 100ft-wide crater, but all they found were pieces of porcelain, and heavy rains kept causing the crater sides to collapse.

In a move guaranteed to make archaeologists facepalm themselves into concussion, Dunfield decided to drill for core samples *after* re-filling the crater. He made four bores down to 190ft, finding a wooden platform at 140ft, 40ft of void, then bedrock. Worse, another property owner on the island, Fred Nolan, now bought the mainland end of the causeway, and neither man would allow the other access to their end of it. Dunfield gave up and returned home to California.

In 1967, Daniel Blankenship and David Tobias decided to buy most of Oak Island for excavation. They negotiated separately with Dunfield and Nolan, to get their experience, and access to both ends of the causeway. They started drilling around 60 bore-holes in the vicinity of the Money Pit, confirming that the island's bedrock was around 170ft below the surface, but that there was also a wooden layer 40ft above that in some areas. They also found porcelain, wood, clay, charcoal and a piece of brass.

In 1969, the pair formed Triton Alliance Limited and started exploring *outside* the Money Pit vicinity. Starting 180ft north-east of the main shaft, they found some samples of metal at 160ft. More metal fragments were found north of the pit over the following year, and a dig at Smith's Cove found a set of logs carved with Roman numerals, which they thought may have been the remains of a coffer dam used to control water during construction of the pit. They also confirmed that the pebble beach at Smith's Cove had been artificially constructed. Additionally they found wrought-iron scissors, a wooden sled, an iron ruler and iron nails and spikes – all of which were dated to before 1790. This was the first evidence of digging before the boys saw those lights in 1795.

The most promising shaft was named '10X', and had a modern casing fitted all the way down to 165ft. Inside were found broken concrete and pieces of wire and chain. A Canadian Broadcasting Company news crew lowered a video camera in, which some people at the time claimed recorded skeletal hands and treasure chests. None of the divers that followed saw any such thing, however.

Fred Nolan found a cross-shaped arrangement of carved boulders around his property, which he believes to have some significance. In time, the various factions began to argue and sue each other, which brought a halt to excavations. The Canadian laws on Treasure Troves were also tightened further in 1989, making it harder to get a licence to explore the Money Pit.

So, the landowners turned to tourism. At first Triton ran the sole Oak Island Exploration Company, but in the 1990s, a public group called the Oak Island Tourism Society tried to get the government to sell the island to them. Instead, it was sold in 2006 to two Michigan brothers, Marty and Rick Lagina, who promptly allied with Blankenship to create Oak Island Tourism Inc. In 2010, the Canadian government changed the Treasure Trove Act again, this time making a specific Oak Island Treasure Act, which states that 'Anyone who wants to search for and recover in Oak Island Nova Scotia precious stones or metals in a state other than their natural state, and to keep them,' would be hit with a lot more red tape, a lot more hoops to jump through, and be heavily taxed on any discovery. That ended excavations at the Money Pit, until reality TV took notice.

In 2014, The History Channel began *The Curse of Oak Island*, in which the Laginas revisit the various excavations with more modern technology, and the aid of Blankenship and his son. So far they have (allegedly) found a single Spanish coin from the 17th century, and this meant the show has been renewed.

Various documentary series about world mysteries and Fortean subjects have featured it, starting with *In Search of...*, hosted by Leonard Nimoy of *Star Trek* fame, which brought the story to a far wider public in 1979. Canadian shows *Northern Mysteries* and *The Conspiracy Show* have both covered the Money Pit, as have more high-profile shows such as *Unsolved Mysteries* and, inevitably, *Ancient Aliens* (guess who they suggest buried stuff there).

The first season of forensic thriller *Bones* included an episode based on a similar money pit, *The Man with the Bone*, and you can take a trip to Oak Island in the videogame *Assassin's Creed III*, in which Captain Kidd has hidden an ancient artefact there.

Books and magazines have also featured the Money Pit, but 1935's *Captain Kidd and His Skeleton Island*, by Harold T. Wilkins, is not one of them, regardless of Gilbert Hedden's conviction that it was. (In fact, Hedden visited Wilkins in England to ask him about his knowledge of Oak Island, only to find Wilkins surprised that an island he thought he'd made up bore such supposed similarities to a real place.)

In 1948, *True Tales of Buried Treasure*, by Edward Rowe Snow, introduced the world to the stone with the cipher on it, which he claimed had been translated by an Irish professor friend – usually presumed to be James Leitchi, Professor of Languages at Dalhousie University – or the Rev A. T. Kempton, of Boston, Massachusetts. In the 1970s children's novel, *The Hand of Robin Squires*, the title character finds that his uncle is a pirate and inventor who was involved with creating the Money Pit.

The 1998 novel *Riptide*, by Lincoln Child and Doug Preston, is openly acknowledged by the authors in the afterword as about a fictionalized version of the Money Pit, though here it's called the Water Pit on Ragged Island in Maine. In the book, the treasure is pirate treasure, including a well-nigh supernatural sword. John Carter's novel *Last Judgement* has the inscription on the tablet lead to a vial of Christ's blood hidden by the Templars.

The closest Clive Cussler has come to the Money Pit is a Chinese-dug pit in *The Silent Sea*, co-written with Jack Du Brul, which does have some similarities to the Oak Island pit, despite having a totally different background. Cussler himself is an experienced undersea explorer and diver, who had led several successful searches for historical wrecks, most famously succeeding in raising the American Civil War submarine, *Hunley*, and has applied for licences to search Oak Island twice in the 1990s, but was refused both times.

## THE TRUTH IS OUT THERE

That the famous pit is a mystery worthy of digging into isn't in doubt, but a lot of treasure-hunting history has obscured the facts, and the site. The Money Pit story is shrouded in confusion, vagueness and outright nonsense, all the way back to the original story of the teenage boys deciding to dig where they had seen a light.

McGinnis and Vaughan were actually both landowners in their mid-30s in 1795, and there's no mention of their treasure hunting recorded anywhere until a newspaper story in 1846. This means the Onslow and Truro companies' stories of responding to a discovery in 1795 are also basically undocumented and therefore unverifiable in a lot of detail. The 1846 version of the tale only mentions a few logs near the surface, with pick-marks and the like at intervals below. Later writers changed this into regular layers of logs every 10ft or so.

The Onslow Company did exist, and the first mention of the inscribed stone with the message about £2 million being buried 40ft below is in its records. This tablet reputedly disappeared sometime in the 1930s, or at least was noticed to not be around, even in photographs. There's no evidence that it ever existed; all illustrations of its symbols derive from drawings published in Snow's *True Tales of Buried Treasure*. Snow never said how Kempton came to be in possession of the tablet's symbols.

According to letters uncovered afterwards, Kempton and Frederick Blair wrote to each other in 1949, after Snow's book came out, as Blair thought that the story in the book was pretty different from what he personally knew. Kempton then described how he got the supposed translation: He had wanted to write a book about the treasure in 1909, and wrote to a minister (religious or government is unclear) to ask if he knew someone who could tell him about the island. The minister found an Irish teacher to write an account for Kempton, which Kempton paid for. He was open in an April 1949 letter that *'The teacher who wrote my MSS. did not give me any proofs of his statements.'* When Kempton went to Mahone Bay later to meet the 'very bright Irish teacher', he found that the man had died some years before.

Kempton had also heard that the stone was now in a museum in Halifax, but never found it. There are stories about it having been in collections, and even used in fireplaces, but Kempton never saw it, and eventually forgot about it, until he showed the teacher's manuscript to Snow, and Snow put the symbols in his book.

Nobody ever reported a first-hand experience of seeing the stone, there are no photos of it, and the translation – which has influenced later searchers to focus on the 130ft-level – was produced by either Kempton himself, or an anonymous teacher having a laugh. It's also highly suspect that the first mention of the stone in Onslow's records comes just as their funding was running out. Suddenly, with the report of an inscription, their investors were back on board.

People have tried to put other interpretations on the inscription. For example, a zoology professor called Barry Fell came to believe in the 1960s that the inscription means *'The people shall not forget the lord, to offset the hardships of winter, and the onset of plague the Ark, he shall pray to the lord,'* and that this means that Coptic Christians from the 1st century AD hid the Ark of the Covenant there. In 2007, a researcher named Keith Ranville claimed that the inscription revealed that the treasure is actually buried on Birch Island, nearby.

The links of gold chain supposedly found in 1849 were originally described as being 'as if torn from an epaulette,' but this description has changed over time.

Things like iron objects or the occasional copper coin have been found, but the site has been so churned and mangled by years of expeditions that there's no way to tell when any of them were actually deposited there. Carbon-dating can only tell when an object originated, not when it was placed somewhere. People have been working on the site for 200 years, and equipment from previous digs keeps turning up in newer ones.

As for the video shot by the CBC news crew, that footage is very blurry, and the water filled with floating sediment which obscures almost everything, but there's nothing that really looks like a skeletal hand, or treasure chest, as people thought at the time. There is an object that convincingly resembles a miner's pick, but that's exactly what you'd expect to see in a shaft that has been dug and re-dug for decades. More recent footage in the Laginas' History Channel TV show, using modern HD cameras, shows no such objects.

One important thing that has been established is that the five 'finger drains' at Smith's Cove do not connect up to the

Money Pit. They were actually part of an 18th-century salt works, filtering salt from seawater and drying it out for commercial and industrial use. In fact, nobody has ever definitely found any flood tunnels leading water into the pit, and the reason for that was established by the Woods Hole Oceanographic Institute in 1995. These foremost scientists on the subject of seawater discovered, by means of pouring dye into the pit, and observing its behaviour, that the flooding is caused by tidal pressures on the island's porous limestone geology.

Oak Island is mostly limestone and anhydrite, which is notably porous, and dissolves quite easily. Salt water infiltrates the porous rock, reacts with both the anhydrites and the oxygen that gets in when the water recedes with the tides, and dissolves the limestone. It then subsides, trees around the edge fall into it and storms bring in other pieces of debris. In 1878, a woman fell 12ft into a sinkhole about 40 yards from the Money Pit, landing in a small limestone cavern. In the 1950s, some men digging a well hit flagstone at 2ft, and then layers of spruce and oak logs. At first people thought it was another Money Pit, but it turned out to be a sinkhole.

What of the coconut fibres, you may ask. Coconuts are not native to Newfoundland, and opinions vary on how far they might drift before they rot away. Some of the fibres were carbon-dated in 1975 to around AD 1200, and suddenly that Templar treasure idea looked more promising – but only for about 20 years, until it was established that the seawater throws carbon dating off by about 450 years, planting those coconut fibres firmly in the 17th to 18th centuries. That's still pirate prime-time, however, and the matting was used as a sort of naval bubble-wrap for cargo at the time, so it could well have been brought by ship and buried deliberately.

# WHERE IS IT NOW?

Nobody's managed to move the island since its discovery, seeing as the Dharma Initiative have yet to get involved, so Oak Island is still in Mahone Bay on the southern coast of Nova Scotia.

The real question is 'was there any treasure at all, and if so, what is it?' After more than 200 years of excavations, you'd think if there was a hoard down there, it would have been found long ago.

It's a lot easier to say what the treasure definitely *isn't*. It's certainly not the hoard of either Blackbeard or Captain Kidd. Blackbeard never operated so far north, and Captain Kidd's treasure is accounted for.

It's also not going to be any of the really loopy suggestions, such as the Ark of the Covenant, or proof that Francis Bacon wrote Shakespeare's plays. Incomprehensibly, some people think that the parchment with 'vi' on it constitutes such proof. Nobody can convincingly explain how the idea works, beyond the fact that letters on parchment are writing, Shakespeare and Bacon were writers, and Bacon described a self-flooding water trap in a work he wrote.

Another far-fetched idea is that the treasure is Marie Antoinette's missing jewels, somehow smuggled to a remote island by a maid, who then hired the French Navy to bury it, for no readily apparent reason.

So what *is* any potential treasure likely to be? There are two main possibilities that still hold up. Three, if you count 'bugger all' as a possibility.

The first option is that the treasure is simply whatever bits and bobs were left behind, or traded, by visiting ships. The area was always relatively busy, with ships stopping off to and from Europe, and there have been settlements on the island in the past. If this is the case, there could be any random mix of coinage from roughly the 16th century onwards, which ordinary, non-famous sailors may have hidden or lost at various times over centuries.

The second possibility is that military payroll was hidden there during the Seven Years' War in the 1750s, or the American War of Independence. Opinions vary on whether it would be British or French payroll, though the Royal Navy is the more popular suspect. The idea is that either the French slipped out of the siege of Fort Louisburg in 1758, and buried the fort's treasure on Oak Island, or that the Royal Navy's engineers buried payroll for the British troops in the War of Independence. The latter theory, however, usually presumes that the navy buried it in the autumn, but then returned and retrieved it in the following spring.

There is some possible evidence for this inasmuch as there was a Royal Navy base close by at Hamilton, and some of the old mining equipment found during expeditions has turned out to be Cornish mining gear, which was issued to Royal Navy engineers in the 18th century. However, it was also considered the best in general, and so was not exclusively used by the navy. Another strike against the theory is that there's no documentation of such a payroll burial.

The third possibility, of course, is that there is no treasure, and that the so-called Money Pit is just a natural sinkhole.

## THE OPPOSITION IN YOUR WAY

This is Canada, so there aren't hostile militaries to worry about, and the island is free of dangerous wildlife – you're unlikely to run into any grizzly bears.

The artificial obstructions start with the history of the site itself. The site is ludicrously contaminated by previous digs to the extent that, not only does equipment from those earlier digs keep turning up, but there is still doubt over exactly which shaft is the original Money Pit. Modern technology such as ground-penetrating radar, or electrical resistance geophysics gear, won't be much help, because it will only show that there are plenty of anomalies on the island – which there are, because of all those previous digs.

The other problem is the legal disputes. Actually getting a licence to excavate for the treasure is difficult enough, and then you'll be faced with a legal minefield of various different people – such as the Laginas, Nolan, etc. – who have different ownerships and rights over different parts of the island. They're all reluctant to let freelance treasure-seekers dig all over the place. It's perfectly possible to trespass on the island without notice, but not to bring in the sort of equipment you'd need to excavate the shafts.

It's also a ridiculously expensive business. So many people and companies have gone bankrupt searching for the treasure that the Money Pit gave its very name to any project that requires an unreasonable influx of cash to keep running without effect. Usually it refers to DIY – there's even a Tom Hanks movie entitled *The Money Pit* about such a house – but it also echoes Mark Twain's epigram defining a gold mine as 'a hole with an idiot at the bottom'.

# GEOPHYSICS

Everybody with even the slightest interest in digging up treasures from the past, whether by beachcombing themselves, or simply from watching TV history shows such as *Time Team*, will have noticed the use of what's called geophysical surveying equipment, whether it be in the form of hand-held metal detectors on the beach, electrical resistance meters used in fields, or even ground-penetrating radar.

Most of these technologies were originally developed as military equipment, and later adapted by first the utilities and construction industries, and then by archaeologists and treasure hunters. Since their use has been modified from their original intentions, their efficacy varies according to the use to which they are put.

The very first metal detectors came about in the late 19th and early 20th century almost by accident. Engineers working on mechanisms for radio direction-finding found that their results were skewed by interference from iron-ore deposits and soon began working on systems to detect ore-bearing deposits on purpose. The way they work is basically something like this: an alternating current is passed through a metal coil producing an alternating magnetic field. Any conductive metal close enough to this coil will have eddy currents induced in it, producing a corresponding magnetic field. A second coil, a magnetometer, will then detect the alteration in this magnetic field, proving that a metal object is there.

The first practical uses for these metal detectors were, obviously, in looking for pipes underground where people wanted to dig foundations and for detecting mines either buried in the soil or floating at sea.

The second major type of technology used for detecting buried valuables is electrical resistance tomography. This technique involves passing electrical current between electrodes that are jabbed into the ground. Different materials have different electrical resistances, which will show up on a graph or printout as different densities or different colours.

This does have the advantage of showing more than just metallic objects, as any disturbance to the earth will have a different electrical resistivity. This means that walls, wood, pathways, even the sites of fires, can all be detected. That said, it needs a trained and experienced interpreter to make sense of the results.

The third form of technology for seeing what's hidden underground is ground-penetrating radar. As the name implies, this relies simply on transmitting radar pulses into the ground, and seeing what they reflect back from. As with the electrical resistance imagery, every material will absorb a different amount of the transmitted waves and so reflect back a different amount.

Again, the results will vary according to local conditions. GPR will go hundreds of feet through ice in Antarctica, up to about 50ft through solid dry rock or concrete, but only a few feet at best through moist soil like loam or peat.

Basically you'll need to be filthy rich, and on good terms with high-powered business and contracts lawyers.

The island isn't hard to get to and isn't in an extreme climate, but it is, geologically, made of dissolved limestone caves and tunnels, like the bubbles in an Aero bar, between the surface and the bedrock 180ft down. This means that the shafts are prone to flooding, sinkholes, landslides and similar dangers to anyone trying to dig down.

The obvious modern solution would be to pump cement down the shafts until it sets, then drill down the centre to get at whatever is thus encased, but that would risk damaging any artefacts, and also be an appallingly brutal practice. The various authorities and licence holders would never give permission for it.

# THE BEALE TREASURE

✖ THE BEALE TREASURE

## WHAT IS IT?

A cache of gold and silver, mined in Colorado between 1819 and
1821, which was then hidden in or around the town of Bedford,
Virginia. The treasure's nature and location were encoded in three
ciphers by one Thomas J. Beale. When decoded, they gave the
following description:

> 'The first deposit consisted of ten hundred and fourteen pounds of gold,
> and thirty-eight hundred and twelve pounds of silver, deposited Nov.
> eighteen nineteen. The second was made Dec. eighteen twenty-one, and
> consisted of nineteen hundred and seven pounds of gold, and twelve
> hundred and eighty-eight of silver; also jewels, obtained in St. Louis
> in exchange for silver to save transportation, and valued at thirteen
> thousand dollars.
>
> The above is securely packed in iron pots, with iron covers. The
> vault is roughly lined with stone, and the vessels rest on solid stone,
> and are covered with others.'

# HOW MUCH IS IT WORTH TO YOU?

Since Beale conveniently gave exact details of the treasure, it's easy enough for you to check the price of a pound of gold or silver online. At the time of writing, however, those amounts would equate to $53 million in gold, $1.7 million in silver, and about a quarter million in jewels. So, let's call it a nice round $55 million.

# THE STORY

In May 1817, 30 men left Virginia for St Louis, Missouri, in order to form an expedition to hunt buffalo and bear. Under advice from local guides, they organized themselves into a militia, captained by Thomas Jefferson Beale, so that they were more prepared for any trouble with local tribes.

They headed south and spent the winter in Santa Fe, in what is now New Mexico. In the spring of 1818, while hunting somewhere 250–300 miles north of Santa Fe, they stumbled across a ravine with rich seams of gold and silver ore. By 1819, they had mined a fair amount, and decided to find somewhere to store until they were ready to take their shares and go their separate ways. They also traded some of it for jewellery, which was lighter and easier to carry. The men knew of a cave near Buford's Tavern in Bedford County, Virginia, which might suit their purpose. While 20 men continued digging, Beale led ten to visit Bedford for a month.

They discovered that the cave was used by local hunters and farmers, and cached the treasure they had so far in a different spot. It then occurred to Beale and company that if anything happened to the group, their relatives would never know where their inheritance was. So, they decided to find a trustworthy person who could hold some form of information for safekeeping.

Beale then spent some time getting to know Robert Morriss, innkeeper of the Washington Hotel in Lynchburg, Virginia, and thought he was just the bloke to be entrusted with such documentation. Beale stayed there over the winter of 1819–20, before returning to the mysterious ravine, where his cohorts were still digging. He returned to the Washington Hotel in early 1822, having deposited more gold and silver in its secret hiding place, and entrusted Morriss with an iron strongbox. He told Morriss to open the box and pass on the details to the men's next of kin if they didn't return within a decade. A few months later, Beale sent Morriss a letter from St Louis, saying that the strongbox contained details of the nature and location of the treasures they had discovered, and the identities of his company. He also said that a second letter would come from a friend of his, and would contain the key to the cipher in which the documents were encoded.

Morriss never heard from Beale again, and no second letter ever arrived. Despite the temptation of the location of a huge stash of gold, he basically forgot about the box for two decades. In 1845, he opened it, and found three papers covered entirely in numbers of between one and three digits. According to the letter, the first paper gave the location of the cache, the second gave the details of what was stashed, and the third listed the people involved. There was no cipher key, however, and Morriss wasn't up to cracking the code himself, so he forgot about it for another 20 years.

In 1862, Morriss knew that he was dying, and passed the box on to a nameless friend, who spent (you guessed it) 20 years trying to decipher the papers. Eventually, he realised that the code was a book cipher, meaning the key was in the form of an existing text. In this case the text was the Declaration Of Independence. Using the Declaration as a key, the second of the three papers gave up the plain text translation describing how roughly 3 tons of gold and silver are stashed within 4 miles of Buford's Tavern. The first and third papers, however, kept their secrets.

In 1885, the anonymous translator enlisted one James B. Ward to make the story and ciphers public, perhaps in the hope of prompting an appearance of the missing cipher keys, in the form of a pamphlet. The pamphlet was expensive – a dozen pages for the equivalent of $15 today – but it was also very successful. So successful, in fact, that people have tried to crack the other two ciphers ever since. So far nobody has succeeded, despite the best efforts of both professional and amateur cryptographers from around the world.

Despite this failure, some of those people, and others just taking wild stabs in the dark, have also been digging up Bedford County ever since. This has brought plenty of tourist dollars in to the County economy, but has also proved something of a pain for local residents, who are doubtless heartily sick of the attention by now, and envy those who need only worry about moles or gophers.

## PREVIOUS SEARCHES IN FACT AND FICTION

Over 130 years there have been many searches for the Beale treasure, however most of these have not involved metal detectors, libraries, or fights and car chases with rivals. Rather, most seekers of the Beale treasure have gone the route of simply obtaining copies of the three published cipher papers and trying to crack the code. The first attempts are actually mentioned in the pamphlet itself, as part of the story. What Morriss did in his attempts to decode the ciphers isn't described in detail, but his nameless friend says that the Declaration of Independence gave 'assistance by which that paper's meaning was made clear'.

In 1898, two brothers named George and Clayton Hart became interested in the pamphlet's cipher, and began poring over it to try to find a solution. As well as trying a variety of texts as keys to the cipher, the Wards approached a psychic, who claimed to contact Beale's spirit, in order for Beale himself to narrate his burial of the treasure. The psychic also described seeing Beale consult a large Bible, which has also been a popular choice for cryptographers looking for keys to this and other ciphers. Beale's ghost didn't bother to reveal the cipher key, or anything about the contents of the two untranslated papers.

Clayton Hart also met the publisher, James Beverly Ward, and his son in 1903. Hart particularly wanted to ask whether Ward had written the pamphlet himself, but Ward and his son insisted that this was not the case. Neighbours of the Wards gave character references, reassuring the Harts that Ward was respectable, not a liar. The Wards also confirmed that Morriss had been the owner of the Washington Hotel in Lynchburg from 1819 to 1862.

Nothing came of the brothers' researches, and Clayton gave up interest in the Beale treasure in 1912. George, however, continued the search for answers until age and infirmity got the better of him 40 years later. He came to the conclusion that the hoard was buried in the vicinity of Goose Creek, a few miles east of Roanoke, Virginia. In 1964, George published the story of their study of the cipher, in a 67-page booklet. This brought the story of the treasure to a new generation of treasure hunters, and also gave the modern age its first look at the pamphlet, all the originals of which were thought at the time to have disappeared and been forgotten. In fact, the Harts' booklet says most of them were destroyed in a fire at the printers, Job Printworks, in 1883.

In 1934, the Library of Congress made a study, but decided that the pamphlet was simply a hoax, and that there was no true cipher, nor any evidence that any of the story had ever happened.

In the 1960s, the Director of Computer Sciences at Sperry-RAND, the builders of UNIVAC machines, was one Carl Hammer, another Beale Cipher fan. Hammer was convinced the story was true, and that history will not record the name of the first person to crack the code – 'We will learn only the name of the second person to crack it – the one who follows directions to Beale's underground vault, and finds it empty,' Hammer once said. He spent the next couple of decades having UNIVAC computers try to crack the code, and formed a study group to examine the text in 1968.

This became The Beale Cypher Association a few years later, and membership cost $25, which entitled members – mainly academics, and amateur cryptographers – to a quarterly newsletter, access to seminars, and the chance to publish articles and theories on the matter. The Association eventually folded in 1996.

By 1979, Hammer's computers came to the conclusion that the cipher was genuinely encoded, not created by coin-flipping or random number tables, and not just a random jumble of numbers. Hammer felt the person who encoded paper B2 was sloppy, not a professional, 'learned by doing', and hadn't bothered to evolve his technique. Crude or not, the cipher still hadn't given up any English translation.

In the late 1970s, however, cryptographers such as Jim Gillogly used the Declaration of Independence to confirm that the first and third ciphers were, at least, not random gibberish. Several strings of letters appeared when the Declaration was used as the key, which the cryptographers assure us would not happen if the cipher was random.

The ciphers were even made part of the training programme for the US Signal Intelligence Service, because its then boss deemed them to be of 'diabolical ingenuity, specifically designed to lure the unwary reader'.

Some treasure hunters dispensed with the task of deciphering the papers altogether, and resorted to more speculative action. Groups of people routinely get arrested in Bedford County for unauthorized digging on private property. One woman even dug up the cemetery of a local church in 1983, convinced that Beale had hidden the treasure there.

This was at the top of Porter's Mountain, which is exactly 4 miles from Buford's Tavern. The landowners in this area are now painfully aware of treasure hunters and anybody wishing to dig here must apply for permission.

Surprisingly, the Beale treasure wasn't a plot point in either of the Nicolas Cage *National Treasure* movies, nor in Dan Brown's similar *The Lost Symbol* novel. It wasn't even in *Cryptonomicon*, Neal Stephenson's novel centring on codes and ciphers. In fact, although people have been trying to dig it up for 150 years or so, it has made relatively little appearance in novels, comics, games, or movies.

There have been plenty of documentaries mentioning the ciphers and the supposed treasure, particularly over the past decade or so, in TV shows such as *Mysteries* and *Brad Meltzer's Decoded*, but fiction has stayed strangely away from the legend.

The Beale story has influenced treasure-hunting media and stories in general, though. Ciphers leading to the locations of lost treasure have actually been fairly common plot elements, but these tend to have been – in franchises such as *Assassin's Creed*, and novels by the likes of Dan Brown – couched in terms of Freemasons and Masonic codes and conspiracies, rather than the Beale papers.

That said, the trope of the 'Lost Dutchman's Mine' may itself be a folkloric evolution of at least part of the Beale story; the part about men having found rich seams of precious metals and kept the location a secret. This is a folktale that grew up in the US around 1891–92, after the death of Jacob Waltz, a German immigrant (the term 'Dutch' is a corruption of 'Deutsch') who had claimed to have found a rich seam of gold in the American south-west, and opened a mine, but kept the location a secret, as did Beale and his men.

Waltz in fact was a farmer, whose business was ruined when his land was flooded, and he became ill. He then lived off tales of this lost mine, which he had told to his nurse. She sold pamphlets and maps to the location for $7 each. Nobody seemed to mind that no-one had ever come back with the loot. This story probably would have been forgotten in favour of the Beale story if not for the death of Adolph Ruth in 1931. Ruth had gone off into the wilds to search for Waltz's mine, and when his body turned up six months later with two bullets in the skull, people assumed he'd been murdered for the discovery. Thus a new, more popular, legend was born. By the 1970s, there were several times as many books and pamphlets about the Lost Dutchman's Mine than there were about Captain Kidd's treasure.

It's not so surprising that something like the Beale papers, which required mental investment on the part of the reader, were largely forgotten.

# THE TRUTH IS OUT THERE

First off, the original pamphlet is out there to read for free. You can find it online at the Internet Archive: http://www.archive.org/details/TheBealePapers.

Although James Ward and Son assured the Hart brothers that Morriss had been proprietor of the Washington Inn from 1819, they lied. In fact Morriss took the hotel over in 1823, according to documents at the time.

Another theory, championed by a researcher called Robert Ward (no relation), is that the papers given to Morriss were written by Edgar Allan Poe. Poe was known as an amateur cryptographer, and had in fact first popularized the idea of using coded clues to treasure in his 1843 story *The Gold Bug* (which also involves a literal gold insect, whose bite compels the treasure hunt). His only novel, *The Narrative of Arthur Gordon Pym of Nantucket*, published in 1838, also had the characters decode some mysterious hieroglyphs. Poe also left a number of ciphers – the Edgar Allan Poe Cryptographic Challenge – for later generations to attempt to decode. So he certainly has the form for it. Some Beale treasure hunters think that he left the Beale papers to his sister, Rosalie, who sold off bits and pieces of his memorabilia before she died in 1874. The theory goes that she sold the original Beale letters and ciphers to James Ward sometime around 1862.

So, an analysis of writing – 'stylometry' – was applied to a Poe story, *The Journal of Julius Rodman*, which is about an expedition across the Rockies, to the William Morriss parts of *The Beale Papers* pamphlet, and to the Beale papers. According to this test, the writing in all three samples was the product of the same person, i.e. Edgar Allan Poe.

There's a bit of a problem with this, as inimical to the theory as spring-loaded spikes are to adventurers, and that is the fact that the text of the pamphlet refers to the Civil War, which didn't start until a dozen years after Poe died. This means that either Poe was *amazingly* prescient; somebody else wrote the Rodman story; or this 'stylography' thing is a load of rubbish.

Interestingly, even the guy who invented this stylography process warns that it's problematic for author identification, and that it needs a lot of samples to work – neither the Poe story nor the pamphlet are large enough samples, and you'd have to compare Poe's entire output to an equivalent amount of Beale to get a significant result.

The letters also refer to 'stampeding', and many skeptics point out that the word stampede didn't originate until around the 1840s. (Prior to that, there was only the Spanish word 'estampedo', meaning a commotion.) The skeptics are only half right, though; the noun 'stampede' wasn't coined in print until 1844, but the intransitive verb 'to' stampede appears as early as 1823, and this is the sense in which the word is used in the letter from Beale, so it isn't actually really a point against it having been written in 1822. The other word seized upon by skeptics is 'improvise', supposedly not coined officially until 1826. However, 'improvising' had been a musical term for an unpredicted turn since the end of the 18th century, and 'improvisation' had been a fancy word for an unforeseen occurrence since the late 15th century. Again, it's far from impossible that the reverse-engineered verb 'improvise' could have been around five years before its first 'official' appearance.

Another, more practical, problem is that the third cipher, purporting to give the details and addresses of 30 men, only runs to 618 characters – that's a fraction under 22 characters for each man's details. Clearly this isn't enough to contain the information it's supposed to.

As with so many conspiracy theories, it didn't take long for people to start pointing their fingers at the Freemasons, who are always a popular choice for the shadowy figures behind America-centric historical mysteries, especially when codes and symbols are involved. There are some Masonic connections to the story. Firstly, there's the description of the treasure being located in a vault of stone, which is part of a Masonic legend about the Biblical character Enoch. Also, the Freemasons are known for using codes and coded tales as lessons. Thirdly, James B. Ward was a Mason from 1862 to around 1867 (after which he was kicked out for spending too much time with those other code-loving robe-wearers, the Ku Klux Klan). Notice that 1862, when Ward became a Mason, is also when the pamphlet claims Morriss suddenly started hinting to people that he had secret knowledge.

All of the people named in the story historically existed in more or less the roles they have in the pamphlet, with one fairly major and obvious exception: Thomas Jefferson Beale himself.

No census record of a Thomas Jefferson Beale exists from the period, although records for some areas are missing or incomplete. That said, his forenames are obviously taken from the founding father of the same name, though these were presumably popular names for boys in the late 18th century, when he would have had to have been born.

Another problem with the story is that gold and silver ores do not look to the naked eye like what we'd recognize as gold and silver. They have to be refined and processed, unless they're found as nuggets in sediment – in which case, because of their differing geological origins, they are never found together. Such a find would have also been one of the biggest in US history – certainly the biggest in what would later become Colorado – and would have sparked a huge gold rush.

Assuming *The Beale Papers* is a work of fiction, then the name Beale probably derives from the sailor, explorer, Presidential surveyor, and (eventually) US Ambassador to Austro-Hungary, Edward Fitzgerald Beale. This Beale had been born in 1822 – the year when Thomas Beale supposedly brought the box with the ciphers to Morriss – and had led all manner of expeditions across the continent. He had even carried genuine treasure, smuggling proof of gold deposits in California across what was then still part of Mexico, in 1848, so as to deliver it to the Federal government.

In 1883, large chunks of Lynchburg, Virginia, were affected by a fire, and one building that was totally destroyed was the home of both *The Virginian* newspaper, and the Job Printing Works – the latter of which was run by one James Beverly Ward.

Both the paper and the printing firm suffered financially; their equipment was destroyed, and their workers laid off while repairs were conducted. Some form of income was needed to help get the businesses and their workers back on their feet.

The cipher key was the Declaration of Independence; and the cipher was solved by taking each number from the code, and counting to that number word in the Declaration. The first letter of that word would be a letter of the decoded message. There is an interesting fact about this decoding, however: Whoever encoded it made some mistakes in the count, and so the words the reader is supposed to get to are not always the correct ones. And yet Ward somehow made the exact same mistakes in order to decode it. In other words, the person who encoded, and the person who decoded it, are one and the same. Ward created the whole thing as a puzzle fiction to raise funds for the wrecked business and its workers.

You'd think that if the pamphlet is a fiction, and it was written in 1885, then the answer to the question of where the treasure is now must be 'nowhere, because it never existed'. There's logic to that, but there's also a *But…*

There were actually local tales of buried treasure in Bedford County that predate the Beale papers. Ward didn't simply make up the whole thing out of his own imagination. He combined some existing folktales with a dash of Poe's popular cryptography and a few fashionable elements of puzzle.

Basically, in 1819 a guy called Thomas Read, and some friends, borrowed a wagon with a block and tackle from a man called Sheriff Isaac Otey of Bedford County, according to Bedford County court records, to move pots of silver. In the process, they broke the hoist and damaged the wagon. Read then went off west somewhere when Sherriff Otey tried to claim compensation of $20–$25.

Two years later, Read came back as part of a wagon train, but a mail courier spotted him in route and warned Otey, who put together a posse of friends and family, including several Bufords. There were even armed slaves in the posse, which intercepted Read near Apple Orchard Overlook, on what is now the Blue Ridge Parkway. Sheriff Otey arrested him on charges of damages to his property.

Read and some men in the wagon train decided to resist arrest – it was the Wild West, after all – and several of the men were Native Americans, which meant that the posse were more than happy to slaughter and bury them at the roadside. The posse then looted the wagons and bodies, finding some gold, silver and jewels. They then buried the white bodies in a field owned by one of the posse, named Luck.

Paschal Buford, who was Otey's brother-in-law as well as a horse farmer, and owner of Buford's Tavern, later recommended that his grandson William buy Wilkerson's Mill, on Goose Creek. William in turn was a friend of, yes, James Beverly Ward, and the pair bought the Mill together. Ward was married to Harriet, a grand-niece of Sheriff Otey, who was also a grand-niece of Robert Morriss. Funny how all these familiar names are connected, isn't it?

The other inspiration for *The Beale Papers* was a story in *The Virginian* newspaper in 1879. This retold a story, from a Kentucky newspaper, of a man who had left coded instructions to where he had buried gold, silver and jewellery in a sugar kettle in a cave in the early years of the Civil War. Robert Willis had stashed this loot on his farmland in Kentucky, in 1861, before going on a cattle drive to Nashville. Willis was killed, but his widow kept the secret, living off it for 18 years. Before she died, she owned up to the secret, and left instructions that a large chunk of what was left – $65,000 in gold and silver, and $10,000 in jewellery – be given to charity and to keep her now-aged servants comfortable.

There's a lot of commonality between this and the Beale story: similar amounts of the same types of treasure, stashed in iron pots in caves, with a single person keeping the secret...

The Beale treasure, then, isn't quite imaginary, but also isn't quite real. It's a confabulation of an exaggeration of the valuables carried by Thomas Read, and the Willis treasure of 1879, which was of a comparable size and value.

Unfortunately this means that, while there *is* treasure associated with the Beale ciphers, it's not treasure that can be found by cracking the code. It was simply the inspiration for the Beale story.

## WHERE IS IT NOW?

The Willis treasure, obviously, was found in 1879, and returned to the local economy. Likewise, the valuables carried by Read were either stashed in Wilkerson's Mill – in which case William Buford and James Ward will have dug it up – or else was the capital with which the two men bought the property. Either way, it too was returned into the Bedford County economy nearly 150 years ago.

It's still a fun challenge to work out where Ward intended the treasure to be located – there have been treasure-hunting games, published as books, which led to prizes, so perhaps Ward might have at least hidden a congratulatory message somewhere, for whoever solved his puzzle.

Any search, sticking to the information known from the pamphlet, needs to be within a 4-mile radius of the site of Buford's Tavern. This is hard to find nowadays, but is a decrepit house visible from Route 460 (the West Lynchburg–Salem Turnpike), a few miles south-west of the village of Montvale. On rougher maps that don't show Montvale, it's about 8 miles west north-west of Bedford and, from the other side, about 11 miles north-east of Roanoke.

The nearby Goose Creek is a good location for a treasure hunt (there's a nice hiking trail along it) but it doesn't fall within the 4-mile range from the site of Buford's Tavern. However, there is also an outcrop of hills called Goose Creek Peaks, which is well within the 4-mile limit.

Mountain View Cemetery, dug up by a woman in 1983, is 4 miles east of the Buford site, and about half a mile south-west of Montvale. That said, over the years, there have been reports of individuals and groups excavating in every cemetery in Bedford County – and a little bit beyond – just on the off-chance.

## THE OPPOSITION IN YOUR WAY

Technically, none, since the Beale treasure is fictional, and the two hoards that inspired it were recovered long ago. That said, if you plan to go digging up cemeteries, you ought to be prepared for opposition from the local police and sheriffs' departments, as well as annoyed local residents.

The area is home to brown bears, so do be careful not to get between an adult bear and her cubs, as that is the best way to get attacked. Making noise when walking through the woods is usually enough to alert the bears to your presence, and will encourage them to stay out of your way. If you have an urge or tendency to move quietly so as not to disturb animals, forget that habit in bear country: the second-best way to get attacked by a bear is to sneak up and surprise it.

Snake-wise, there are northern pine snakes, which are harmless but grow up to 7ft long. They have green/brown patches on a white or cream base colour, and will play dead rather than attack. There are also eastern hognosed snakes, which will hide and sometimes spray musk at you, but are otherwise harmless, and eastern king snakes, which have red markings.

This part of Virginia is also a hotspot for Bigfoot sightings, if that sort of thing worries you.

As for human predators, the Lynchburg area is rated as more crime-ridden than average for the State by the FBI, with a crime rate higher than 86 per cent of the rest of Virginia – but it still has only average crime for the US as a whole.

It's worth noting, if you are a fan of bourbon, that this Lynchburg is *not* the home of Jack Daniel's. *That* Lynchburg is in Tennessee.

ORG. IV. MEER

OCEAN

(SÜDLICHES EISMEER)

80

R. T FORSCHTES

SÜD · POL

Westliche Länge von Greenwich

180 v. Paris

Anzeichen von hohem Land

en Südpol erreichte Breite 78°10'
Ross, Febr. 1842

Senkrechte Eiswand, 150–200 F. hoch

Beaufort I.

Franklin I.
600 F.

Anzeichen von hohem Land

Offenes Meer

Viele Walfische

Packeis,
Ross März 1842

# TREASURES

# OF ASIA

# KUSANAGI AND THE HONJO MASAMUNE

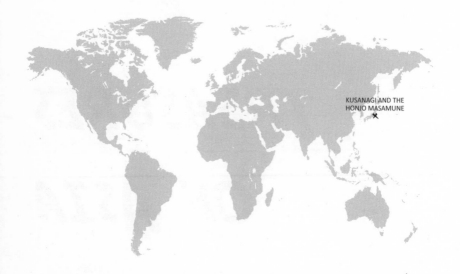

KUSANAGI AND THE
HONJO MASAMUNE

## WHAT IS IT?

These two treasures are particular kinds of specialist antique: historic swords.

Kusanagi-no-Tsurugi, which means Grasscutter-sword, is one of the three pieces (the others are a curved jewel and an eight-sided mirror) of the Japanese Imperial Regalia, which are supposed to be used in imperial coronation ceremonies, but which haven't been seen in public for centuries. Kusanagi was, according to legend, given to the Twelfth Emperor of Japan by the goddess Amaterasu.

The Honjo Masamune is a more recent sword; a katana made by the swordsmith Gorō Nyūdō Masamune sometime around AD 1300. It actually became known as Honjo Masamune 300 years later, after the 16th century General Honjō Shigenaga took it as a spoil of battle, and it went on to be a physical symbol of the

Shogunate throughout the Edo period. It is considered by some historians, and lots of admirers of Japanese culture, to be the finest sword ever made. It was last seen in 1946, being handed over to an American soldier at a police station in the Mejiro district of Tokyo.

## HOW MUCH IS IT WORTH TO YOU?

Kusanagi's worth is difficult to estimate, as it has an essentially mythical origin. That said, there have been actual physical versions of the sword, dating back to around the 8th century. An intact sword of that age – in any culture – would be worth millions.

Likewise, the Honjo Masamune, a katana dating from the 14th century, would be worth around $5-$8 million today, just as an antique – that's the kind of range in which other swords of similar vintage have been valued. Given its history, and its sacred place in Japanese culture, however, it should actually fetch a lot more.

## THE STORY

Kusanagi is a sword from legend, like Excalibur. Rather than a Sword in the Stone, however, it was the Sword in the Snake, having been torn from the body of an eight-headed hydra-like serpent, which had been slain by Susa-no-O-no-Mikoto, the god of storm and sea. (He defeated it by the simple expedient of getting all eight heads drunk on rice wine, and then cutting them off. Unsporting, but effective.) The sword was originally called Ame-no-Murakumo-no-Tsurugi, and Susa-no-O gave it to his sister, the sun goddess Amaterasu, who in turn gave it to the 1st century warrior Yamato Takeru. Yamato was then lured into a trap by a demonic enemy, who set the grassland around him on fire, intending to burn him alive. Yamato, however, used the sword to cut away the grass and scatter it to the winds, and so the sword acquired its new name – Grass-Cutter sword.

For centuries, the sword has been considered the symbol of valour in the Imperial Regalia, despite having been stolen at least once, lost in a sea battle at least once, and was last seen uncovered in the Edo period (somewhere between the 16th and 19th centuries!)

Since then, it has always been covered up in sacred wrappings, as have the rest of the Imperial Regalia. They're all said to be housed in the Atsuta Shrine in Nagano Prefecture, though not on public display, and Kusanagi hasn't been seen in centuries. The Japanese authorities have long kept the world guessing about the reality and ownership status of Kusanagi by this means.

The Honjo Masamune was made around 1326 by the master swordsmith Masamune. According to legend, he had a competition about it with his great rival (and some say prodigal student), Sengo Muramasa. Each smith hung a sword they had made over a stream. The Muramasa cut clean through everything that touched it, including fish, sticks and leaves, while the Masamune only cut the leaves, but deflected the fish aside. Muramasa claimed victory, as his sword had cut more, but a watching monk disagreed. The monk said this test had proved the Masamune's superiority, because it was as good at deflecting things aside, and didn't cut things unnecessarily, by which he meant it didn't slice up innocent bystanding lifeforms like the fish.

This, incidentally, led to another Samurai sword legend – that a blade drawn must taste blood. The tradition became attached specifically to Muramasa blades, after the monk declared Muramasa's blade as potentially evil, as it was indiscriminately bloodthirsty. Over time, that idea spread to other parts of the culture.

The Honjo Masamune got the 'Honjo' appellation from General Honjō Shigenaga, who, at the tender age of 21, won it as booty in the Fourth Battle of Kawanakajima, in 1561. Shigenaga was one of Japan's most famous historical badasses – the previous owner of the sword that now bears Honjo's name actually used it in the battle to split Shigenaga's helmet clean in half. Amazingly, however, it didn't do the same to Shigenaga's head, and he was able to kill the guy and take his sword.

The story ensured the sword would always bear his name, but, sadly, Shigenaga wasn't as good an accountant as he was a badass, and four years later he sold it to the Toyotomi Shogun, ruler of Japan. Five years after that, Tokugawa Ieyasu kicked out the Toyotomi, and founded the legendary Tokugawa Shogunate.

Ieyasu was so impressed with the sword – since by this point

Masamune was already long-established as the greatest smith ever in Japanese culture – that he made it a symbol of his dynasty, and it remained so until the shogunate ended in 1868. His descendants still kept it, however, until World War II, when the sword was owned by Tokugawa Iemasu, President of the House of Peers (the Japanese equivalent to the UK's House of Lords). After the surrender of Japan in 1945, the Allied Occupation Authority decided that swords were all cultural weapons of war that needed to be impounded and destroyed. They were to be given to police stations, who would turn them over to the appropriate Allied officials.

Iemasu, to settle angrier voices, and perhaps thinking that they would be returned as historical artefacts, happily turned over the whole Tokugawa sword collection, including the near-legendary Honjo Masamune, which was then considered the most famous and valuable sword in Japan. He took 15 historical blades to the Mejiro police station in Tokyo, in December 1945. From there, they were handed on to a US 7th Cavalry sergeant named on the station's paperwork as Coldy Bimore. None of them were ever seen again, and it turns out that no Coldy Bimore has ever served in the US military.

# PREVIOUS SEARCHES IN FACT AND FICTION

Kusanagi hasn't been the subject of much treasure-hunting in real life, as opinion is fairly split between those who feel it isn't lost (and lives at the Atsuta Shrine), and those who feel it never existed in the first place. Neither of which are good motivators for searching for it.

That said, about a decade ago, a news team from NHK, Japan's national TV network, did try to gain access to the sword in order to film it and verify its condition. Negotiations broke down, however, and the film crew was turned away when they arrived at the shrine.

Its legendary status, however, means it has been used a lot in fiction, especially in manga, anime and videogames. It's especially prevalent in the *Final Fantasy* series of videogames, as well as in the *Naruto* and *Usagi Yojimbo* franchises. It appears in *Okami*,

*Sailor Moon* (in the guise of the Space Sword) and can be acquired in *World of Warcraft*. It's also used by one of the villains in *The Darkness II*. In most of these, it doesn't remotely resemble the correct type of sword, but is usually depicted as either a katana or some kind of glaive.

In western culture, it's one of the three holy swords that contain a nail from the crucifixion in Jim Butcher's *Dresden Files* novels, and is stolen in the Steve Martin movie *The Pink Panther 2* (in which it's a katana).

It also gave its name to the main protagonist of the *Ghost In The Shell* franchise, just as its supposed owner, Yamato, gave his name to the world's biggest battleship in World War II. The sword has also recently given its name to the largest wooden building in Japan, the Kusanagi Sports Complex Gymnasium.

The Honjo Masamune has been the focus of searching for decades, but this has mainly been in the form of online research, sifting through libraries, and so on.

Sword and treasure-hunting Internet forums are occasionally enlivened by people claiming to have found it, and sometimes even showing photos or videos as an attempt at proof. However, the Honjo has, like all handmade swords, individual characteristics and blade markings (you can see the 1945 drawing of the markings here: http://ericwrites.com/wp-content/uploads/2015/01/honjo.jpg), and none have yet matched, nor indeed turned out to have Masamune's signature (which few of his blades do, but the Honjo is one of them).

There is a Masamune that's known to have come back to the US in March 1946, brought by General Walter Krüger of the 6th Army. This one was presented to President Harry S. Truman, on behalf of the Japanese government, and is held in the Truman Library. It's unsigned but authenticated and so, no, not the Honjo, but it is one of only ten known surviving Masamune blades.

In 2014, the Shimazu Masamune, another signed blade, turned up in Kyoto, having previously disappeared during the war. It wasn't one of those that Iemasu had turned over in 1945, as his family had gifted it to Princess Kazu in 1862.

The Honjo, like Kusanagi, makes frequent appearances, with appropriate special powers, in manga, anime and videogames. It is the focus of an episode of *Warehouse 13*, in which it has the power to make the wielder invisible because it is so sharp that it actually cuts light.

# THE TRUTH IS OUT THERE

While Kusanagi's origin is obviously mythical, sword development in Japan does go back a long way, centuries before the first katana and tachi style swords – what Westerners tend to think of as Japanese swords – came about.

It's known from finds at places such as Misasagi, the old imperial mausolea, and various other ancient burial sites, that swords of the form matching Kusanagi's description have been made from the 2nd century BC, through to the 8th century AD. Prior to the 8th century, there was no standard cultural sword design in Japan. By the 6th century Chinese, Korean and Japanese smiths were producing swords with blades running from 2ft to 4ft, with different types of hilt. They were all straight-bladed, whether single- or double-edged, and the tip curved inwards on both sides to a point – pretty much like Bronze-Age swords from other parts of the world. This type of sword was known as Tsurugi in Japanese, and later as Ken – the Japanese pronunciation of the Chinese ideogram, which remains as the root for the words kendo and kenjutsu, Japanese sword-fighting arts.

After that point, the influence of mainland Chinese and Korean swords began to take effect, and the tsuba type of guard, and curved blades, became the dominant form. Around this time, quality steel became more widely available, and the best swords in Japan were imported from the Chinese kingdom of Eastern Wu, which the Japanese called Kure (no relation to the present day city of Kure, which is in Hiroshima Prefecture, and was founded in 1902). These were considered the most valuable swords of the period, both as weapons and as ceremonial status symbols.

Circa AD 702, the sword Kogarasu Maru was made by the smith Amakuni, and this is pretty much the first true tachi, with a curved blade, signed on the tang. This would launch the reputation of the katana and tachi style blades as being of superior quality and artwork.

This is also the era in which the 7th century *Kojiki*, one of the earliest Japanese texts, was written. Like the original Norse myths, or the British tales of King Arthur, or the Greek myths, this text is not particularly historical, hence the completely fantastical tale of the sword's discovery, which the text sets somewhere probably around 100 BC. Kusanagi was famous even by this point, though it was said to have been stolen by a monk from either China or Korea, and the loss having killed off the tenth Emperor. This is mentioned in another early text, the *Nihon Shoki*, written in the early 8th century which, although it also includes fantastical elements such as Creation myths, soon gives way to reportage of 7th century events. In this text, Kusanagi was stolen in the 660s, and returned about 20 years later, at which point it was given into the care of the Atsuta Shrine.

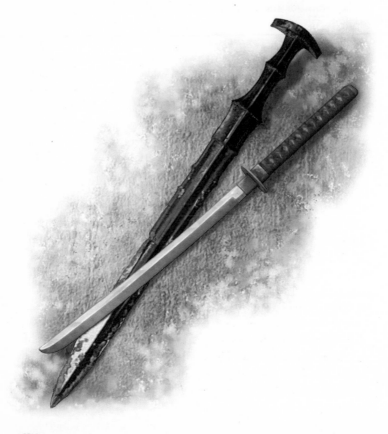

It's next referred to in *The Tale of the Heike*, having been lost at sea in the 1185 Battle of Dan-no-ura. It's also, however, in the 13th century that the first replica of it is confirmed to have been made, in 1210. That makes this the closest thing to an original Kusanagi, being the first definitely-existing physical version. From here on in, there is something that the Atsuta Shrine can actually have in storage. A monk in the Edo period was able to describe the sword as 33in long, well maintained and with a white metallic sheen to it.

Now things get interesting: in the 19th century, a second (at least) replica was made for the emperor to have with him. This replica existed until at least 1945, owned by Hirohito. After the war, however, it disappeared; it probably would have been handed over to the occupying forces, or taken as a prize, but perhaps not. Either way, the focus on the occupying forces has always been about a different sword...

The 14th century artisan Gorō Nyūdō Masamune experimented for years to find a way to make a blade that couldn't be dinged, at least under normal circumstances. His work brought apprentices to his door from all over the empire, wanting to learn his secret. In the end, his ten apprentices all became famous masters of sword-making in their own right, and the golden age of the 'samurai sword' was in full swing.

Masamune's process amounted to the ability to temper blades at a much higher temperature than anyone had before. Smiths who had reached such temperatures found that their blades would crack or warp when quenched. Masamune was able to acquire better quality materials for all parts of the forging process, not just the steel itself. He was then able to make his blades by a process called *nijuba*, which involves annealing and tempering the blade by heating and quenching it twice.

Signed Masamune swords became rarer as his life went on, as apparently he went into a level of conceit in which he felt he didn't need to sign blades, as he insisted that they were so superior that anyone seeing one would recognize it at once. This, of course, is another reason why the Honjo Masamune would be so valuable, as it is one he did sign on the tang, somewhere around 1326 (he died in 1343).

There's no truth to the story of his rivalry with Muramasa, whether as master and apprentice or otherwise, as Muramasa lived two hundred years after Masamune.

After World War II, General Douglas MacArthur ordered a total disarmament of Japan, which was by then occupied by Allied forces. This disarmament was to include swords, partly because they were such a part of the warrior culture there, which meant they were thought to inspire resistance (and if you think that couldn't happen in Western countries, the Union government did it with bagpipes after the Jacobite Rebellion, for the same reason!), and partly because mass-produced swords had been issued to the military during the war.

There was a difference between the crude rolled-steel swords made in the 1930s and 1940s – which the Japanese didn't consider true swords – and the historic hand-made antiques. To the Allies this meant modern cheap ones should be destroyed – and many were melted down or dumped in ocean reefs – and that the antiques were great souvenirs for officers.

The fate of such weapons was the responsibility of the Foreign Liquidations Commission of the US Army Forces Western Pacific. They would collect swords from police stations and take them for appropriate analysis, storage and disposal. Naturally this process often actually ended up with soldiers of the unit weeding out the best blades to give as gifts and souvenirs to higher-ranking officers, who would bring them home to the US when their service finished.

Tokugawa Iemasu had handed in the Honjo Masamune and 14 other swords in December 1945. In January, they were picked up by 'Sgt Coldy Bimore', who, as we know, never existed. The name is the product of a botched translation – either phonetic, when the Mejiro policeman tried to write it down, or in transliteration back from kanji, the Japanese pictographic script.

If it's a pronunciation issue, then it means the name could have been Cody someone, or Cole somebody, or even Colonel D somebody. If it's a kanji transliteration issue, though, then actually it could have been something like Dickson or Dickerson as a surname, rather than Bimore. Some people have wondered if he simply could have been planning a scam, and asked 'could I buy more?' rather than giving a name.

All that said, there is a name that's at least phonetically similar, and whom records show was serving in the right place at the right time: Cole D. B. Moore, a Technician 4th Grade attached to the Foreign Liquidations Commission, service number 34681402. Score another match for 'Coldy Bimore', as, although Moore wasn't a sergeant, the T/4 grade insignia was three chevrons over a T – which anyone would simply assume meant sergeant because of three chevrons. Moore was demobbed in April 1946, but why didn't people link Bimore to him sooner? Probably because his service records were among millions destroyed in a fire at the National Personnel Records Center in 1973.

The National Archives, however, says Moore was a farmer from Wilcox County, Georgia, in civilian life. Sadly, Moore died some years ago, and is buried at the Christian Home Cemetery in Pitts, Wilcox County. His widow died in 2012, but they also had five children and numerous grandchildren.

## WHERE IS IT NOW?

The original Kusanagi most likely never existed as an actual pre-8th century sword, though there have been several replicas to that style of manufacture over the centuries. At least one replica was housed at Atsuta from the 13th century onwards, and another in the Imperial Palace until 1945. Since then, neither have been seen uncovered, and it's possible that either or both were taken by the Allied occupation forces and either brought home as a war prize or destroyed.

Clearly the fact that the Atsuta one has remained covered up ever since means there's something iffy going on – at best, time is taking its toll on the 13th-century blade and nobody wants to show it off in that state. Perhaps, however, it's actually the Victorian replica, or a new one, or simply an empty container with no sword remaining. The shrine was heavily bombed during World War II, and rebuilt afterwards. Although it contains thousands of historic artefacts, who knows how many were destroyed?

If there was a Kusanagi prior to the one made in 1210, it was probably made somewhere in the late 7th century, in between the writing of the *Kojiki* and the *Nihon Shoki*. Lost at sea, it will

## CONSERVATION AND CARE

The conservation and care of antiques and antiquities is a very specialist matter – and every type of artefact has its own special requirements.

These, however, are not really matters for the treasure hunter, as it's your job to find the things, not to look after them. It will be the responsibility of the ultimate owner, whether that be a museum or private individual, to take care of the artefact. That said, it's always worth being aware of the fact that there will be an issue.

In the treasure hunter's case the important thing will be to make sure that the treasure is recovered safely, which will be dependent on both its nature and the environment in which it is to be found. Organic material submerged in the right depth of water might well be preserved, due to the lack of oxygen available to rot causing bacteria. In such a case, bringing it to the surface will cause it to rot, and you don't want that. For example, anyone who remembers the media coverage of the raising of the Tudor warship *Mary Rose* will remember that the wood of the ship had to be kept wet with salt water so that it would not dry out and rot and crumble.

The biggest likely problem with treasure found on land will be fragility. Even gold jewellery can be fragile, and a piece will be worth far more intact than in fragments, so the utmost care must be taken when unearthing anything. Always be gentle. It also helps to follow the archaeological procedure of documenting your dig with pictures before you pick it up, so that if an object does break as you bring it out of its location, you have a record of how it should be put back together.

Care and restoration of your discoveries, however, is really a matter for professionals, be they museum conservators or jewellers. Never be tempted to get scrubbing with a brillo pad. Also always be wary of exposing new finds to direct sunlight, especially if they are textiles or papers or parchments, as there is a risk of their fading.

have rusted away to nothing in the Shimonoseki Strait, under the Kanmonkyo suspension bridge in the city of Shimonoseki, as that is what's now on the site of the Dan-no-ura battle.

The Honjo Masamune, on the other hand, definitely did exist, and suffered one of two fates. One possibility is that Cole Moore simply did his job, and delivered his consignment of swords to the furnace, to be melted down. If so, then it – along with the other 14 antique masterpieces – is gone forever.

The other possibility is slightly more likely. The difference in quality and value between the mass-produced military katana of the 20th century, and centuries-old antique heirlooms, was obvious to anyone. It was standard unofficial policy for US soldiers to give their superior officers gifts of quality swords. It was also official policy that soldiers were allowed to keep one sword and one firearm as war trophies. This means it's most likely that Moore would have kept one sword, and gifted the others to other officers.

There is, however, no way to tell which sword went where. It's unlikely that Moore kept the Honjo Masamune, as researchers have tried putting his descendants in touch with the Japanese authorities, and nothing has come of it. The Japanese made their own inquiries, and so Moore either wasn't Coldy Bimore, or, far more likely, took home a far less important sword, and gifted the Honjo Masamune to someone else, probably in that three months before being demobbed.

In short, then, the Honjo Masamune is almost certainly (unless it has been pawned or sold) somewhere in the home of a descendant of an unknown officer in the US Army Forces, Western Pacific, who probably never even knew how important a sword it is. Sadly this means there's a very uncomfortable likelihood that this priceless medieval relic has been ruined by being played with by several generations of children. Whoever now has it most likely doesn't know what they have – it's just grandad's or great-grandad's dusty old relic, lying in the attic, or propped in a cluttered basement or garage corner.

## THE OPPOSITION IN YOUR WAY

The big problem with either sword, if you find it outside Japan, is that it can only be properly and officially authenticated in Japan – at which point, being a national treasure, they'll refuse to let it back out!

The Atsuta Shrine is in Nagoya City – 1-1-1 Jingu, Atsuta Ward, Nagoya, Aichi Prefecture 456-8585 – and is open to the public. It's a lovely place, 200km$^2$ of paradise surrounded by a 16th-century wall. It's also got excellent security, hordes of tourists, and the anonymous lump that may or may not be a Kusanagi isn't among the goodies on display, unless there's an imperial coronation when you visit.

# Peking Man

✗ PEKING MAN

## WHAT IS IT?

This treasure is a set of fossils found near Beijing in the 1920s and 1930s. They belong to a subset of human ancestor species Homo Erectus, and are classified as Homo Erectus Pekinensis.

The main pieces are 15 pieces of cranial bone that make up the front half of the skull, plus 11 jawbones and a few limb bones. In total they seem to come from a total of 12 individuals, of different ages. A lot of teeth and stone tools were also found, and several of those teeth actually still exist, at the Palaeontological Museum in the university at Uppsala, Sweden.

A number of prehistoric Homo Sapien skeletons were also found at the same site.

## HOW MUCH IS IT WORTH TO YOU?

In monetary terms, not that much. A reward of $5,000 was offered in 1972, which would equate to about $29,000 today, and a new set of expeditions to search for new specimens has been running for several years.

In terms of historical interest, especially for collectors, the pieces could sell for thousands each, if ever they turn up. As for their anthropological and palaeontological value, they're priceless. They are, after all, the only known examples of Homo Erectus Pekinensis, which is considered to be one of the first – if not the first – tool-using ancestor of modern humanity, as well as being evidence towards the theory that all humans evolved from Africa and then migrated.

## THE STORY

In 1921, Swedish geologist Johan Gunnar Andersson and American palaeontologist Walter Granger went to the area of Zhoukoudian, in China. They were looking for fossils, and were directed by workers at a local quarry to a site whose name translates as 'Dragon Bone Hill' – a sure clue to the presence of ancient bones and fossils.

Andersson recognized that the site was an ancient quartz mine, and that there could be human, or at least hominid, remains in the vicinity, and perhaps their tools. The pair began excavating, but it was their assistant – an Austrian by the name of Otto Zdansky – who found a fossil tooth, which he believed to be human. More pieces were found in 1923 and 1924, and these were sent to Uppsala University, where it was discovered in 1926 that fossilized teeth of a new species of hominid were among the artefacts.

The race was then on to dig up a whole skeleton, even though there were arguments over whether anyone could really have identified a new species from a tooth.

Armed with funding from the Rockefeller Foundation, a 1928 expedition turned up a jawbone, as well as more teeth, and some bits of skull, which led to the foundation of the Cenozoic Research Laboratory at what was then called Peking Union Medical College. By now the digs were being supervised by a team of Chinese Palaeontologists – Yang Zhongjian, Pei Wenzhong and Jia Lanpo – and over the next decade they excavated a couple of hundred fossils, mostly teeth and pieces of skull and jaw – six almost complete. Studying them suggested that they came from at least 40 different individuals. This continued for a decade or so, until the Japanese invaded Manchuria in 1937, and started the Sino-Japanese War.

As the Japanese progressed across China, the authorities became concerned about the safety of the fossils. In November 1941, just a couple of weeks before the Japanese attacked Pearl Harbor, the Cenozoic Research Lab's Hu Chengzi packed them up in two crates for transport to the US. The crates were then taken in a US Marine Corps truck to Camp Holcomb, a Marine base at Qinhuangdao, on the Gulf of Pechili. The intent was to sail the fossils out to Singapore, and then on to the US, eventually to be delivered to the American Museum Of Natural History in New York City.

However, despite the presence of assorted trucks, ships and trains all at the port, and the presence of both Chinese military and US Marine escorts, the crates of fossils were simply never seen again.

## PREVIOUS SEARCHES IN FACT AND FICTION

The Chinese government – both the Nationalists prior to 1948, and the Communists since – have long sought to find the fossils, as they are a prime national treasure. Likewise, the Rockefeller Foundation and the American Natural History Museum have pored through thousands of documents and witness depositions over the years, to try to piece together what happened.

In fiction, the story is probably the inspiration for elements of the plot of the highly entertaining B-movie, *Horror Express*, which involves a crated-up fossil ape-man found in a Chinese cave (but which turns out to be a zombie-creating alien brain parasite that can't stand up to the powerful combo of Peter Cushing and Christopher Lee). It may also have been an influence on *Quatermass and the Pit*.

A $5,000 dollar reward was offered in 1972 by Christopher Janus, a Chicago financier, and president of a charity called the Greek Heritage Foundation. At first the FBI contributed to searching for leads, as did the CIA (let's face it, it's a good cover story for nosing around in China). Janus actually got a response, from a woman claiming to have the bones, but who asked half a million dollars for them.

A writer named Harry L. Shapiro also got involved with Janus's search for the relics, and believed that the mystery woman who asked half a million for the fossils was the widow of a Marine interned at Tianjin, who knew where the crates were hidden. In fact she provided a picture of a box containing skull fragments, but the picture was unclear, and she soon disappeared. In fact she may never have existed, as Janus turned out to be two-faced. In 1981 he was convicted of fraud: a scam he based upon the idea of getting funds needed to make a movie about Peking Man. It'd be interesting to know if he also sought funds to pay the half-million to the person claiming to have the bones. Needless to say, he wasn't actually doing anything about making a movie.

In 2000, the magazine *Guangming Ribao* interviewed Zhou Guoxing, who worked at the Beijing Natural History Museum. He claimed that an American naval officer and Embassy guard had seen two people burying a crate in the grounds at the rear of the American Embassy on the evening before Pearl Harbor, and that he had suspected the contents to be the fossils of Peking Man. Zhou then discovered that a garage had been built on the burial site, and that neither the US nor Chinese governments would allow it to be dug up.

Zhou's story seems to be a variation on something else that happened in 2000 – a Qing-era tomb was found on the grounds of the US Embassy. This, however, was excavated, recovering coins and ancient makeup. No fossils were included.

More interestingly, Zhou Guoxing found a Japanese trail. In 1992, he was visiting an exhibition of fossils in Osaka, and met up with Iketani Senshi, a professor at Shizuoka University. Iketani had been a student of Takai Tōji, who had visited the fossils at the Peking Union Medical College (PUMC). Iketani revealed that that Toji had reported the fossils missing not on his first visit, in 1941, but his third, in August 1942. He and his assistant (now Professor) Nagakai claimed that the fossils had definitely not been taken to Japan, but to America. How this could have happened in August 1942 from occupied China is something he didn't try to explain. Zhou admitted it didn't add up.

The story of the burial in embassy grounds is hearsay, and doesn't fit the timeline. Nor does it make sense for the Japanese to have let the Americans ship stuff out of Qinhuangdao. The Japanese, however, were known to have shipped fossils of Solo Man and Java Man from the Dutch East Indies to Japan. Which brings us to a former Japanese soldier, Nakada Hironami. He claimed that he saw a fossil skull of Peking Man both in Changchun, which, during World War II, was the capital of the Japanese puppet territory of Manchukuo, and in Japan in 1948. In both cases, the skull was in a box owned by his father-in-law, Endo Takaji.

There is a problem with the story, in that the witness claimed to have seen a complete skull, and no such example of Peking Man has ever been found. Only partial bones were recorded and cast, but the inventory for the two crates lists several intact skulls, just to confuse everyone.

It has become a popular theory in recent decades (based on a newspaper story in the *Guangming Daily*) that the fossils went down with a ship named the *Awa Maru*, sunk in 1945. Despite the popularity of the theory, one has to wonder why the Japanese either waited so long to ship them out, or recorded them stolen in 1942.

In 2005, on the 60th Anniversary of VJ Day and the end of World War II, the Fangshan provincial government set up the *Xunzhao Beijingren Tougaigu Huashi Gongzuo Weiyuanhui*, or 'Working Committee to Locate the Fossilized Skulls of Peking Man'.

This committee has been open about being certain the fossils are either in China or Japan.

The committee's 63 stated leads have been paper-thin, however, generally consisting of half-remembered memories of relatives who claimed to have seen skulls or witnessed boxes being buried. One person claimed to have seen a transcript from a US report placing the skulls in Japan, while others claimed to have been shown them by doctors at the PUMC, or to have seen neighbours who worked at the PUMC bring home skulls and bury them.

Oh, and just for fun, China has its own share of creationists, who believe that the fossils are those of monkeys, and that it was an anti-religious hoax all along.

# THE TRUTH IS OUT THERE

As well as the Peking Man fossils, the excavations turned up skeletal fragments of other early hominids and, in the highest cave at the site, ancient Homo Sapiens. These pieces may have helped confuse the issue as to which bones seen by witnesses may have actually been Peking Man fossils.

Originally the fossils were dated at 300,000–500,000 years, but more recent studies have pushed their date back to 700,000 years or more. Clearly the site was occupied for a very long time, as the modern human skeletons there date from around 150,000 years ago.

By 1941, a man called Franz Weidenreich was in charge of the fossils, and he had plaster casts made of all the specimens. This is fortunate, as the casts survive, and so exact accurate replicas have been made of the fossils, which can still be studied today. Weidenreich is the one who arranged for the originals to be transported back to the US while he was returning there, approaching the US Ambassador and Marine Corps to help. They, at first, refused.

He kept trying, however, and after several months, the US authorities agreed, because the Natural History Museum in New York was so interested. In November 1941, Hu Zhengzhi's team had packed everything into two crates, and dropped them off at the Peking Union Medical College's Controller's Office, where they were supposed to have been stored in the No. 4 strong room in Building F. The crates should have then been sent to the US Embassy, and from there transferred to Camp Holcomb and shipped out of Qinhuangdao.

However, the whole area was controlled at the time by the Japanese army, and as of 8 December, the US and Japan were at war. The Japanese immediately took over control of the Peking Union Medical College and started interrogating the American staff. The Japanese were also interested in the fossils, among other loot, and sent two archaeology professors—Hasebe Kotondo and Takai Tōji – to check them out. When Kotondo arrived, however, and went to open up Strongroom No. 4, the fossils were gone.

Now the Chinese and Americans blamed the Japanese army for looting them, and the Japanese blamed the Chinese and Americans for smuggling them out. But which of them were right? Actually, both. Evidence provided by Chinese anthropologist Pei Wenzhong suggests that the two crates were sent to Camp Holcomb via the US Embassy at the end of November 1941. The Marines transporting the crates, however, were interned in Qinhuangdao on 8 December, before being forwarded on to a prison camp in Tianjin.

Two of the Marines, Herman Davis and a Dr Foley, have described how they hid the crates in the Swiss Warehouse, the Pasteur Institute and with various Chinese contacts, all in Tianjin. This adds up to more than two crates – but they also admit to not having looked in the crates, and so may have simply not known which crates in their truck were the ones with the fossils. Unfortunately the bigger problem is that the nearest Pasteur Institute – even in 1942 – was in Bangkok, Thailand. There wasn't one in China.

There was a Swiss consulate, and lots of warehouses owned by many different nationalities, but no building by the name of 'Swiss Warehouse'. It's possible that it was a local nickname for a particular warehouse, or a Marine Corps codename for a location, but the two ex-Marines' stories are on shaky ground.

What of the skulls seen by witnesses in 1948? Endō Takaji was an archaeologist, but was studying the remains of Zhalainur Man, found in Manchuria, and it's far more likely that his son-in-law saw a skull of this hominid, not Peking Man.

Which brings up another interesting element. There have been a lot more fossil discoveries in China over the years than just Peking Man, and so many of the leads could be accurate to stolen fossils without being Peking Man. The committee to find them did issue the most complete inventory of the cargo, which reveals that the two crates contained a total of seven boxes, and are filled with hundreds of teeth and skeletal fragments, including four (partial) skulls of Peking Man, as well as intact skulls, teeth and fossilized bones of a *different* hominid – the 18,000-year-old Upper Cave Man (Shandingdongren), examples of which had also been excavated at Zhoukoudian.

## WHERE IS IT NOW?

There are a couple of partial answers to this. You can see very good replicas of the fossils, and reconstructions of the hominids as they may have looked in their lifetimes, at Zhoukoudian Museum. Copies can be seen in various museums around the world, such as at London's Natural History Museum. In fact, you can even buy your own accurate resin castings from commercial suppliers to museums, who trade online.

Several of the original fossil teeth survive at the Palaeontological Museum of the University of Uppsala, in Sweden. That doesn't count, as far as finding a lost treasure is concerned, though.

Looking at the different stories that the witnesses and people involved have given over the years, it seems most probable that somewhere along the line the fossils got mixed in among other hominid fossils from China, and that this probably happened at the Peking Union Medical College in or before August 1942.

That means that some of the fossils could well be in private collections or museums, mislabelled as similar relics, such as Upper Cave Man, or other general subtypes of Homo Erectus. In that sense, they're probably as lost as it's possible to be, without being buried in a hoard somewhere. Of course, the converse is

# ARTEFACT OR ARTY FAKE

You'd think that fake artefacts aren't something you have to worry about when searching for lost treasures. After all, if it's been buried in a tomb for a thousand years, it can't have been knocked off in a sweat-shop somewhere and be for sale on eBay. To some degree this is true, but just because something dates from the period of an old treasure, that doesn't mean to say that it wasn't faked back in the day.

People have been faking valuable objects and materials for as long as there have *been* valuable materials and objects. There have been a couple of forgery-heavy periods in history. In medieval times, religious iconography and artefacts were big business, and Christian dioceses all over Europe were churning out relics of Saints, pieces of the 'True Cross', lances, grails, shrouds and so on. Since most claimants to being Christian artefacts tend to date from around that era, the chances of them being fakes are high. The other big period of fakery is the 19th century, when people around the world began to take a really big interest in history and started making reproductions of older stuff – which is why a lot of purportedly antique and ancient arms and armour turn out to be Victorian reproductions.

The greatest chance of running into faked artefacts and treasures, of course, is when you think you've tracked down lost treasures that have been hoarded in private collections or have been gathering dust in museums. These may well turn out to actually be fakes created by some previous seller at some point in the past. Likewise, it is estimated that 90 per cent of antiquities put up for auction – especially online – are fakes. This is as good a reason as any to go out and find the things in situ where they were lost.

That said, you can still discover fakes. Some scientists believe that the Baghdad Battery may be an example of a primitive tool used to electroplate objects of less valuable metal with silver or gold. Gold and coinage from any period could be, and was, counterfeited, so even if you find a hoard of gold coins buried in a Southern vault since the Civil War, they could still be fake even if they're the actual objects that were lost at the time. Genuine fakes, so to speak.

Most people have now heard of carbon dating and gas spectroscopy. The former can tell the age of an object, and the latter what materials it's composed of; however, you should be aware that both of these techniques destroy a sample of the piece, and so must be carefully considered before use. A better thing to look for, whether with coins or more complex objects, is a thin raised line encircling it, or a change in texture where such a line has been sanded away. This is a sure sign of a mould seam, where the two halves of a mould have been pressed together, to produce multiple copies from a single original piece.

also true – if there is a hoard stashed somewhere, it's as likely to have those other types of fossils – for which we have other extant specimens – mixed in to complicate things.

Thankfully, there is actually another way to discover this treasure: Simply find new specimens in situ in the cave system at Dragon-Bone Hill, near Zhoukoudian.

In fact, this has sort of happened already – a piece of jawbone thought to belong to Peking Man was found there in 1959, and quickly hustled away to a secret archive just in case. Since then, the search for new specimens has continued, but everything that has been found has turned out to belong to other, later, hominids and proto-humans.

## THE OPPOSITION IN YOUR WAY

Zhoukoudian is in the Fangshan district of Beijing, a suburb south-east of the city. The Chinese government's and Fangshan government's regulations and red tape are going to be your biggest problems if you want to dig stuff up, but there is a museum, and parts of the site are open to the public. Also, because excavations are still going on, if you're a student it may be possible to apply to get in and join a dig, just like any other regular field archaeology site.

Accessing the caves is a different matter, both because more of them are closed to the public, and because the area is prone to mudslides – there is a danger of collapse. Poking around in cramped underground excavations are always a matter of some risk.

This is also an UNESCO World Heritage Site, so the UN would be annoyed with illicit digging. Not that there'd be much point in taking along geophysical equipment, as the soil is not suited to them, and the layers in which finds have been made are deep enough to be out of range. It's old-fashioned naked-eye digging all the way.

If you are mad enough to try being Lara Croft, you should bear in mind that you'd be bringing down the ire of local police, the PSB (Public Security Bureau, essentially the Chinese KGB) and the world's largest army and air force.

Zhoukoudian is heavily forested, but the most notable wildlife is avian – in particular a local form of black stork. These are not dangerous, but they are protected by law, so you'll want to be careful around them.

The area is a hotbed of artefact smuggling, which is the most common crime in the district. Be careful what you pick up or carry for anyone. Beijing as a whole is actually one of the safest cities in the world for what we'd consider 'proper' crime, and foreigners are not targeted any more than locals. That said, pickpockets and clip-joint teahouses (where you'll be lured in and then hit with massive fees) have been on the increase for some time. Otherwise, it's always wise to take the same precautions as anywhere else – don't flash valuables, make sure your bag is secure, and so on.

RG IV. MEER

OCEAN

(SÜDLICHES EISMEER)

R. FORSCHTES

SÜD · POL

Westliche Länge von Greenwich

80 · 10 · 0 · 10 · 20 · 30 · 40 · 50 · 60 · 70 · 80 · 90 · 100 · 110 · 120 · 130 · 140 · 150 · 160 · 170 · 180 · 80

Anzeichen von hohem Land

en Südpol. erreichte Breite (78°10')
Ross, Febr. 1842

Senkrechte Eiswand 150–200 F. hoch

180° v. Paris

Beaufort I.

Franklin I.

600 F.

Offenes Meer

Viele Walfische

Packeis,
Ross, März 1842

Coulman I.

# THE TREASURES

# OF EUROPE

# THE HOLY GRAIL

✖ THE HOLY GRAIL

## WHAT IS IT?

According to legend, myth, the beliefs of millions, and Indiana Jones, this is the Cup of Christ, the cup from which Jesus drank at the Last Supper, before his crucifixion, and also the cup in which Joseph of Arimathea subsequently caught some of Christ's blood during the crucifixion.

It has supposedly become imbued with spiritual grace and is a direct connection to the Son of God, which is capable of sustaining the lives of men without food, of healing any sickness or wound, and of even granting eternal life – not just to those who drink from it, but even to those who are able to spend time in its radiant presence.

## HOW MUCH IS IT WORTH TO YOU?

An artefact that could heal any illness or injury, let alone confer immortality, would be priceless beyond imagining. It would also probably be the object of a whole bunch of wars by governments wanting to get control of it for themselves and bury it in a secret vault.

As a historical artefact, however, it would surely be on a par with any crown jewel in the world, worth at least several hundred thousand pounds. Any finder could name their own price, and have both religious organizations and private collectors engaged in a bidding war the likes of which the world has never seen.

Of course it'd also be worth your life, as there are doubtless plenty of people who'd kill for it, at least if the movies are to be believed.

## THE STORY

The most prevalent modern take on the Holy Grail is that Joseph of Arimathea picks up Christ's cup from the Last Supper as a sort of souvenir, which he then uses to collect droplets of blood from the crucifixion. Joseph is then thrown in jail, but somehow manages to hang on to the cup. He is visited by a vision of Jesus, who tells him that the cup will have wondrous properties, that he must make sure the cup is guarded forever, and that a line of keepers of the Grail must be formed, so that only the most pious and spiritual person would be able to find it and enjoy its powers. When he gets out, Joseph puts together a group of friends and family – and the occasional spiritual follower – and travels west.

Since it was heavily associated with King Arthur's Knights of the Round Table, it was commonly believed that Joseph brought it by way of Italy and France to England. Supposedly he planted his staff in the ground at Glastonbury, and it took root and grew, proving that he had brought the Grail to the country. The Grail was then hidden in the castle of a wounded king, surrounded by waste lands and guarded against all comers, who must prove their worth to view it.

Sir Percival (and, in some versions, Bors and Galahad) is allowed to be in proximity to the Grail, during a feast in the castle of the Fisher King. There, the worthy watch a ceremony in which innocent youths carry the holiest relics of Christianity – including the Holy Lance, which supposedly pierced Christ's side – around between courses. The final relic, carried by a beautiful girl, is the Grail. Although this is a massive feast, the Fisher King himself subsists on only one wafer, otherwise kept alive by the power of the Grail. Percival later finds out that if he'd said the right thing when he saw the Grail, it would have fully healed the injured king and probably made Percival immortal.

Aside from the myths of Arthur, the fate of the physical Grail is fragmentary. St Peter is said to have taken it to Rome in the 1st century AD, and St Lawrence followed that up by taking it with him to Spain, where, 1,000 years later, it had to be defended against the Islamic invasions from North Africa.

They may not have succeeded, as several tales from the time of the Crusades suggest that various groups of Crusaders claimed to have found it during their exploits. An emerald chalice taken at Caesarea Maritima on the coast of Israel was the subject of one claim, while the Knights Templar are said to have found it, along with the Ark of the Covenant, and umpteen other lost treasures, in the Temple Mount while they occupied Jerusalem.

On the Islamic side, there are some Arabic documents, written in Cairo at the time of the later Crusades, which suggest that the Holy Grail was taken to the city of Leon, in Spain, in the 11th century.

## PREVIOUS SEARCHES IN FACT AND FICTION

The most famous search for this legendary vessel was the great Grail Quest of the Knights of the Round Table. This is a set of myths and romances written in the 12th and 13th centuries, harkening back to the post-Roman era, in which Arthur's greatest defining action is his commissioning of the quest for the Grail.

The first story to feature the Grail is Chrétien de Troyes' *Perceval: Conte del Graal*, or *Percival: Story of the Grail*, around 1180. Percival, raised by his widowed mother, is desperate to be a knight, and goes to Arthur's Court, where he variously gets bullied, trained and married, in more or less that order. On his way home, he encounters the lame Fisher King, who invites him back to the castle for a party.

There, he sees the procession of various holy objects between courses, including the Holy Lance, and 'a grail' – a rather unspecified serving dish. The next morning he finds himself alone, and returns home to find his mother has died. Back at Camelot, a 'loathly lady' reveals that had he asked whom the Grail served and why the Lance bled, the Fisher King would be healed, and the lands around the castle returned to a bountiful state. We also later hear that the Grail contained the single sacramental wafer which could sustain life indefinitely.

The Knights of the Round Table were then tasked with various quests, including to find the Grail, and de Troyes' story is on the receiving end of what today we would call fanfic continuations, with several writers adding to the hunt for the Holy Grail. The first of these focuses on Sir Gawain, who, annoyed at his sister's forthcoming marriage, rides off and finds himself in a totally different Grail castle, in which he learns of a broken sword that can only be mended by the sufficiently full of Grace hero who will find the Grail, and heal both the Fisher King and his lands. (Tolkien fans may be more familiar with this one – not only is the broken sword Aragorn's, but Gawain's brother takes a trip in a swan-shaped boat too.)

Wolfram von Eschenbach's 13th century *Parzifal* and Sir Thomas Malory's 15th century *Le Morte d'Arthur* really became the big hits of the Middle Ages, which codified all the previous variants and poems into the story as we know it today.

Oddly, however, the Grail romances were then largely forgotten, partly because the Renaissance encouraged storytellers and their audiences to rediscover the classical tales of Greece and Rome, and to develop their own politically-charged fictions.

The story of the Grail then returned to popularity in the 19th century, thanks to Alfred Tennyson's *Idylls of the King* and Wagner's operatic adaptation of *Parsifal* (which saw the 'z' in Parzival exchanged for an 's'. *Parsifal* was also the first Grail movie, in 1922.

*Parzifal* is also responsible for a lot of the real-life searches for the Grail over the past century. Even before the war, *Parzifal* was German archaeologist Otto Rahn's favourite Grail story. It has the Grail be a dark stone in a reliquary, and says that whoever owned it or was near it would have eternal life. Rahn was Germany's leading expert on Arthurian myth, and was sure that Eschenbach's *Parzival* tale was true, and that the Grail castle of Munsalvaesche really existed.

Rahn thought that the medieval dualist Cathar sect – who were wiped out at Montségur in France during the Albigensian Crusade in the 13th century – had the Grail, and that they'd smuggled it out and hidden it in caves and tunnels under and around the Montségur area. After all, the troubadours sang about it, the name is similar enough to Munsalvaesche…

He took over the lease of a local hotel and began exploring the caves, which are the largest limestone cave system in Europe. In one cave, called the Bethlehem Cave, he found skeletons he believed were Cathar, and a pentacle-shaped alcove in the wall large enough for a person to stand in. He thought Cathars stood there as a part of an initiation ceremony. He then ran out of money and went back home to write a book about his experience.

Enter Gestapo and SS supremo Heinrich Himmler, who offered Rahn 1,000 marks a month to find the Grail, and to write a book about his search. Himmler was a folklore fan, who wanted to bring back his version of pagan rituals from which to create his own SS religion, and who thought he was a reincarnation of King Heinrich I, or Henry the Fowler (who in fact was one of the nicer guys, as Dark Age kings go). Himmler was trying fantasy world-building for real. Contrary to popular belief and Hollywood movies, Himmler, not Hitler, was the one obsessed with the occult. He was obsessed with Arthurian Grail quests, and named rooms at his castle in Wewelsburg after elements from Arthurian myth.

Himmler's grand-a-month offer had one condition, which was somewhat awkward, given that Rahn was gay and half-Jewish: he would have to join the SS, and wear the uniform. Rahn did so, being appointed to the Ahnenerbe, as an Unterscharfuhrer (roughly halfway between a corporal and a sergeant). The Ahnenerbe was a unit of academics set up by the Nazis to 'prove' Himmler's theory of Germanic superiority and Aryan history. Said theories, of course, being all total bollocks, they then had to try to find proof of stuff that wasn't true. Himmler even wanted to prove that Jesus couldn't have been Jewish, and take Jews out of the Aryan Bible. This was nonsense that would later be used as holocaust justification.

But the money was good, so Rahn kept his trap shut, wrote another book, and continued searching for the Grail around most of Europe's pagan sites, from the Externsteine in Germany to Iceland. He even didn't rock the boat when he found that Himmler had inserted anti-Semitic propaganda into the 5,000 leather-bound copies of his book, to be given out to Nazi officers.

After two-and-a-half years of travelling on expeditions, Rahn finally noticed that something was very wrong with the SS; that they were really into brutality, oppression and mass murder, and that they were almost a culture unto themselves. He also therefore noticed that his own days were numbered if he didn't turn up a Grail soon.

In 1937 Himmler stripped him of his rank and sent him to be a guard at Dachau. Freaked out by what he saw there, he quickly became an alcoholic and repeatedly sought to leave Germany and live in France, but this was denied.

SS members were supposed to prove their Aryan racial purity four generations back – he'd been able to delay it while off grail-hunting, but once he was back in Germany the jig was up. In 1939 it came out that he was a gay Jewish SS officer, which was basically suicidal. He had hoped they'd let it slide if he found the Grail, but his searches had been fruitless. On 16 March 1939, on the anniversary of the execution of Montségur's Cathars, he went to the below-freezing Alps on the Austrian border with a bottle of scotch and some sleeping pills, and froze himself to death.

The Nazis reported this as 'the tragic death of an outstanding SS officer and scientist', with a posthumous promotion to Obersturmfuhrer, equivalent to 1st Lieutenant. Despite the death of their expert, the Nazis still kept looking for the Grail, and in 1940 Himmler and Hitler went to Barcelona to try to persuade General Franco – whom they had helped out in the Spanish Civil War a few years earlier – to come into the war on the Axis side. They also, however, wanted to check out a new lead to the Holy Grail.

They went to Montserrat Abbey in the Pyrenees, built on the foundations of a previous castle. SS researchers had found an old Catalonian song about a 'mystical font of life' at the castle, and Himmler now thought that Munsalvaesche might be Montserrat rather than Montségur. Himmler found a German-speaking monk at the abbey, Andrew Ripple Nobel, to help him with the quest, but the monk refused to tell him anything.

According to the writings of the American Howard Buchner, that didn't stop Himmler, and that he now thought the Grail was in the French Pyrenees, near Montségur, and sent Otto Skorzeny to look for it in March 1944. Nobody had been able to figure out how the Cathars could have got stuff out of Montségur, until Skorzeny figured they must have abseiled down the sheer cliff side, taking the least likely route.

On 16 March, locals marked the anniversary with a ceremony, and a German plane made a cross in the sky above them – which Buchner took to mean the Nazis were showing that Skorzeny had found the Grail, or so says the story.

Unfortunately, it's not true. Skorzeny is known to have been in Yugoslavia in March 1944, and the fact that Buchner has the Grail eventually taken by U-boat to a secret Nazi base on Antarctica takes it well into the realms of fiction.

As the 20th century went on, the Grail became ever more popular in fiction. *The Silver Chalice*, by Thomas B. Costain, was one of the earliest populist novels on the subject and was filmed in 1954.

Bernard Cornwell, creator of *Sharpe*, has written a series called *The Grail Quest*, set during The Hundred Years' War, while Michael Moorcock's *The War Hound and the World's Pain* has a spiritual Grail quest in the Thirty Years' War.

Marion Zimmer Bradley's *The Mists of Avalon* uses the Grail as a symbol for the element of water, while Peter David brings the Arthurian Grail quest to modern New York in *One Knight Only* and *Fall of Knight*. On a more literary note, the Grail is a major element in Umberto Eco's *Baudolino*.

King Arthur and the Knights of the Round Table have been the subject of many movies, especially through the 1950s and 1960s, but most simply dealt with the adventure side – the rivalry with Lancelot over Guinevere, and the battle against Mordred – rather than with the quest for the Grail. That had to wait until the French film *Lancelot du Lac* in 1974, which was closer to the Troyes version of the story.

The first really successful Grail story for movie audiences was a rather different beast: *Monty Python and the Holy Grail*, in which the surreal comedy troupe took a tour through Dark Age and Arthurian Myth to great effect. Such great effect, in fact, that it was rebooted as the stage musical *Spamalot*. Both of those are fairly thick with medieval grime. John Boorman provided a definitive Arthurian Grail quest in 1981's *Excalibur*. This reintroduced the idea of the Grail as a spiritual concept by which the king and the land are connected.

Terry Gilliam's *The Fisher King* also revisits this idea, in a surrealist modern context, but, let's be honest, most of us are going to be thinking of *Indiana Jones and the Last Crusade* when we think of movies about searching for the Holy Grail. And why not?

TV has covered the legend, both in many documentaries, and in settings as diverse as *Stargate SG-1* and *Babylon 5*. The Grail has, obviously, been studied in plenty of non-fiction books as well, whether giving a psychological or spiritual interpretation to the Grail Quest (as Carl Jung and Joseph Campbell did), or, as has become more popular in recent years, in terms of historical conspiracy theories. For example, in *The Sign and the Seal*, Graham Hancock suggests that the Grail is actually a fictionalized Ark of the Covenant, while *The Holy Blood, and the Holy Grail*, famously goes with the idea that the Grail is the bloodline of Jesus Christ's descendants (and thus inspired *The Da Vinci Code*).

## THE TRUTH IS OUT THERE

Why would the Grail Romance writers, or later believers such as Himmler, have got the idea that the Grail should have such power of eternal life? Not from the Bible, certainly; there's nothing in there that would lead to such a speculation.

There is, however, precedent in earlier European pagan lore; specifically there's the mythology of the Celts of Ireland. In Irish Celtic mythology there was a king called Bran the Blessed, who had a cauldron imbued with many magical powers.

Among other things, the Cauldron of Bran could supply enough food to feed a whole army from whatever little ingredients were put into it. More impressive still, it could revive any corpse that had been placed inside it – even one which had been chopped to pieces. The slain so placed in the cauldron would be revived whole and healthy.

That this element of the Grail myth was borrowed from the Celtic myths is no secret, though it was largely forgotten by post-medieval writers and Grail fans. That the tale is borrowed is acknowledged right there in Chretien de Troyes' original texts, in the form of the Fisher King.

The Fisher King – named Bron in this version, to really rub it in – is the king who at some point in the past was charged with looking after the Grail, in his castle in the wastelands. He had at some point been wounded in the legs (this is also why Sir Percival is the one to find the Grail – the name derives from per cheval, meaning pierced thigh, which means he has the same traits as the Grail's guardian), and can't move on his own. He doesn't exist in myth or literature until Chretien de Troyes pretty much invents the Grail Quest in *Perceval, le Conte du Graal*, in the second half of the 12th century.

Is there even such a thing as an actual Holy Grail? Well, that depends on how you define the term 'Holy Grail'. Let's take the different elements separately:

*The Cup used by Jesus at the Last Supper*: Logically there must have been some form of drinking vessels at any meal in Biblical times. So, that would mean you'd be asking on whether the story of Jesus is true, for him to have used whatever crockery was around, and that's a whole different debate.

That said, this actually wasn't originally referred to as the Holy Grail, but the Holy Chalice, while the Grail was originally written to be a flat dish or stone. In the last few centuries, however, the two have become conflated.

There are several alleged Holy Chalices around, including one in St Peter's in Rome, which is used in papal masses – though nowadays more than one chalice used by the Pope has become tagged as being the 'official' one.

*The vessel used by Joseph of Arimathea to catch Christ's blood*: Never existed. In the Bible, and other related religious texts from the era, Joseph is one who takes custody of Jesus's body after the crucifixion, and prepares it for burial – which would involve washing all the blood, sweat and dirt off the body. Nobody mentions him having any sort of vessel to carry it in until the 12th century, when Robert de Boron introduced him into the Arthurian cycle as bringing the Grail to Britain. (At other times, his son, Josephus, is tagged with that duty.)

*A cup or goblet granting healing and/or immortality*: Outside of Indiana Jones … These powers derive from the Cauldron of Bran, in Welsh mythology.

Interestingly, the Nazis did try making their own new Nazi Grail, which was more the size and shape of a soup tureen, and had figures around the rim, in the style of the Celtic depictions of warriors that harken back to the tales of Bran's cauldron.

*The bloodline of Jesus through the Merovingian Kings*: No. Just, no. Aside from the Sangraal/sang real mistranslation, the simple fact is lineage spreads as it descends. Even if we assume a surviving Jesus, who has kids, you've got 80 generations (usually said to be 25 years), with an average of 2.4 kids – multiplied exponentially. That's 2.4 to the power of 80. It's a *lot* of descendants, not just one secret family leading to a French girl who needs protection.

*The object sought by Arthurian knights in the Grail Quest*: Hold on, folks, because this is where things get a little strange.

Strange in the sense that although we're talking about fictional characters, some of whom may be loosely based on figures from centuries earlier, on a spiritual quest for a magical object in a set of acknowledged fairy tales ... This is still the one that absolutely, yes, does exist.

Sort of.

There are four main medieval Grail Quest stories: those by Chretien de Troyes, Robert de Boron, Thomas Malory's *Morte d'Arthur*, and Wolfram von Eschenbach's *Parzifal*, which, as the title implies, is somewhat of a knockoff of de Troyes's earlier *Perceval*. Eschenbach produces the most refined and, dare we say, efficient version of the story. He also gives us much more straightforward detail about where the quest leads to and what it is.

Best of all, he bases his story's Grail on a real object in a real place. And that object actually still exists.

To save you poring through either a lot of Latin, medieval German, or potentially bad English translations, Eschenbach has the Grail found at the castle of Munsalvaesche, an invisible castle. At first the idea of an invisible castle sounds like a mad idea: castles are enormous stone fortresses dominating the countryside, with towers visible for miles, and all that. How could it be invisible? The obvious conclusion is that Eschenbach is using a bit of magic in his tale, with sorcery or supernatural powers making things difficult for the questing knights.

In fact, however, that isn't really what he meant. What he actually meant is that there was a well-defended fortress which didn't loom over the countryside, and which people didn't really perceive as a castle at all.

## WHERE IS IT NOW?

Wolfram von Eschenbach's actual, genuine Holy Grail is viewable behind a panel of bullet-proof glass in the Iglesia Catedral-Basílica Metropolitana de la Asunción de Nuestra Señora de Valencia, alternatively known as Saint Mary's Cathedral or just Valencia

Cathedral. The address is Plaza Almoina, s/n, 46003 Valencia, Spain. It's really not a secret; it's just that nobody really notices it. Probably this is because it doesn't glow, and none of the people who occasionally get to touch it in the religious duties have become noticeably immortal or returned from the dead. That sort of thing would get news coverage, probably.

That said, this *is* the Grail that Eschenbach wrote into *Parzival*, and which was subsequently appropriated by various other medieval writers. Until the turn of the 20th century, this Grail was held at the monastery of San Juan de la Peña, located at the south-west of Jaca, in the province of Huesca. It has also been occasionally used by the Pope as the Holy Chalice as well – most recently by Benedict XVI in 2006.

This, of course, is also the Grail that Himmler was after during World War II, but which, thankfully, was never allowed to fall into his hands.

If you know your Eschenbach, you should also know that, of the relatively few people who know of this Grail as the Holy Grail at all, most of them focus on the wrong bit. The golden chalice is impressive, and has been used as a papal chalice as recently as 2006, but the part that Eschenbach cast as his Holy Grail is, in fact, the upturned chalcedony bowl that serves as a base, and not the golden and agate goblet. The base is thought to date from around the 4th–1st century BC, while the upper cup dates from no later than AD 262 (it's mentioned in a Roman inventory from that year).

There are various other cups and dishes around which have been claimed as the Grail, but have all turned out to be later medieval creations. One now in Genoa was captured from the Saracens in the 12th century, while another now held in New York's Metropolitan Museum of Art was made in Antioch, but no earlier than the 6th century AD.

## THE OPPOSITION IN YOUR WAY

Unlike a lot of the famous treasures you might hope to find, this one does actually have some rightful owners – the Catholic Church of Spain – who would not be best pleased if you try to

# ARTEFACT SMUGGLING

It's currently estimated by archaeological authorities (after a worldwide survey of archaeologists) that looting and smuggling is endemic in 103 countries. Not just war-torn ones, either: 90 per cent of Iron Age sites in Turkey have been dug up by looters.

There are laws in most countries about the transport and ownership – and especially the sale – of artefacts and treasure. In general, the laws in countries from which artefacts tend to be taken are more punitive than in receiving countries. Get caught smuggling stuff into a modern Western country, and you'll probably face a hefty fine, a loss of licence and business opportunities, and maybe a few months in jail. Get caught smuggling artefacts out of a country where they've been found, and you're likely to end up in a roach-infested dungeon for which they've thrown away the key. Unless you've paid the appropriate backhanders and bribes, obviously.

There are two reasons for the severity of laws about artefact smuggling. The first reason is that historical and treasure artefacts tend to be part of a country's cultural heritage, so stealing it amounts to demeaning the nation and its people. The second, and more prosaic, reason is that there's often a crossover with the drugs trade, as both types of trafficking require the employment of a talent for smuggling. This also means that if you're suspected of smuggling artefacts, you'll also be suspected of drugs smuggling first and foremost.

In various parts of the world, artefact smuggling is also increasingly associated with terrorism, as such organizations seek to raise funds for buying arms by looting historic sites and selling the treasures off to private collectors. The collectors who buy looted artefacts see the looting and smuggling as a victimless crime, but that's overlooking the fact that so many of the smuggling networks – especially in the Middle East – are run by terrorist and insurgent groups.

The way it tends to work is that a group of bandits or bribed soldiers will force locals at gunpoint to help them access the artefacts on-site. They will then be handed over first to representatives of a criminal gang in the nearest city, who will arrange for them to be taken across the border to a neighbouring country. From there, the pipeline is taken over by a dealer equally at home with gangsters and art collectors, who will supervise the advertising, sale and transport of the antiquities.

He also arranges for the laundry of the artefacts. As with money laundering, the pieces have to be made to seem legitimate, either by forging their provenances, and licences to export, or by outright physically disguising them.

As with all forms of smuggling – be it drugs, rare animals, or people – the organized smugglers are constantly coming up with new ways to disguise their activities and protect themselves, while the individuals are more likely to be caught.

make off with it. That would mean you'd be lumbered with the full force of Spanish law enforcement and military coming down on you like the proverbial ton of bricks.

So, the Spanish police, army, navy and air force would all be somewhat miffed if someone tried to walk off with it, no matter how good they look in spandex or a fedora.

As a treasure to make money out of, you'll have problems. There would be some issues in trying to get a decent price for the Valencia Grail simply because being a known tourist attraction means it's pretty recognizable to the authorities, and therefore could not be sold on as easily as simple gold. Likewise, breaking it up to disguise its nature and origins would also destroy most of its value, to the point where it wouldn't have been worth the bother.

The trick, therefore, would be to sell it to some private collector who is willing to pay a huge amount for something they know they can never show off to anyone, or even admit that they own. This, again, is somewhat counterproductive, as collecting such historical treasures does tend to be about bragging rights for private individuals.

On the other hand, if you simply want to see it for youself, then the only things standing in your way are the ticket prices for a trip to Valencia, and any queues in front of you.

# THE TEMPLAR TREASURE

✘ THE TEMPLAR TREASURE

## WHAT IS IT?

A matter for debate to start with. At the very least you can expect coinage, title deeds and personal belongings held by the Order, since members were required to hand over their family fortunes – or at least their individual shares of such – as part of joining up. The amount of coinage would surely be considerable, as the King of France was in debt to them, and very much annoyed that the Paris Preceptory alone was, apparently, richer than his court.

However, over time, stories have evolved which imply the potential for them to have also owned various other more exotic and unique treasures – many of which have their own chapters in this book. In recent decades especially, many people have come to believe that the Knights Templar had uncovered treasures from the Temple of Solomon while they were in Jerusalem; treasures such as the Holy Grail, and the Ark of the Covenant, not to mention gold that had been given to Solomon by the Queen of Sheba.

In any event, the main targets among seekers after this particular treasure are the glittering cargoes of 18 ships under the Templar flag.

## HOW MUCH IS IT WORTH TO YOU?

Eighteen or so shiploads of gold coinage alone would be worth billions of dollars – or indeed pounds – today, even before looking at any specific valuable historical artefacts which the Templars, according to legend, supposedly dug up in the Holy Land.

This could potentially include the Holy Grail and the Ark of the Covenant – you can check the chapters on those artefacts for the sort of value they carry.

## THE STORY

Long story short, in 1119, a French knight called Hugues de Payens formed a posse with eight other knights (all of whom were his relatives) and set out to provide protection for pilgrims travelling to and from the Holy Land. Soon, King Baldwin gave them permission to set up an HQ at the Al-Aqsa Mosque, which is on the site of Solomon's Temple.

From this HQ, the Templars got their name, in various slightly different translations that average out to 'Poor Knights of Christ and the Temple of Solomon'. They weren't a big noise, even in the Crusades, until the Council of Troyes in 1129, at which they got the official nod from the Church (thanks to being bigged up by influential Abbot Bernard de Clairvaux, who just happened to be the nephew of Andre de Montbard, one of the original nine knights) to be a proper monastic Order. In fact, St Bernard here codified the Templars' rules as the ideal Christian life.

This gave them the right to seek donations (of cash, lands and titled sons as recruits), and the popularity to get them. Recruits would give up all their worldly goods to the Order, while other donors could feel confident that they were not just helping defend Jerusalem from Islam, but were buying a place in Heaven after death.

Although the Order had been founded in the Holy Land, it had a foothold back home in Europe within a couple of years, first in Portugal, and then in Spain, France, England and elsewhere. In 1139 they really hit it big when Pope Innocent II proclaimed that the Templars could cross all borders, pay no taxes and submit to no authority other than the Pope himself. This meant that they could keep all their income, without turning it over to any kings.

Over the course of the next few decades, the order got into banking – having started by safely escorting pilgrims, the Order evolved into escorting their valuables, by basically inventing the promissory note, or bearer bond. Travellers and pilgrims could deposit funds at the nearest Templar Preceptory in return for a note of what the goods were worth. This could then be taken to any other preceptory and redeemed in full, or in part. The practical upshot of which was that the Templar Preceptories would be full of gold and the travellers wouldn't have to carry inconvenient bandit-bait.

Eventually, however, things began to go awry. Firstly, the Templars got their asses handed to them by Saladin at the Battle of the Horns of Hattin. Rival orders, the Hospitallers and Teutonic Knights, got into the banking game, and European Royalty really didn't like the idea of there being an independent private army allowed to cross borders freely, and whom they were funding blindly.

The man most worried about this was King Philippe IV of France. The Order's founders were French, his kingdom was their homeland and they were beginning to fancy the idea of having a country to themselves – following the lead of the Teutonic Knights, who had founded Prussia. In 1306, the Order facilitated a coup on Cyprus, and Philippe felt they might try to topple him. He also owed them money, and the royal coffers were empty. A good heresy charge would strip the Order of its riches...

So, on 13 October 1307, Preceptories were raided, the members of the Order arrested for trial by the Inquisition and their assets seized. Philippe had issued secret orders for the arrests, with the intent of rounding up every Templar in France, as well as having sent requests for other nations to do the same, with the backing of the newest Pope.

Over the next few years, the Templars were charged with assorted heresies and treasons, such as idolatry and sodomy. During their trials, it emerged from the testimony of a Templar called Jean de Châlon that a Gérard de Villiers had put to sea with 18 galleys, and that a Templar Preceptor from Champagne, Hugues de Chalon (brother of Jean), had taken the hoard of Templar treasurer Hugues de Pairaud to these ships on 50 horses.

The ships then sailed out of La Rochelle for parts unknown, immediately before the raids, leaving King Philippe fuming that so much of the Templar assets had escaped his clutches.

## PREVIOUS SEARCHES IN FACT AND FICTION

The Templars have been a subject of fascination from the 18th century onwards. Most of this fascination, however, has been about their character and their exploits, rather than about the treasure they may have spirited away.

From here on in, the legend of the missing Templar treasure has become big business, and the Templar connection has been appended to several other treasures and supposed locations that originally had nothing to do with them – Oak Island, for example.

In later years the Templar treasure got associated with the stories of treasure at Rennes-le-Château, in the popular book, *The Holy Blood and the Holy Grail*.

This story supposedly started in 1892, when the local priest, Bérenger Saunière, dug up some parchments with clues to a buried treasure. Cue mysterious influxes of cash and the restoration of the local church, with its strange devil-carving, and a trail of coded art pieces throughout history … Throw in secret societies and Freemasons, and you're halfway to the idea of surviving Templars already.

This has all spawned a veritable industry of Templar-themed conspiracy and treasure books, such as Steve Berry's novel *The Templar Legacy*.

## THE TRUTH IS OUT THERE

Let's get the Rennes-le-Château stuff out of the way first. In fact the Saunière story originated with a Belgian named Roger Crouquet, in *Le Soir illustré*, in 1948. Crouquet had visited friends in the area and heard from locals about how Saunière preferred debauchery to his priestly job, and how, at the turn of the century, he decided to fund his lifestyle by putting ads in foreign newspapers saying that the poor priest of Rennes-le-Château lived among heretics and the place was in dire need of funds and repairs. Crouquet said that an old woman told him it was Saunière, 'changed into a devil'.

A few years later, Noël Corbu, who had opened a restaurant on Sauniere's former estate, started telling stories that Saunière had dug up parchments in 1892 (while renovating the church), which led to a treasure. However, in Corbu's version, the treasure was that of Blanche of Castile, and amounted to 28,500,000 gold pieces. This was nothing to do with the Templars, though she was around in the first half of the 13th century. The money was supposedly raised by Blanche to pay the ransom of St Louis, a prisoner of the Saracens. Corbu, of course, had it that Saunière had only found a small part of the treasure.

A decade later, Pierre Plantard and Gérard de Sède expanded upon this into their hoax Priory of Sion, which supposedly descended from the Templar Grand Masters, and so brought the Order into the myth. But they never actually had anything to do with it originally.

The first question you need answered is how rich the Templar Order actually was in 1307. Unfortunately, and perhaps surprisingly, the answer is 'not very'. None of the military orders really were, and for a simple reason: they were in a very expensive business, which ate through funds very quickly.

Although the Order was partly funded by donations from members, churches and nobles, these donations didn't come permanently or without changes. Over time, two things happened to this income. Firstly, it decreased, partly because of changing politics at home, and partly because the focus of how people gave their money had changed from giving to the Church as an institution, to giving as patronage to individuals, nobles or knights. Secondly, a lot of kings and princes, jealous of the amounts that the Church were amassing, began to forbid donations of land to the Church or military Orders without express permission from the Crown. In the era, religious authority could often overrule secular royalty, thanks to Innocent II's ruling in 1139, but the crowned heads of Europe were by now able to argue that when Innocent II proclaimed that the Order(s) only owed allegiance to the Pope, he really just meant himself personally, and that now that he was dead, the rule had expired.

This restriction was a problem because the orders also made their money from trade, brewing and farming – all things which required the ownership of land. For extra fun, the turn of the 14th century was already experiencing what we'd now call horrific inflation, so that the value of the income from rents, trade, etc. that the order got was greatly reduced.

The Kings of Aragon were also unhappy with all of the military orders' lack of actual military ability and delivery, because their warriors kept being hauled away to fight in papal wars in Sicily, leaving castles and preceptories undermanned. Which was a bit of a problem as Berbers were making huge advances into Christian-held territory at the time.

So, although the Order had a reputation for riches despite its professed vows of poverty, the fragmentary records that survive seem to indicate that the vows were more accurate than the reputation. In Acre in 1275, William de Beaujeu wrote that the Order 'was in a weaker state than it had ever been, with many expenses and almost no revenues, as its possessions had all been plundered by the Sultan'.

Combine these territorial and manpower losses with a fall in income, and it's no surprise that things were running on a low logistics budget. In Huesca, the preceptory could only arm seven knights and three sergeants. Remember that a 'knight' in this context is supported by squires, grooms, a sergeant and a platoon of men-at-arms, so here we see a situation where they can only afford to run a full crew for half the knights available (people writing conspiracy-themed books often ask how 'nine knights' could protect however many miles of road. The answer, of course, is that 'nine knights' actually means about three hundred fighters, when the sergeants and men-at-arms are counted in).

After the Templar Order was raided and shut down, an inventory was taken of its properties. Not only did this survey not turn up piles of hidden loot, but in fact it showed that Templar properties were, in general, what modern folks would call fixer-uppers, or, frankly, falling to bits.

All Templar property that could be found was seized, of course, but even that inventory shows that the quality and values of materials seized were on a par with ordinary people's – peasants' – belongings, rather than the sort of bling expected to be found in places frequented by the nobility.

The next question is the size and nature of the Templar fleet. Most people assume by the word 'fleet' that there must have been a lot of ships, able to carry multiple cargoes of treasure. When you do your research (the first rule of treasure hunting, remember?), you'll find lots of different numbers for how many ships the Order had. Some sources are more reliable than others, but since no record giving a number of ships has survived from the Order, even the reliable sources aren't guaranteed to be right.

The more wide-eyed, conspiracy-minded, or gullible, treasure and Templar fans have come up with a range of ridiculous numbers – up to 181 ships, according to one website. Most historians, however, seem to plump for there being 18, which supposedly left La Rochelle with the treasure, as per de Chalon's story. This is unfortunate, as it later turned out that de Chalon's testimony was as Douglas Adams might have said, apocryphal, or at least wildly inaccurate.

We know they had ships, of course, because they had income, lands, resources and recruits in Western Europe, and had to get them to the Holy Land somehow – which meant crossing the Mediterranean. The Order could also make little on the side by ferrying pilgrims, which makes sense since the Order was founded to protect pilgrims on their journey. The Templars actually had two 'fleets' – the pilgrim fleet taking pilgrims from Marseille to the Holy Land twice a year (at Easter and August), which consisted of two or three ships, depending on whether the Easter and August ones were the same ships, plus one kept in port, plus their proper business and war fleet at La Rochelle, which included ships named *La Templere* and *La Buzzard*.

There are also some records mentioning ships; Section 119 of *The Rule of the Templars*, circa 1187, mentions the Order having ships at Acre (but annoyingly doesn't give descriptions or numbers). The records of the port of La Rochelle also do show that the Templars exported wine by ship from there. (They owned many vineyards in the area at the time.) It was, however, usual for the military Orders to charter ships from their captains, rather than own them outright, and the ships exporting wine were simply hired. Overall there's no way to know how many ships the Templars owned outright, even if we could tell how many they used. That said, we know that Henry III of England hired a Spanish Templar ship (called *The Great Ship*, which suggests the Templars didn't stay up for long hours thinking up ship names) in 1224, which he later bought outright. Since the Templars in Spain were willing to part with it, presumably they did own enough others for their purposes. However, it was also possible for countries to assign ships to the Templars if they needed a Templar naval trip – for example in England it was a duty of the Constable of Dover Castle to give them a ship.

The surviving records and tales of Templar maritime activity don't show much skill or experience in the matter. When King James I of Aragon asked the military Orders to send warships to accompany him on a Crusade in 1269, the Templars sent only one ship, and its rudder broke. The Templars didn't follow the normal naval practice of carrying a spare rudder, and so had to borrow one from the king's own ship, much to the disbelief and annoyance of his crew. There are also reports of Templar ships being famous for not carrying enough drinking water for their voyages.

The first mention of a war 'fleet' comes in 1292, when Pope Nicholas IV ordered both the Templars and Hospitallers to build up fleets of warships. The following year, the Templars teamed up with Venice to send a battle fleet to protect Cyprus. The Templars contributed two war galleys. You read that right: *two*.

The actual Templar records of their fleets don't survive intact, but those of the other military Orders at the time do, and show, for example, the Hospitallers owning only four ships. It's logical to suppose that that the Templars would have had a similar number. So, there may have been 18 ships in the Templar port at La Rochelle on that day, but we can safely say that at least 14 of them will have simply been hired.

So why didn't the king or the Inquisition go after the fleet that de Chalons mentioned?

Because they knew he was talking rubbish. They had already impounded and inventoried the contents of the Paris Preceptory and, in actual fact, even de Chalons had only mentioned the taking of 50 horses and the personal fortune of Hugues de Pairaud. A far cry from a huge hoard looted from the Holy Land and then smuggled out of Paris.

## WHERE IS IT NOW?

Basically, most of it will have been returned back into the medieval economy in trade, in purchases, and when former Templars joined other Orders. It was standard for personal possessions to be tithed to an Order by a member of it, and the various Orders also did exchange regalia from time to time.

The idea that every piece of bling the Order owned would be

lumped together in a single hoard is based on a number of logical fallacies. Even if the Templars had, say, 18 ships, and they all sailed before the arrests, there has never been any evidence to suggest that any of them had a treasure cargo. Even if one or more of them had, there's nothing to say they all sailed for the same destination. In fact, if the Order loaded multiple ships with valuables – be it gold, jewels, relics, or documents – in order to keep them out of the hands of the French king's men, it would have made a lot more sense if they scattered to different destinations. Putting all your eggs in one basket is never a good idea when you know someone is dead-set on taking the basket.

What we can be pretty certain of is that it's *not* in the various places that popular culture tells us to expect to find it in.

Rosslyn Chapel in Scotland is a complete blind, because it wasn't built until 150 years – that's six generations of any Templar family at the time – after the Order ended. Worse still, as far as that bedtime story goes, the legend that it was built by descendants of a Templar called William Sinclair is untrue. There *was* a William Sinclair involved with the last days of the Order, but not as a Templar; in fact he was one of the blokes who testified against them at their trial. That makes it pretty unlikely that he would have had his descendants keep Templar secrets in any way, let alone an overly elaborate way.

The Church of Mary Magdalene in Rennes-le-Château was excavated in the late 1950s, by the way. A skeleton was found, but no sign that anything had ever been cached there.

If you want to have a reasonable chance to find some Templar goodies, the places to look are the vicinity of Templar Preceptories, but probably not on the actual grounds of the Preceptories, as this would be the place the king's men will have focused their search upon.

What you need to do is find yourself a Templar who survived the dissolution of the Order and returned home. Find out where this person lived, and search on the lands of his family estate – because if he snatched a bag of coins or artefacts on the way out the door, or was entrusted with them to take care of, he will have buried them on his land, just like everybody else did back in the day.

There are doubtless pieces of the Templar treasure – at least in the form of gold and silver coinage and ingots held by the Order – still out there, but there's no evidential reason to assume it would all be together in one hoard. It's going to be scattered across Europe in personal holdings cached by former Templar members. Most of them, however, simply transferred over into other Orders, especially the Hospitallers. So, really a lot of individual Templar possessions will have ended up belonging to them, and trying to search for it in Templar locations will set you onto a trail to nothing from the start.

## THE OPPOSITION IN YOUR WAY

The main obstacle to your search is basically popular opinion, as all it offers is misleading disinformation. That and the fact that the Order's area of operations and influence was so wide – there could be a little pot of Templar coinage almost anywhere in Western Europe, the Mediterranean, or the Middle East.

As for the big haul – the opposition you'll face is its lack of actual existence. The Templars simply weren't the rich secret society in 1307 that modern populist pseudo-history tells us they were.

# Nazi Gold

✖ NAZI GOLD

## WHAT IS IT?

Basically, gold bullion.

Of course the Nazis looted plenty of other treasures as well – artworks, jewels, precious metals and so on – plenty of which is still missing, but much of which has been recovered or whose fate is at least known.

Bullion is a more intriguing treasure because it's a mix of both looted gold, traded gold from foreign banks before the war and the country's own gold reserves. For the most part when the phrase 'Nazi gold' comes up what is being referred to is the national gold reserves held by Nazi Germany's central national bank, the Reichsbank, rather than looted gold – but it's often difficult, if not impossible, to separate the two.

## HOW MUCH IS IT WORTH TO YOU?

It's difficult to put a price on what Nazi gold may be out there, simply because nobody's quite sure how much of it is still hidden and awaiting discovery, and also because the Nazi government back in the day outright lied about how much they had to start with.

That said, it was estimated in 1997 that they had looted about $8.7 billion worth of gold in total, and any time the subject comes up in the news media, the figures quoted tend to be in the half a billion to a billion pounds range ($0.75 billion–$1.5 billion).

Those figures are probably over-optimistic, however, as the largest recovered Nazi gold hoard – found at Merkers in 1945, amounted to 100 tons, or about half a billion dollars today, and this is generally thought to have been almost half of the country's total gold holdings. Another 40 tons or so have been discovered in various places over the years – mostly in 1945 – which would leave at least another 60 tons or so floating about somewhere, waiting to be found. At the same value per ton, that would come to around $300 million, or £175 million.

## THE STORY

In 1945, the war is clearly over for Nazi Germany. Their forces are retreating back into the mountains and forests of the Fatherland, while the Russians press them from one side, and the British and Americans from the other.

As they retreat, they take with them all the material that they don't want the Allies to get their hands on – weapons, ammunition, documents about who did what in the Holocaust, cash printing plates and the country's gold reserves – quite apart from all the art and treasures they had looted from conquered peoples over the previous decade.

The Reichsbank gold wasn't the only Nazi gold hidden at the end of the war, but it is the central treasure that's still missing, and some of that other gold from elsewhere was added to it during its journey.

In April of 1945, the President of the Reichsbank – a man named Funk – and Nazi Reich Minister of Propaganda, Joseph Goebbels, agreed to send the gold reserves of the bank south, to prevent it falling into Allied – and especially Russian – hands.

Funk put the bank's Chief Cashier, Georg Netzeband, in charge, while Goebbels assigned a police escort headed by Georg

Kruger. Kruger also brought his daughter along, to get her out of the soon-to-be-overrun-by-vengeful-Russians Berlin. The two Georgs were given orders to take the loot south to Bavaria, but these orders were not particularly specific about exactly where.

Goebbels's propaganda, however, had been making a big deal out of the Alps in Bavaria being a perfect and impenetrable natural fortress from which to defend the Reich. It must have seemed quite logical to Netzeband and Kruger to head for this great fortress.

The little convoy went first to Dresden, then through Bohemia to Pilsen, and thence to Munich. They travelled mainly at night, to avoid Allied air attack, and the trucks were sufficiently overloaded that they had trouble traversing some roads. The convoy then reached Munich, where it picked up more financial cargo, to the tune of 96 bags of British and American banknotes.

It then drove south into Bavaria, and essentially disappeared. Rumours began to fly about where it could have ended up: at the bottom of Lake Toplitz, or indeed any Alpine lake; smuggled out of the country by plane or U-boat; deposited in Swiss banks … The possibilities are many, and almost every town and village in southern Germany, Austria and the Czech Republic eventually acquired a local folktale or two about the SS or other German units hiding crates of loot, either for personal retirement or to fund a potential resurgence of Nazi warmongering.

## PREVIOUS SEARCHES IN FACT AND FICTION

Searching for Nazi gold, and any other valuables, started in April of 1945, when a couple of Military Police soldiers with the US Army's 90th Infantry Division stopped a couple of out-of-place French women in the town of Merkers. The women told of how they and other civilians had been drafted in to help stash gold in the local Kaiseroda Salt Mine. The Americans soon had this tale confirmed by other soldiers, and Allied POWs who had been released from local camps and who had also helped move the gold. They then interrogated the highest ranking captured German official on-site, who was actually a director at Berlin's National Galleries. He was there to look after looted art treasures stored in the mine – paintings were his speciality – but he also knew that gold reserves had been transferred there from the Reichsbank in February. He thought this was the entire reserve, but in fact it wasn't quite, as Netzeband's consignment was still in transit.

Just within the mine's entrance was found half a billion Reichsmarks in paper currency, in 550 bags. Behind a steel blast door was a 150x75ft vault containing 7,000 bags of around 60lb each of bullion, in ingots and coins (including $17,775,000 in $20 coins). That's 250 tons of bullion. There were also bales of paper currencies (nearly 100 million French francs, and two and a half billion Reichsmarks), cases of gold and silver teeth, jewellery and other valuables looted from Holocaust victims. The rest of the mine's 30 miles or so of tunnels and galleries were filled with paintings, statuary and other art from all over Europe.

Over April, the Americans shipped the gold, currency and art to a surviving Reichsbank vault in Frankfurt, under intense security. It probably goes without saying that it was immediately rumoured locally that one truckload of gold disappeared en route, and people have been looking for it ever since.

Documents in the mine also set the Allied intelligence agencies on the trail of other caches of loot, in the form of gold and silver bars, other precious metals, another $25,000 in US gold coins, a million Swiss Francs, and another billion or so French Francs. All of these were returned to the Allied clearing centre at Frankfurt.

Many of the documents also provided a paper trail of where Nazi money had been spent, or siphoned off to, either by the State or by individuals. While vital in itself, that side of things doesn't involve actual treasure hunting, though.

In 1946, the US Treasury and the OSS (the Office of Strategic Services, forerunners of the CIA) looked into some of these documents also, and figured out that at the beginning of 1945, the Vatican Bank had snagged over $80 million of Nazi gold in Swiss francs for 'safekeeping', though the British military had managed to catch about a third of it on the way across the Austrian border.

The next big development came in 1959, when a diving expedition to Toplitzsee – Lake Toplitz, in Austria's Salzkammergut, in the Alps near Salzburg – found a layer of logs hiding something in a layer near the lake bottom. Since the lake was a known Nazi site – it had been used for torpedo testing and suchlike during the war – and since it was common knowledge that the Nazis had gone to a lot of effort to hide loot, it didn't take long before people started putting those two things together and coming up with the thought of sunken bullion.

The lake is now the most famous of the supposed dumping grounds for Nazi gold, and attracts tourists and treasure hunters from around the world, and has done so for many years. The 1959 expedition, and others since, have recovered interested bits and pieces from the lake, including counterfeit banknotes and the equipment to print currency, plates and printing presses.

Despite the popularity of the lake among treasure hunters, there has never really been much evidence that any gold was ever sunk in it. Certainly none has ever been found there, despite many people's assumptions, and many adventure stories – especially in the 1960s and 1970s – being based around the idea.

In fact it seems to have been Ian Fleming's *Goldfinger* which really cemented Lake Toplitz as a depository for Nazi gold in the public subconscious, as the gold bar which Bond wagers in his game of golf with Auric Goldfinger is said to have come from there. Ironically, this identification is given by Smithers, a secretary to the treasury; the same British government department which was actually happy to trade and buy Nazi gold in the run-up to the war – and maybe afterwards, but that's still to come. Stay tuned.

Helen MacInnes' novel *The Salzburg Connection* also has Nazi gold recovered from there, while the novel and TV series *Private Schulz* takes a more accurate view by having the characters' supply of fake British fivers dumped there.

Oddly enough, the popular action-adventure TV shows of the 1960s especially in Britain, such as *The Saint*, *The Champions* and *The Persuaders* – basically everything made by ITC – tended to mix and match their Nazi gold plots, with each show usually having at least one 'Nazi gold in Lake Toplitz (or equivalent)' and one 'Nazi gold in former mine' episode.

The Clint Eastwood movie *Kelly's Heroes* takes the far more sensible approach of the Nazi gold sought after by the protagonists being stored in an actual bank.

Now, it's true that lots of Nazi materiel *was* deposited in the lake at the end of the war, but so far this has proved to be munitions, printing presses for banknotes, and British and US currency counterfeited by Operation Bernhard – a project that recruited concentration camp prisoners to forge Allied currency in order to destabilize the British economy. In other words, stuff that was, at best, of no further use to the fleeing Nazis, and may have been of more use to the Allies, if only as evidence of wrongdoing.

Materials, in other words, that they could no longer use after the war, and didn't want the Allies to be able to use. Gold, on the other hand, is something that is always useful and so must be hidden for later recovery.

## THE TRUTH IS OUT THERE

The Nazis, of course, were quite clever about hanging on to their precious yellow bricks, with some help even from their enemies, because bankers being in a class of villainy all to themselves isn't a post-2008 phenomenon.

After the Anschluss and occupation of Czechoslovakia in 1938, the Nazis grabbed the Czech and Austrian national banks' gold reserves and added them – about $71 million in 1939 value – to those of the Reichsbank. In 1939 they decided to sell off what was then £5.6 million worth of gold to raise currency, and this they did through the Bank of England.

Some £4 million of the gold went to banks in Belgium and Holland, with the rest sold in London. In 1939, when war broke out, Chancellor of the Exchequer Sir John Simon asked the Governor of the Bank of England if they were holding any of this gold. The governor said they held gold at times for the international banking system, and had no need to know who it actually belonged to, honest guv, straight up. At the same time, some of it was already being shipped off to New York.

Ex-Prime Minister David Lloyd George commented that, 'Germany had no more right to the gold than a burglar.' Note how most of this gold ended up in Belgium and Holland. Guess what happened when those countries were overrun by Germany in 1940? Yep, the same gold found itself reclaimed by the Reichsbank again, along with the Belgian and Dutch reserves, which amounted to $223 million and $193 million respectively. Early in the war the Reichsbank also grabbed about $550 million worth of gold reserves from the countries Germany occupied.

How much the Reichsbank started the war with is, as you see, hard to estimate, as their records show that they outright lied all along, in international banking circles, about how much they had. Then there's the question of how much they spent running the war – trying to conquer the world is an expensive business. Fortunately for the Nazis, paper money was in proper use. They did most of their purchasing of raw materials with countries like Spain and Portugal, and paid in various currencies. Partway through the war, the Portuguese figured out that about three quarters of it was counterfeit.

Anyway, fast forward to the end of the war, and the issue of how much gold was left.

Netzeband, being both a well-trained and conscientious cashier, and aware that being responsible for the gold and currency meant it would be his head on the block – literally – if every penny didn't get to wherever it was going, made a detailed inventory of the cargo. This inventory, known as the Netzeband Report, has been a central tool for treasure hunters ever since.

Netzeband listed the cargo as 10 tons of gold, which was to be shipped south in three trucks. This gold was in the form of 770 ingots in 385 money sacks – two ingots to a bag, with paper currency stuffed in as well. Printing plates for banknotes also went along with them.

When the convoy reached the Alps – specifically a checkpoint in the village of Forhund, near the town of Garmisch – the two Georgs were somewhat disappointed in their hopes of finding the gateway to a secure fortress. Instead, the officer in command, Major Possinger, told them that the region was in fact full of refugees displaced by Allied bombing. He sent them to the Alpine Division base at Mittelwald, which is apparently known as the violin capital of the world. The Alpenkorps base there was commanded by a Colonel Franz Pfeiffer.

There, the gold was unloaded into the Officers' Mess. Colonel Pfeiffer took command of it and decided that it must be hidden. Pfeiffer decided to hide the gold from everybody, not just the

Allies. He then put the convoy and its cargo under the orders of a Captain Rüger, who took Netzeband and the trucks to the nearby Alpine village of Lake Wachensee. Not, you'll notice, Lake Toplitz.

The first thing Rüger did was to have the money loaded back onto the trucks and moved to a more secure space than the Alpenkorps' dining room, in which everybody could eye it up and think about how to grab a share. Taking Netzeband with him, Rüger moved the gold to the small village of Einseidel, at the southern end of the lake. At Einseidel is a three-storey alpine storage building called 'The Forest House'. This had been built around the turn of the 19th century, for the farmers and villagers of the area to store supplies and equipment over the winter.

Rüger and Netzeband first put their valuable cargo in the hay loft of the Forest House. At this point, Georg Netzeband thought his job was done, and his responsibility for the gold and currency had been discharged. Unfortunately, this wasn't quite the case.

While the Reichsbank funds were being stashed in the Forest House, other trucks carrying more gold and currency were arriving at Mittelwald. These trucks were sent by the SS, the Abwehr and the Foreign Ministry. How much gold, cash and other valuables were among these shipments isn't known, because Colonel Pfeiffer doesn't seem to have been much interested in keeping records that could be used by the Allies. This worried Georg Netzeband, as this other treasure was being mixed in with his cargo when stored at the Forest House, which meant the total hoard now did not match his inventory. Worse still, Pfeiffer consistently refused to give Netzeband a receipt for delivery of his cargo, which meant he would be held responsible for any discrepancies. Since there were now undocumented cargoes turning up at Mittelwald, there were definitely discrepancies aplenty.

Meanwhile, the villagers around Wachensee began to get restless as April 1945 drew to a close, as they heard rumours about gold being stored and hidden in the area. By 26 April, all the gold that was coming had arrived, and Colonel Pfeiffer began having his men move the hoard to a series of hiding spots in the mountains surrounding the area. Witnesses reported seeing mule trains laden with crates being led up Mount Steinriegel and Mount Klausen-Kopf on that date and returning in the morning unladen.

Although the local villagers reported that the mules were escorted by ordinary conscripts, later interrogations of the Mittelwald personnel after Germany's surrender showed that these men were actually the highest officers on the base, dressing down in rank to disguise themselves. Led by Captain Rüger, they spent three nights transporting the hoard to a number of caches on the mountains. According to Rüger's interrogation at the hands of US forces, the officers moved the 770 gold ingots brought by Netzeband from the Reichsbank, the 96 bags of Allied currencies from Munich and 56 crates sent to Mittelwald by the SS, Abwehr and Foreign Ministry. These crates consisted of 36 crates of gold ingots and coinage, and 20 crates of other materials – probably documents. This treasure was placed in several specially dug pits, three metres square, the sides lined with wooden planks, at various points amidst these mountains.

The treasure was buried just in time, as the US Army turned up at Major Possinger's checkpoint on the road into Garmisch on 30 April, just a day after the treasure burial was completed. Possinger told the Americans that that the region was full of refugees, and persuaded them to call off a bombing raid that would have flattened the town. Far from being an impenetrable fortress, Garmisch actually was just about the easiest town in Germany for the Allies to take, as the populace were more than happy to hand over the running of the town and get back to a peacetime way of life.

Since the Allies were already chasing down Nazi Germany's resources, and the local populace had witnessed parts of the hoard being taken into the woods and mountains, the Americans quickly brought in one of their special 'Gold Rush' teams of searchers to interrogate the personnel who had been taken prisoner from the Mittelwald Alpenkorps base.

Georg Netzeband, under interrogation, maintained that he didn't know the final location of the treasure. Colonel Pfeiffer disappeared for several weeks, but in the meantime his officers, including Captain Rüger, had been questioned and had spoken about some of the locations in which the gold and currency were buried.

Rüger was put in the care of the 55th Pioneer Battalion, who collected his mountain gear from his billet, and took him up Mount Steinriegel so that he could lead them to the loot, which he did. He took them to three caches on the mountains Steinriegel and Klausen-Kopf, where the soldiers dug up 728 gold ingots. This is indisputable – they took pictures of themselves goofing around with the gold bars, and you can easily find them on the Internet.

These were all from Netzeband's cargo of 770 ingots. So, what happened to the remaining undocumented crates from the SS, Abwehr and Foreign Ministry, and the 96 bags of Allied currency from Munich?

According to a death-bed confession by one of Pfeiffer's Alpenkorps lieutenants, Pfeiffer and a few other officers returned on the night of 29 April and removed the 96 bags of currency to a new hiding place on a third mountain, away from both Steinriegel and Klausen-Kopf. They left Netzeband's gold where it was because it was too heavy for them to spirit away on their own. Since all the caches on those two mountains were thoroughly swept clean by the 55th Pioneers, it's logical to assume that the other crates not from Netzeband's cargo were also hidden on a third mountain.

They then met on Klausen-Kopf and agreed to tell any American interrogators who asked about the missing cash that the SS had taken it south to Tyrol.

Colonel Pfeiffer stayed at large in the woods for several weeks before turning himself in and sticking to the story about the SS taking any remaining treasure to the Tyrol. Despite this, he was somehow able to bribe US troops with dollar bills. The ordinary American soldier was earning a mere $20 a month for his troubles, so it's unlikely that he was getting large sums of dollars from them. However, if he had, say, 96 sacks worth of US banknotes to play with … After the war, he lived quite comfortably in Argentina for many years, before retiring to Germany in the 1980s. He died in 1994.

So, 770 ingots were buried, but only 728 were recovered, leaving 42 ingots unaccounted for. Plus 36 crates of gold and 20 crates of who-knows-what.

Part of the reason for Lake Toplitz becoming associated with the gold is probably because the Netzeband Report listed printing plates and currency among his cargo, and printing plates and (counterfeit) currency were found in Lake Toplitz in 1959. However the plates and fake Allied currency dumped in Toplitz had come not from the Reichsbank in Berlin, but from Operation Bernhard, which had originally operated from Sachsenhausen concentration camp, but had been transferred to Mauthausen in Austria – not far from Lake Toplitz – in early 1945.

Toplitz had been used as a naval testing station for mines and torpedoes and suchlike throughout the war, and so was judged a suitable secure location to dump the equipment from the counterfeiting operation. (The personnel, all concentration camp inmates, were transferred to Ebensee concentration camp to be murdered, but a revolt at the camp saved them.)

The two completely different sets of printing plates and currency were then conflated in the minds of those investigating missing Nazi loot.

Other sites seem to have been used by retreating Nazis during the last stages of the war.

In the Czech Republic, in 1962, an intelligence officer named Helmut Gaenzel went undercover in prison for three months to eavesdrop on jailed Nazi general Christoph Klein. According to Klein, crates were brought by train to the vicinity of the town of Štěchovice.

Three hundred French and Russian prisoners were used to unload the crates and transfer this cargo to a series of tunnels known as 'The Snake'. The silence of these prisoners was then ensured by their being by 11 SS soldiers – who, in turn, were shot by General Klein's driver, just in case any of the prisoners had let anything slip to them.

The location of 'The Snake' is rather vague, but ground-penetrating radar suggests there are earthworks under a field on the outskirts of town, which had been used as a landing strip during the war. The Czech government, however, is of the opinion that the field is more likely a mass war grave, and refuses to allow permission for any excavation, as they don't want to either disturb a war grave or upset descendants of whoever might be in it.

There was also an SS barracks and mess hall in Štěchovice, linked by a bridge over a narrow gulley. The wife of one of the SS officers there was witness to another set of crates being hidden away in this gulley. According to her, the gulley was filled with crates, including several tunnels branching off it. She did not see what was in the crates, but, of course, treasure hunters immediately jumped to the conclusion that mystery crates = Nazi gold. In this case, two of the tunnels have subsequently been discovered, but the boxes and crates found therein were all filled with weapons and ammunition, not treasure of any kind.

It is most likely that this material was intended for use by an insurgent/guerrilla campaign after Germany's surrender, which never actually materialized.

Štěchovice isn't the only potential site for Nazi gold in the former Sudetenland of the Czech Republic, however.

In the town of Ziproc, the local castle was built in the 12th century on a hill made largely of jasper, and its dungeons were expanded in the 17th century. Jasper is a natural enhancer of radio waves, so in World War II the SS made full use of this by making the castle a headquarters and listening post, from which they could monitor Allied radio traffic, as well as having better signals for their own communications with Berlin and other occupied areas.

At the end of the war, you guessed it, crates were brought in but never left. Nobody thought much of this at first, and the Czech military took control of the castle in 1947. In 1993 the military left, selling the castle to a private owner. One of the first things the new owner did was to get some of the plumbing fixed and, during the process, the plumbers discovered not just some hidden tunnels in the dungeons, which had been concreted over by the SS, but some boxes stashed in the castle well. The boxes turned out to contain SS weapons and documents, and the occasional grenade-related booby-trap, which failed to go off after 50 years underwater.

There are still other booby traps in the well, and ground-penetrating radar shows there are also still unopened tunnels under the castle. It's unclear how old these tunnels are, as the 17th-century dungeon itself was only rediscovered in the early 2000s.

## WHERE IS IT NOW?

By 'it', the question is: what's the best place to look for the 42 ingots remaining from Netzeband's cargo? Or, more accurately, the best place to look for *40* remaining ingots.

You see, in 1996, two of them turned up in – wait for it – the Bank of England. Basically, the only way they could have got there is if someone had deposited them in a bank somewhere, and they had consequently been used in an international gold swap – a common procedure from the beginning of the 20th century onwards, in which national central banks swap gold back and forth in order to show that they meet central reserve ratio requirements. This is a standard procedure recognized as normal by the International Monetary Fund, but is essentially cosmetic in nature.

At some point, someone swapped these ingots into the Bank of England to make the Bank of England's gold reserves look as if they were at the right levels. At first it was suggested that the bars had been some of the Czech bank gold from 1938, but the serial numbers stamped on them turned out to be part of Netzeband's consignment, meaning they must have come in after 1945. This means some people at at least two national banks have been rather naughty in transferring Nazi gold around Europe instead of shunting it to the clearing system to determine rightful ownership.

The main other banks known to have received large amounts of Reichsbank gold are the Swiss National Bank and the Vatican Bank. The former was Europe's main gold distribution centre for decades, and during the war is known to have received about $440 million in bullion from Nazi Germany (roughly $316 million of which was looted gold, and about $124 million was 'official' German gold reserves).

So, the first answer to 'where is Netzeband's gold?' is most likely 'in a Swiss bank vault', as that's where two of the ingots got to the Bank of England from.

The second part of the answer is: In Argentina, or at least in the Argentine economy. Colonel Pfeiffer retired to there after the war, and as he was the last person known to be in possession of any of Netzeband's consignment, and he lived a more than comfortable life with no visible means of support, it's a logical and straightforward deduction. That said, he also had been in possession of a large supply of (either real or fake) US dollars, which no doubt also helped.

Finally, in terms of where to look for it out in the field: bear in mind that the known hoards of Nazi treasure – including gold – which have been recovered over the years were all stashed in caves and bunkers; usually salt or copper mines. Such locations are protected from bombing, hard to spot from the air, easy to close up with digging equipment or explosives, and – most importantly – able to be accessed again for the gold to be removed by anyone who knows that it's there.

So, as a general rule of thumb, any hoards of Nazi treasure – whether Reichsbank holdings or looted from conquered countries and Holocaust victims – are far more likely to be in caves and tunnels, sealed in by engineered collapses, than at the bottom of lakes. The best option in the area would be the old Riedboden lead mine, which closed down in 1903. If you absolutely must look in a lake, then Walchensee, Kochelsee, or Loisach are all at least in the general area of where the Netzeband gold actually went.

The unrecovered crates are, however, most likely to be still buried in their original hiding places on a mountain somewhere between the mountains of Steinriegel and Klausen-Kopf. Good choices of Bavarian Alps to search would be Altlach-Berg, Simmetsberg and Sintelsberg.

## THE OPPOSITION IN YOUR WAY

As with so many treasure hunting locations, tourists are always around. In fact there are even Nazi-gold tour routes, for drivers, bikers and even historical and battlefield-themed coach tours. This makes it more practical to go and have a look at these sites yourself, but the disadvantage is that, obviously, despite so many people tramping back and forth, nobody has ever actually found anything more.

There have been death threats made to treasure hunters in various parts of the former East Germany and Czech Republic, but none have been acted upon, and it appears more related to the likelihood of them discovering incriminating documents that name names, rather than to do with nicking gold from any modern-day Nazis. (There are neo-Nazi groups who would probably love to lay claim to the loot, but there is no historical line of descent between individual groups in the 1940s and ones today.)

Bavaria and Austria are both very safe areas in terms of crime, though the usual precautions should be taken when travelling. Organised crime – especially from the former Iron Curtain countries – has increased in recent years, but not in any way related to either Nazi gold or the search for it.

In terms of nature, while you're tramping around the mountains in search of burial locations, there are few to no dangerous animals. Bears very rarely wander into the area, and tend to be shot when they do, leaving the occasional lynx as the only real mammalian predator, and they're not big enough to attack people. You may, however, encounter wild boar, which can be stroppy (but are delicious), and will see – but are unlikely to interact with – eagles.

The biggest danger, therefore, is in the form of low temperatures above the snow line and the danger of avalanches. You must bear these in mind, and be sure to get proper local and professional advice about being safe in snow and forest.

# LYCRA CROFT

For those wondering exactly what Lara Croft's beloved lycra actually is, and how many lycans have to die for every pair of leggings, it's actually a copolymer of polyurethane and polyurea created as a synthetic replacement for natural latex (which originates in rain-forest trees.)

Lycra's actually the UK, Irish, Israeli and Antipodean name for what's called Spandex (an anagram of 'expands') in the US, and Elastane in mainland Europe. It was invented by DuPont chemists C. L. Sandquist and Joseph Shivers in 1958, originally under the codename 'K'.

The elasticity and expansion that gave it its American and European names gives the artificial fibres the ability to stretch to up to six times their resting length before tearing, and to return to their original length – and a garment to its original shape – more quickly than natural textiles. This makes it ideal for clothing than can both stretch during activity, and adhere to the body to provide muscular support, and even a level of compression which can assist with controlling circulation, especially at altitude, and thus holding off muscle fatigue for longer. Swimwear – or any other clothing likely to get wet – made of lycra dries far more quickly than other materials, reducing the risk of hypothermia if you still have to wear it after crossing a river.

Though it's useful stuff, much of its practical value goes unrecognized by most people, as fashion and trends have taken over. In fact over 80 per cent of *all* clothing now contains some amount of Lycra, for cosmetic fashion purposes.

The other issues to check out are the laws on treasure hunting and metal detecting. Treasure-trove law in Germany has half the find belonging to the finder, and the other half to the landowner – it's tax-free for both. Searching is allowed in most places, away from historical monuments, but be aware that some areas have been slapped with no-metal-detecting orders, usually because of the amount of World War II ordnance that could too easily be triggered if dug up by an enthusiastic amateur.

# THE IRISH CROWN JEWELS

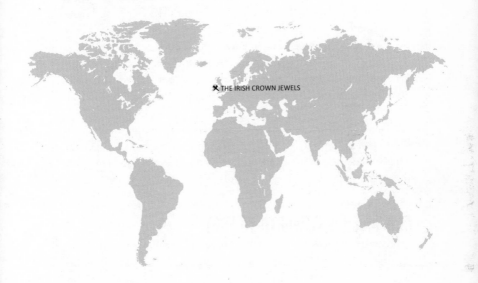

✖ THE IRISH CROWN JEWELS

## WHAT IS IT?

A star and badge, of multiple (394 altogether) diamonds, emeralds and rubies. The Brazilian diamonds used had originally belonged to Queen Charlotte and then George IV, and the regalia were commissioned by William IV. They were intended to be worn by the king, when he was in Ireland, and by the Lord Lieutenant of Ireland when the king was at home in England. The police report on their theft describes them thusly:

'A Diamond Star of the Grand Master of the Order of St. Patrick composed of brilliants (Brazilian stones) of the purest water, 4⅝ by 4¼ inches, consisting of eight points, four greater and four lesser, issuing from a centre enclosing a cross of rubies and a trefoil of emeralds surrounding a sky blue enamel circle with words, "Quis Separabit MDCCLXXXIII." in rose diamonds engraved on back. Value about £14,000.'

'A Diamond Badge of the Grand Master of the Order of St. Patrick set in silver containing a trefoil in emeralds on a ruby cross surrounded by a sky blue enamelled circle with "Quis Separabit MDCCLXXXIII." in rose diamonds surrounded by a wreath of trefoils in emeralds, the whole enclosed by a circle of large single Brazilian stones of the finest water, surmounted by a crowned harp in diamonds and loop, also in Brazilian stones. Total size of oval 3 by 2⅜ inches; height 5⅝ inches. Value £16,000.'

There are also five lost 'collars' awarded to the members of the Order, when they were made Knights. These 'collars' were actually gold and enamelled necklaces with badges of office, valued at £1,050 each.

There are also a few other diamonds which actually shouldn't have been in the burgled safe to start with, whose value is unclear. The 'trefoils of emeralds' are in fact shamrocks made of emerald, this being Ireland.

## HOW MUCH IS IT WORTH TO YOU?

Luckily, as you can see above, we know just how much they were worth to start with: a little over £35,000. Today, the star would be worth, in economic terms, £10.16 million. The badge would be worth £11.6 million, and the five missing collars are now worth £762,300 each. That's a total of just over £25.57 million ($42.5 million) for the set.

## THE STORY

In 1903 a new strongroom had been specially built for the regalia in Dublin Castle, directly adjoining the Ulster King of Arms's library and office, which had just moved from another tower of the castle to the Bedford Tower. The King of Arms was one Arthur Vicars, and he was the chief Herald and Genealogist for Ireland. His ceremonial duties were 'inspecting, overseeing and correcting, and embodying the arms and ensigns of illustrious persons and of imposing and ordaining differences therein, according to the Laws of Arms: of granting Letters Patent of Arms to men of rank and fit persons'. He was also Registrar of, and Knight Attendant upon, the Order of St Patrick.

The regalia themselves, along with other valuables, were stored in a safe for which there were only a limited number of keys. The plans for the strongroom had been prepared by the Office of Public Works but when the work was completed – and it's difficult to resist politically incorrect jokes about Irish builders here, perhaps because this occurrence spawned many of them – the door to the new strongroom was made too small to admit the safe that was supposed to be stored in it, and which contained the regalia.

Vicars therefore simply had the safe put in the library in which his own office was located, where he could keep an eye on it. The safe was pretty well guarded, with both police and soldiers on duty 24/7 and a police inspection every night.

As well as the safe in the library there were several bits and bobs in a glass case in the strongroom; three collars and badges belonging to the Knights of St Patrick as well as two silver state maces, the Irish Sword of State, a jewelled sceptre and two silver spurs. Also, there was the gilt crown, an enamelled badge and a gilt collar which the King of Arms would wear on ceremonial occasions. There was another collar and badge in a drawer too. There were only two keys to the safe, and Vicars had both, but a total of seven people had keys to Vicars's office.

All was well for the next four years, until 15 March 1907, when Lord Aberdeen, the lord lieutenant at the time, wore the jewels for an early St Patrick's celebration. After that event, they were put back in the safe in Vicars's office and were shown there to a visitor – John Crawford Hodgson, librarian to the Duke of Northumberland – on 11 June. They were next intended to be worn by King Edward VII at an investiture ceremony on 10 July, when the king was due to invest the second Baron Fitzpatrick into the Order of St Patrick on the first day of the Irish International Exposition.

On 28 June, Vicars found the latch-key of the front door to the Bedford Tower missing from his set of keys and had to be let into the building by a member of the police (the key re-appeared on Monday 8 July). On Wednesday 3 July, the cleaning woman found the front door of the Bedford Tower unlocked at 7 a.m. She reported this to the messenger when he arrived for work who in turn reported it to Vicars. The latter took little interest in the matter.

On Saturday 6 July, the cleaning woman found the door of the strongroom open when she arrived for work. Though the inner grille was locked, the key was in the lock and attached to it was the key of the bookcases and presses in the library. The cleaning woman locked the strongroom door and left the keys for the messenger's attention. Again the messenger reported the matter to Vicars. Again the latter took little interest in the matter.

On the same day, 6 July, a messenger arrived from Messrs West and Son, jewellers, bringing with him a gold and enamelled collar of the Order of St Patrick which had been worn by the recently deceased Lord de Ros. It was now to be used in the investiture of a new knight. Mahony, the Cork Herald, took possession of the parcel, checked its contents and left them on Vicars's desk. Later, Vicars asked the messenger to place the contents of the parcel in the safe and even gave him his own keys to open the safe door. The messenger found the safe unlocked and empty and went to tell Vicars of this event. Vicars checked the safe for himself.

The king, needless to say, was extremely annoyed, but went ahead with the ceremony anyway.

The Dublin Metropolitan Police launched an immediate investigation, putting out reward posters giving the descriptions and values mentioned above. Scotland Yard sent over Chief Inspector John Kane to take charge, and he wrote up a report which supposedly names the culprit (or at least who he thought was the culprit), but this report was immediately covered up and buried by the Royal Irish Constabulary.

Vicars refused to resign from his position and blamed his deputy, Francis Shackleton, brother of the famous Antarctic explorer Ernest Shackleton. Kane dismissed this possibility, and a Royal Commission decided that Vicars had not done his job due diligence and fired both him and his staff.

Politicians and commentators of both nationalist and unionist leanings accused one another of being responsible and started working up the most complicated conspiracy theories, but the regalia have not been seen since, and no official judgement has been made on what happened to them.

# PREVIOUS SEARCHES IN FACT AND FICTION

The main historical search for the stolen treasure came not in the form of an expedition to dig up possible hiding locations, but in the form of a Vice-Regal Commission of Inquiry in January of 1908.

Lord Aberdeen, the Lord Lieutenant of Ireland, set this up to 'investigate the circumstances of the loss of the regalia of the Order of St Patrick', and 'to inquire whether Sir Arthur Vicars exercised due vigilance and proper care as the custodian thereof'.

Witnesses were examined, and statements read, all in the actual room from which the regalia had been stolen in the first place. The commission was led by Solicitor-General Redmond Barry, and comprised of Judge James J. Shaw, Robert F. Starkie and Chester Jones. It lasted for a mere week, from 10–16 January. This inquiry had no power to subpoena witnesses or question them under oath, while Vicars and Mahony Sr wanted a public enquiry that would do that. As a result, Vicars refused to attend or answer any questions, as did his clerk, Sydney Horlock, and his typist, Mary Gibbon.

This meant that he looked even more at fault, and the search for what happened was missing the most important witness. They did at least have copies of his statements given to the police during their fruitless investigation.

Mahony, Shackleton and Goldney did all attend, as did Vicars's secretary, George Burtchaell. Other witnesses included Assistant Commissioner of the Dublin Metropolitan Police, MV Harrel; Superintendent John Lowe; Chief Inspector John Kane of Scotland Yard; and Sir George C. V. Holmes, Chairman of the Board of Works (who had built the too-small-for-the-safe strongroom).

Chief Inspector Kane told the commission that it was an inside job, and had happened before 5 July.

In 1922, what we now call the Republic of Ireland became an essentially independent country in the form of the Irish Free State, and of course Dublin Castle and all its contents became the new country's responsibility. In 1927, an Irish government memo was written which indicated that 'the Castle Jewels are for sale and that they could be got for £2,000 or £3,000'. This may have been an indication that stolen jewels were up for sale, or that a fraud was being perpetrated in their name, or that someone had found them and sought a reward. There's no sure way to tell, as the memo was declared secret and buried until 1976. Needless to say, the stolen jewels don't seem to have been bought back at this point.

Also in 1927, however, a Dublin jeweller named James Weldon claimed to have been contacted in 1927 by Shackleton, offering to sell him the location of the regalia. That said, this story was brought up by Weldon's descendants as a family anecdote, and there's no written documentation.

In 1983, the Gardai, the Irish police, were given a tip by a woman whose grandfather had been a Republican activist back in the inter-war years. He had told his family stories of how he had been involved in stealing the regalia, and that – having either failed to ransom the jewels, or succeeded in embarrassing the establishment – had buried them in the foothills of the Wicklow (or Dublin, if you're local) Mountains.

The Gardai dispatched a team to search at the location given, but found nothing.

If you're thinking that this sounds like a job for Sherlock Holmes, you'd be right. In fact, Sir Arthur Conan-Doyle was a good friend – and distant cousin – of Arthur Vicars, so it would be surprising if they hadn't discussed the case at some point and given some consideration to what Holmes would have made of it.

The fact they doubtless had such conversations is borne out by the publication in 1908 of the Holmes story *The Adventure of the Bruce-Partington Plans*. This is best remembered both for being more of a prototype spy thriller than a detective story, and for the element of a body found on railway tracks after having been placed on a train's roof (which was actually inspired by another real crime, the unsolved murder of a woman called Mary Money, in 1905).

The theft of the secret plans in the story involves a series of keys all possessed by one man charged with looking after them, and one of the villains being a deputy who is the brother of a famed VIP – in fact a thinly-disguised Francis Shackleton.

A fictionalized account of the case proper – *Jewels*, by Bob Perrin – was published in 1979. This one also casts Shackleton as the insider, going with the Nationalist conspiracy theory that he had been lured into gay orgies by a cashiered British officer, who persuaded him to make impressions of the safe keys while Vicars was drunk and/or drugged. In the novel the culprits all have unfortunate accidents, with the truth covered up to hide the fact that one of the participants in said gay orgies was the Duke of Argyll, brother-in-law to the king.

## THE TRUTH IS OUT THERE

Though called the 'Irish Crown Jewels', they weren't actually crown jewels, but simply expensive jewellery belonging to a chivalric honours roll, roughly equivalent to the Order of the Garter in the UK, founded in 1783. There was, after all, no Irish royal family at the time to *have* crown jewels.

The regalia were first referred to by the term 'crown jewels' in 1905, when the Order's statutes were revised. After the theft, of course, all the newspapers in Britain and Ireland referred to them as 'Crown Jewels' as well, simply because the choice of wording helped the tale sound more shocking and daring – and therefore more worthy of buying a newspaper to read about it.

Oddly enough, the theft of 1907 wasn't the first time that they'd been, shall we say, inappropriately handled. Arthur Vicars had some subconscious determination to be a walking stereotype, and so was known to drink himself to sleep when he was on night duty. This is not the sort of person you want claiming to be keeping an eye on your best bling, as was proved when on at least one occasion he woke up in the morning to find that he was wearing the star and badge. Some prankster among his staff had taken them out of the safe and put them on him while he was out for the count. Why anyone did this before the invention of mobile phones and Twitter is a mystery, because that gag would have gone viral in an instant.

This regalia was presented to the Order by King William IV in 1831, having been made by the jewellers Rundell, Bridge and Company of London. Members of the Order were titled 'Knights Companions' as with the Order of the Garter. The chief herald and genealogical officer for Ireland under British rule, the Ulster King of Arms, was the guy tasked with registering the Order's membership and looking after its regalia.

In 1905, the statutes of the Order were revised, and it was decided that it would make better sense, security-wise, that the jewels, and the collars and badges of the members, should be moved from their original locations (a bank vault in the case of the regalia, and the castle library in the case of the collars) and secured in a thick steel safe in the strongroom of the Office of Arms, in Dublin Castle.

Arthur Vicars had been serving as Ulster King of Arms since 1893, and had already overseen the switching of the Office's location from Bermingham Tower to Bedford Tower in 1903. Under him were the heralds for Cork and Dublin – Pierce Gun Mahony and Francis Shackleton respectively – and one Francis Bennett Goldney, who had the rather strange title of Athlone Pursuivant. Mahony was Vicars's nephew, and Shackleton his housemate, so it's easy to see how they might have fallen into the job so easily.

Things then actually started to go awry on 3 July, when the office cleaner, a Mrs Farrell, found the door unlocked. She told this to the staff messenger, a William Stivey, who told Vicars. Vicars just shrugged with an 'oh, really?' On the morning of 6 July, Mrs Farrell found the doors lying open again, and Vicars again shrugged off the news.

In mid-afternoon that day, Vicars told Stivey to put away the collar of a recently deceased member of the Order in the safe and gave him the key. This was a surprise to the messenger, who had never been asked to use the safe before or given a key. Stivey found the safe was already unlocked and ran to tell Vicars, who found that the Order's regalia and five knights' collars were gone. It wasn't just the official treasure that had disappeared, Vicars had been storing his own mother's diamond jewellery in the safe unofficially, and that had been nicked as well.

The keys to the boxes containing the regalia were kept in the safe with them, which seems a rather unwise decision. Superintendent John Lowe, Detective Owen Kerr and Assistant Commissioner William V. Harrel came from the Dublin Metropolitan Police to investigate.

They determined that the theft had been neat and tidy and had to have taken at least ten undisturbed minutes. Many staff and members of the Dublin Met had keys to the front door, but the only two keys to the safe were held by Vicars. There were also four keys to the strongroom door, and another two to an inner grille, one of which was still in the lock.

Harrel and Lowe then called upon Scotland Yard to help and sent details of the missing jewels around the world. The makers of the safe, Ratner (this was a combination of Ratcliff and Horner, no relation to Gerald Ratner of cheap jewellery store fame), were questioned as were many Dublin locksmiths. The safe hadn't been forced, and the keys had been used. The thief or thieves had deliberately set out to make the robbery obvious by leaving the doors open.

Bedford Tower was searched, but nothing found, and both the lord lieutenant and Vicars convinced themselves it was all a prank – Vicars openly waited for the jewels to be returned by parcel-post.

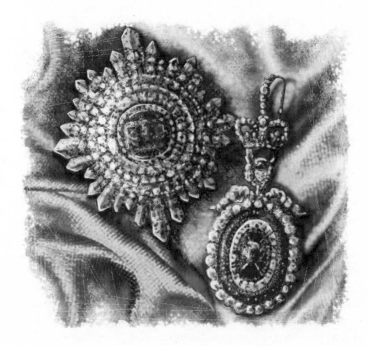

By 10 July, a reward of £1,000 was offered for information leading to the recovery of the jewels and the capture of the thief or thieves, but nobody ever tried to claim it. Detective Chief Inspector John Kane of Scotland Yard arrived on 12 July. He believed that the theft was intended to mess up the royal visit and wrote a report identifying the likely thief – but the Chief Commissioner of the Dublin Met refused to accept the identification and the report mysteriously disappeared when Kane returned to London.

Nevertheless, it was spectacularly obvious to everyone that it was an inside job. Despite this, Vicars continued to pronounce that none of his staff would or could have done it. This means either he was incredibly blind or did it himself. The latter option is easily possible: of the two keys to the safe, one was always on Vicars's person, and the other was a spare he kept at home. One of them was used in the robbery.

Of the available Heralds, Mahony hadn't been in to the office until 4 July, and neither Shackleton nor Goldney had even been in Ireland at any point between 11 June and 6 July, when the robbery took place. This didn't look good for Vicars.

The king, Edward VII, was getting annoyed and also felt it was an inside job. He wanted Vicars out, and although the lord lieutenant was on Vicars's side, he couldn't disobey a direct order from his royal boss. Therefore, on 23 October, Vicars was suspended, as were Goldney, Mahony and Shackleton.

Feeling betrayed, Vicars called for a full public inquiry to be held in an attempt to clear his name. His step-brother, Pierce O'Mahony – Pierce Gun Mahony's father – stepped in to help out. He had been a Nationalist MP and called for the issue to be raised in the House of Commons. Irish MPs refused on the grounds that an inquiry might throw too much light on rumours of gay orgies among the Office of Arms' staff. Eventually, however, the Knights of the Order of St Patrick themselves petitioned the king for an inquiry. The king, under the advisement of the lord lieutenant, established a court of enquiry.

The Crown Jewels Commission (Ireland) was established in January 1908, to investigate the theft and to determine whether Vicars had been negligent. Since the commission was to sit in private, could not subpoena witnesses and could not take evidence under oath, Vicars refused to take part. The commission still had his statements to the police, however. Then the fun really started.

When it comes to looking at the staff of the Office of Arms as suspects, all manner of interesting quirks began to show.

Vicars, as it turns out, had a liking for showing off the regalia to visitors, as well as being prone to drinking on an evening shift and storing his own family heirlooms in the safe. Vicars had also acted as a guarantor for the frequently indebted Shackleton, who was always in hock beyond his means and who lived in the house with the spare safe key; surely a possible motive. In fact Vicars had by now decided to finger Shackleton as the culprit to anyone who'd listen, despite the fact that he hadn't even been in Ireland during the time in which the theft could have taken place. Vicars had even told Chief Inspector Kane that Shackleton did it, but Kane refused to believe this, considering Shackleton's absence from Ireland at the time, and this was not the person he had named in his missing report.

Goldney got involved with this setup, at Vicars's request, becoming a guarantor in dealings with Shackleton's loan-shark. When Shackleton gave his evidence at the Inquiry, he took pains to point out that he had been accused by tabloid newspapers of conspiring with Lord Haddo to commit the theft – Lord Haddo, of course, being the son of the lord lieutenant, who had set up the Inquiry. Needless to say, the solicitor-general quickly decided that this was a side to the case that didn't need to be gone into.

Instead, the commission's verdict was this: 'Having fully investigated all the circumstances connected with the loss of the Regalia of the Order of St Patrick, and having examined and considered carefully the arrangements of the Office of Arms in which the Regalia were deposited, and the provisions made by Sir Arthur Vicars, or under his direction, for their safe keeping, and having regard especially to the inactivity of Sir Arthur Vicars on the occasions immediately preceding the disappearance of the Jewels, when he knew that the Office and the Strong Room had been opened at night by unauthorised persons, we feel bound to report to Your Excellency that, in our opinion, Sir Arthur Vicars did not exercise due vigilance or proper care as the custodian of the Regalia.'

The commission also took great pains to say how much they thought that Shackleton was a really trustworthy fellow, and it was unimaginable that he could have been involved with such a crime. Vicars, Shackleton and Goldney were fired, but Vicars refused to hand over the office keys, forcing his replacement, Neville Wilkinson, to break in in order to start work.

Mahony was allowed to keep his job, and his father started a campaign to protest Vicars's innocence and pin the blame on Shackleton, by leaking to the press stories that the establishment wanted rid of Vicars because he had allowed a man of such low character into the job. Vicars, meanwhile, also continued to blame Shackleton, as well as the Board of Works. He claimed his lack of response to being told that his secure doors were being left open was down to pressure of overwork.

A year after the theft, a Nationalist Irish-American newspaper, the *Gaelic American*, really got things going in a sensationalist way with more stuff leaked by O'Mahony, when it revealed that drunken gay orgies had been held in the Office of Arms rooms. The paper suggested that Shackleton and a Captain Gaudeons had stolen the regalia and got away with it by threatening to expose the identities of establishment figures involved.

Shackleton did have a friend named Richard Gorges, who had been a British Army captain, and his reference to Lord Haddo in his testimony to the commission could easily be interpreted as a thinly-veiled 'I know stuff' warning to go easy on him.

The article was written by a Republican Brotherhood member named Bulmer Hobson, and he bumped into Gorges a few years later. Supposedly Gorges admitted that the main details of this story were true, and said that the regalia had once been stolen as a drunken prank by Lord Haddo, who returned them in the morning. According to this version, Shackleton then took them for real and sold them in Amsterdam.

It's certainly odd that the commission both went to the extent of singling out Shackleton for praise as being trustworthy, and also considered him of sufficiently low character that association with him was a good reason for firing Vicars.

So, who did it? Let's do a Poirot and gather the suspects. Figuring out the truth of the matter will always be difficult, as a surprising number of files and documentation also went walkabout over the years. At least eight Home Office files on the subject were officially destroyed, and the Ulster Office's official correspondence records between 1902 and 1908 are missing altogether (everything else from that office was replaced by the Office of the Chief Herald of Ireland in 1943), as is Chief Inspector Kane's ultimate report.

Shackleton definitely had means and motive: He was a regular debtor, in hock to loan sharks – at one point even his more famous brother Ernest had to borrow £1,000 to help pay off some of his debts – and he was later jailed for fraud (passing a bad cheque) in 1914. He had an office key and lived in the same house as the spare safe key. That said, what he didn't have was opportunity. Shackleton had left Ireland before 11 June, when the regalia were last seen, and didn't return until 9 July, three days after the theft had been discovered. So he definitely didn't take them. It actually appears that most of the vituperation against him was down to his debts and his homosexuality, making him an easy target. That said, he could still have been involved in a conspiracy to commit the theft, perhaps by planning it. There's no evidence to that effect, however, but it doesn't stop even most modern commentators from blaming him.

Gorges has to be a suspect if for no other reason than that he spent a lot of time boasting about having stolen the Irish Crown Jewels to his fellow jailbirds while serving a sentence for manslaughter. None of them believed him, however, as, like Shackleton, he wasn't in Ireland at the time of the theft. According to his boasts, Shackleton had planned it, inspired by an earlier prank theft, and had taken the jewels to Amsterdam to be sold, with the proviso that they not be broken up for at least three years, in case they wanted to buy them back or ransom them.

Vicars, as possessor of both keys, is also an obvious suspect, but his belief that first none of his staff can have done it, and then that Shackleton had, suggests that he was psychologically guilt-ridden over his failure, and relieved to pin the blame on someone. Had he taken the jewels, he'd have had a much more comfortable life after being fired, and would have had no reason to continue blaming Shackleton years later, in his will, as he did.

Pierce Gun Mahony had little means or opportunity. Motivationally, he was from a Nationalist family, and so if the intent was simply to disrupt a British bit of ceremony, then he could still have been involved in some capacity.

That leaves us with Francis Bennett Goldney, and here we have a winner. Shackleton might have more access to the spare safe key, but Goldney's track record as a kleptomaniac (he once took two silver communion cups from Canterbury Cathedral, and sold them to the Metropolitan Museum of Art in New York) means he's the most likely culprit to have actually taken them. He was the newest of the Heralds on the team, having been appointed in February of 1907, and he was the third man in the Vicars/Shackleton debtor's triangle, which means he undoubtedly visited the house often, and knew the financial situation. Since Vicars had at least once been sufficiently stupefied to have the regalia placed on him without his waking up, it's not impossible that the safe key could have been lifted from his pocket and replaced without alerting him.

That Goldney was a thief is not in doubt: he died in a car accident in France in 1918, and when his personal effects and belongings were studied, it turned out that he was in illegal possession of more stolen archive goods – ancient charters and historic documents stolen from Canterbury, and a painting by Romanelli which was the property of the Duke of Bedford until Goldney nicked it.

It's still possible that Shackleton and Goldney could have been in cahoots, and, either way, it was likely Goldney who fingered Shackleton as the culprit to Vicars. (Vicars' statement said a friend had tipped him off about Shackleton's supposed guilt.)

Speaking of Canterbury, folklore there suggests a mayoral connection to the theft. Newspaper publisher J. A. Jennings claimed that an anonymous American millionaire staying with Goldney had had a false bottom added to his car's petrol tank in order to smuggle the jewels in it when they went from Dover to Amsterdam. Interestingly, one John Pierpont Morgan (yes, that J. P. Morgan) was in Canterbury with Goldney in August 1907, and has been retroactively accused elsewhere of smuggling Etruscan artefacts to the Metropolitan Museum of Art.

In the end, Shackleton changed his name to Mellor after his release from prison, and died in 1941.

Gorges was hit by a train in 1944.

A very bitter Vicars retired to Kilmorna House in County Kerry, married a Gertrude Wright in 1917, and was murdered by the IRA in 1921. His will wasn't published until 1976, when it turned out to contain this paragraph: 'I might have had more to dispose of had it not been for the outrageous way in which I was treated by the Irish Government over the loss of the Irish Crown Jewels in 1907, backed up by the late King Edward VII whom I had always loyally and faithfully served, when I was made a scapegoat to save other departments responsible and when they shielded the real culprit and thief Francis R. Shackleton (brother of the explorer who didn't reach the South Pole). My whole life and work was ruined by this cruel misfortune and by the wicked and blackguardly acts of the Irish Government.'

Pierce Gun Mahony was, ironically, given his middle name, shot in a supposed hunting accident in 1914.

As for the 1927 memo about the jewels being for sale, of course when the Irish Free State had been created in 1922, the remaining non-stolen pieces belonging to the Order of St Patrick also became property of the new country, and it's more likely that these were being offered to Britain for sale – and indeed they were returned to Britain during the 1940s.

## WHERE IS IT NOW?

There is a popular view, especially among Irish Nationalists, that the regalia was secretly returned to the British Royal Family shortly afterwards by Loyalists who had taken it to blame on Nationalists. This makes no sense today, with royal regalia being a driving force of the UK tourism industry – such spectacular pieces would draw too many crowds of paying customers to keep secret.

There are basically two possibilities: the pieces were broken up and the gemstones fenced individually, or, they are still in the hands of the family of some private collector, and after over a century it's entirely possible that such descendants don't even know that the pieces in great-granddad's study actually *are* these historical artefacts.

Logically, the former option is more likely. Most jewel thefts are for the cash value of the pieces, and even if the theft was politically motivated by Nationalists, since no ransom demand or propaganda was made of the pieces, it is reasonable to assume that so many gemstones would buy a lot of guns/bribes/printing/whatever. Regardless of whether the motive for the theft was for the cash or for political purposes, the pieces would be very recognizable at the time and very risky to try to sell intact. Dismantling them and taking the individual stones to different fences and buyers would be far safer.

That said, it isn't impossible that the pieces could have been stolen to order for a collector for a set price.

For what it's worth, the old Ulster's office library still exists at Dublin Castle (now shared with a conference centre). The Ratner safe from which the jewels were taken was returned to the castle in 2007, but is now in the Garda Museum there – which, funnily enough, is in the Bermingham Tower, where it began its life before the move to Bedford Tower in 1903.

You can also still see the house shared by Vicars and Shackleton, in St James's Terrace, Clonskeagh.

## THE OPPOSITION IN YOUR WAY

The loss of various reports and documents is a big problem, but really it's virtually certain that the jewels will no longer be in the same recognizable form. They will have been split up and distributed over half of Europe before the World War I.

On the upside, those of you who don't like snakes should have no problem in Ireland…

RG IV. MEER

OCEAN
(SÜDLICHES EISMEER)

R. FORSCHTES

SÜD
POL

Westliche Länge von Greenwich

80
10 0 10
20
30
40
50
60
70
80
90
100
110
120
130
140
150
160
170
180
80

20
30
40

80

140
150
160
170

180° v. Paris

Anzeichen von hohem Land

en Südpol erreichte Breite 78°10' Senkrechte Eiswand 150–200 F. hoch
Ross, Febr. 1842

290

410

Beaufort I.

Franklin I.

600 F

190

1842

Offenes
Meer

Viele
Walfische

Packeis,
Ross, März 1842

Coulman I.

# TREASURES OF THE MIDDLE EAST

# THE ARK OF THE COVENANT

✕ THE ARK OF THE COVENANT

## WHAT IS IT?

Depending on whether you're an adventure movie fan, a believer in visits to Earth by ancient astronauts, or a religious believer, your answer could vary between 'a radio for talking to God', some kind of *Star Trek*-style replicator that supplies food, or a sacred vessel for holding the literal power of God within it.

Basically, however, it would be safest to say that it is a wooden box, covered inside and out with gold sheeting, which is supposed to contain the actual stone tablets graven with the Ten Commandments.

The Ark was – or is – a wooden box, two cubits long, by one and a half deep, and one and a half wide. The exact size can only really be estimated as an average because the original dimensions are in cubits, and a cubit was defined as the distance from a man's elbow to the tip of his middle finger. Since everybody is a little different, the exact dimensions would vary according to the person making the box. Nowadays, however, the cubit is usually averaged out to mean 18in, which would make the box 3ft long, 2ft 3in deep, and 2ft 3in wide.

The wood is sandwiched between sheets of gold, inside and out. There's a gold ring on each corner, oriented as two rings on each side. Two wooden staves, sheathed in gold, go through the gold rings for carrying the Ark.

The lid, or 'mercy seat', is two and a half cubits (3ft 9in) by one and a half cubits (2ft 3in) of pure gold, and has two cherubim beaten out of a single piece of gold. These cherubim are at opposite ends of the lid, facing each other, with their wings held stretched out towards each other. There's no mention of how thick the lid is, but it'd have to be around a quarter of an inch thick.

The Ark isn't supposed to be empty, of course, but should contain two stone tablets, the *luchot HaBrit* in Hebrew, on which the Ten Commandments are engraved.

## HOW MUCH IS IT WORTH TO YOU?

Even before getting into the historical value and religious signficance … a *lot*. At the time of writing, gold is worth $937 per troy ounce. From the Biblical dimensions of the Ark, the lid – the 'mercy seat' alone, not even counting the cherubs, weighs in at around 10,966.4 ounces – that's $10.28 million at today's market rate.
Just for the lid.

Add, say, a couple of million for each side, and the floor, and, yeah, $15 million in gold alone? Plus the additional cultural and historical value. Plus, if you believe the religious texts, the ability to talk directly to God and demolish cities.

## THE STORY

According to the Biblical book of *Exodus*, when Moses stayed on Mount Sinai for 40 days to commune with God in a cloud, he was given the instructions for constructing the Ark of the Covenant, as well as given the stone tablets of the Ten Commandments, which would be kept in it. He was also given instructions on creating the Tabernacle – the temple that would house the Ark when they were encamped – and all the furniture it would need, and how to properly handle it. It even had to be kept behind a curtain.

Although Moses came back downhill with the Ten Commandments after 40 days, it took a year before the Ark was ready. The Israelites then carried it at the head of their march for 40 years between Egypt and the Promised Land. As well as providing food in the form of manna when supplies ran short, it also parted the River Jordan, so that everybody could walk across without getting their feet wet.

When the Israelite army reached Jericho and needed to bring down the city's walls, as well as the horns that were blown by seven priests on a circumnavigation of the walls each day, the Ark was borne around as well.

Eventually, Joshua set it up in a permanent Tabernacle at Shiloh, but things soon went awry. The Israelites decided to take it as a weapon to the Battle of Gibeah, but still got beaten. The Ark itself – or God, whose power energized it – tended not to work for them when they tried to use it as a weapon without God's prior instructions to do so, and this occurred both at Gibeah, and later on, when the Philistines came calling. Normally after a defeat, such as at Gibeah, or at the Battle of Ai before that, the Israelites would consult the Ark and mourn at it, but when they fought against the Philistines, things changed.

Once again, the Ark refused to work for them during this unauthorized weaponization, and it was then captured by the Philistines. When Eli, the Israelite priest in charge, heard the news, he dropped dead with shock. The Philistines, in turn, hung on to it for only seven months, during which time it caused them nothing but trouble. They tried putting it into the temple of their god, Dagon, and found that the statue of Dagon kept breaking, falling in front of the Ark. Before they knew it, the Philistines were afflicted with plagues of boils, mice, and ... er, hemorrhoids.

Keen to be able to sit comfortably again, the Philistines decided to return the Ark to the Israelites, though it first stopped off in Beth-shemesh, where 70 or so townsmen came to look at it and got struck dead. Eventually, however, it made it home, pulled by a couple of oxen, and was put in a Tabernacle at Kiriath-Jearim for 20 years, until the legendary King David came to be in charge.

David had it transferred to Zion, which would become Jerusalem, but on the way a guy tried to steady it when it toppled, and got zapped by it for his trouble. In the end, though, it was put in its permanent Tabernacle there. David wanted to build a new temple to hold it, but God talked him out of that, and so the people held their services at the Tabernacle, where they made sacrifices to the Ark, and were given out food in return.

The priests who worked with the Ark – the Levites – had to wear special gear to do so, and it was more like armour than anything else, with a special breastplate and a rope tied around their waists. This latter was so that if the Ark zapped them, their bodies could be pulled back out of the Tabernacle without risking anyone else's life.

The Ark was still carried as a mix of standard and weapon by the Israelite army, but David took it with him when he legged it during a conspiracy against him. He then sent it back in the care of Zadok the priest. Zadok would later crown Solomon king, and, as a result, would later have the anthem written by Handel for British royal coronations named after him.

King Solomon, when not flirting with the Queen of Sheba, and getting mines erroneously named after him, had a prophetic dream in which God promised him wisdom and this prompted him to regularly worship at the Ark. He also had it placed in a special chamber, the Holy of Holies, in the temple he built. When the temple was dedicated and the Ark installed, the temple was filled with a cloud like the one Moses had stayed in on Mount Sinai.

For some reason Solomon decided that the presence of the Ark in the city made the entire city so holy that he couldn't let his wife live there, and had to leave her in a house out in the countryside. At some point, however, the Ark was removed from the temple, as the later King Josiah puts it back there (in 2 Chronicles 35).

In 597 BC, the Babylonians invaded and trashed the Israelite kingdom. They ravaged Jerusalem, and looted Solomon's Temple. What happened to the Ark from here on in depends on who you want to believe. According to the Greek version of the book of *Ezra*, the invaders 'took all the holy vessels of the Lord, both great and small, and the Ark of God, and the king's treasures, and carried them away into Babylon'. However, according to the *Second Book of Maccabees*, the prophet Jeremiah had been sent a vision by God that warned him to take the Tabernacle and the Ark to safety. Jeremiah, therefore, took the Ark to 'the mountain from the top of which Moses saw God's promised land'.

Once there, Jeremiah stashed the Ark, the Tabernacle tent and a few other bits and bobs in a cave, whose entrance he then blocked up. And that's the point at which the Ark vanishes from Biblical scripture. Ordinarily you could say this is when it vanished from history, but outside of scripture it has never really appeared in any historical documentation.

Technically, there are two other references to the Ark later in the Bible, but the first (in *Hebrews*) is a back-reference to the Ark prior to its disappearance, and the other (in the book of *Revelations*) is a description of the Ark in Heaven, of which the Ark built by Moses was only a physical copy.

## PREVIOUS SEARCHES IN FACT AND FICTION

Searching for the Ark of the Covenant actually began right at the time when Jeremiah hid it, circa 597 BC. According to the same *Maccabees* text, some of Jeremiah's friends decided to put markers to show their own people where the Ark was hidden, so that it could be recovered safely once the Babylonian threat had gone. However, they couldn't find the cave, and when they mentioned this to Jeremiah, he was annoyed with them and told them: 'The place shall remain unknown until God finally gathers his people together and shows mercy to them. The Lord will bring these things to light again, and the glory of the Lord will appear with the cloud, as it was seen both in the time of Moses and when Solomon prayed that the shrine might be worthily consecrated.'

Needless to say, he didn't bother to mention to them where he had put it, and none of them had had the sense to just follow him.

The Knights Templar are said to have searched for this, as well as other Biblical and historical artefacts, both on the Temple Mount and on Mount Sinai in the 12th century, and to have possibly brought it back to Paris, or Malta, or Warwickshire … This motivation for their activities, however, is ascribed by modern writers. The earliest Templar connection is in Louis Charpentier's

1966 *The Mysteries of Chartres Cathedral*, in which Charpentier claimed the Templars brought the Ark back and buried it in a vault at Chartres.

The idea of the Ark being in Ethiopia first made its way to Europe in the 16th century, and first appeared in English thanks to James Bruce's travels in search of the source of the Nile in the 18th century. An 1813 edition of his book contained the first partial English translation of the *Kebra Nagast*, which tells how the ancient king Menelik switched out the Ark for a fake, and brought it south to Ethiopia.

In 1798, however, an antiquarian called J. Salmon wrote in *A Description of the Works of Art of Ancient and Modern Rome, Particularly In Architecture, Sculpture & Painting, Volume One*, that the Ark had in fact been taken to Rome (probably in AD 70), and had been stored in the Basilica of St John Lateran, in Rome, but had been destroyed by a fire in the 14th century. (In fact it burnt to the ground twice in that century, in the Templar-quashing year of 1307, and again in 1361.) There's a certain sense to this Regency theory, as the Romans did sack the Temple in AD 70, and there is an apparently Ark-like rectangular object being carried out of the Second Temple on the triumphal Arch of Titus. The Basilica in question wasn't built until the 4th century, but the site had previously hosted the Emperor Constantine's palace, and before that a Praetorian Cavalry unit. The main thing going against Salmon's theory is that the image on the Arch of Titus has later been shown to be a different artefact, the shew-bread table, used for making offerings of bread as part of rituals in the Temple.

In 1899 a loose aggregation of what were called British Israelists got into the Ark-hunting business. These were a group, originating around 1870, who believed that all European peoples were descended from the Tribes of Israel, and that the British Royal Family, despite all the historical evidence, were direct descendants of the Biblical King David. Oddly, they didn't rush off to the Middle East in search of the Ark, but decided instead to dig up the Hill of Tara, an Iron Age hill fort in Ireland. They poked around there unsuccessfully for the next three years, before the Irish Antiquities authorities managed to put a stop to them, but not before they had done considerable damage to the site. (In

1919 the Israelists would form an official group, which in turn founded the Ark-themed publisher, Covenant Press, in 1921.)

Later in the 1920s, there was a period of belief that the Ark had been found in Tutankhamen's tomb, in the form of a perfectly preserved large rectangular box, carrying staves on either side. However, this proved to be a portable Anubis shrine, and is only half the size of the Ark's dimensions.

Oddly, despite the Nazi attempts to locate the Holy Grail, and the plot of a certain Hollywood movie, the Nazis never did actually go looking for the Ark. The Ark's imminent rise to popular fame would actually be mostly due to a completely different type of subject matter: the rise of pseudoscience books promoting the 'ancient astronaut' theory, that ancient myths were actually tellings of how aliens had interacted with ancient civilizations. So, according to the likes of Brad Steiger, Erich von Däniken and other writers, artefacts like the Ark could have been examples of advanced technology, indistinguishable from magic.

In particular George Sassoon (son of the famous poet Siegfried) and Rodney Dale decided to cast the Ark of the Covenant as a nuclear-powered alien machine designed to feed the Israelites for 40 years, and went to the trouble of designing its workings and figuring out what the chemical composition of the magic food manna should have been. They originally published this as an article in the 1 April 1976 edition of *New Scientist*. Note the date. They then expanded it into a paperback called *The Manna Machine* in 1978.

That got the Ark noticed by Spielberg, which got it the position of Indiana Jones's MacGuffin and launched the modern era of Ark hunting. Once *Raiders of the Lost Ark* brought it into the public consciousness, suddenly lots of people wanted to find it.

Hardly had the end credits rolled on *Raiders* than Ron Wyatt – former anaesthetist and Seventh-Day Adventist turned searcher for Noah's Ark – claimed to have found the Ark of the Covenant. In 1982 he said that he had found a network of tunnels under the hill of Gethsemane, which were filled with items from Solomon's Temple, including the Ark. He wasn't however, able to provide any photographic proof or bring it out with him. He also claimed that Jesus's blood had drained through a crack in the rock and onto the Ark.

In the late 1980s, British travel journalist Graham Hancock followed the trail of the Ark to Ethiopia, and wrote up his tale in *The Sign and the Seal* in 1992. Hancock's theory is that the Ark went to Egypt first, then travelled down the Nile to Lake Tana and eventually went to Axum.

In 1998, Bob Cornuke, who had founded a group called the Biblical Archaeology Studies and Exploration Institute, also decided to embark on his own exploration of the Ethiopia link. Cornuke researched the story that priests of the time of Jeremiah took the Ark back to Egypt, a reversal of the Exodus, to keep it out of Babylonian hands. It spent a century on Elephantine Island (now sited on Lake Nasser, and home to an unfinished luxury hotel and a *lot* of crocodiles), and then was taken to Lake Tana Kirkos in Ethiopia. Cornuke found that the monks on Tana Kirkos still carried out the same rituals as priests of the Old Testament era, and was shown items used alongside the Ark. Cornuke was told by the Tana Kirkos monks that the Ark remained with them for 800 years, before being moved around AD 400 to the then capital, Aksum, when the Ethiopians became Christian.

Just to be really awkward, there's a fourth variant of the Ark's trek down into Africa, but this time further than Ethiopia. In the mid-2000s, writer and Professor of Modern Jewish History, Tudor Parfitt, heard about the tales of Lemba people of South Africa, whose folklore says they brought the Ark – known to them as the 'Voice of God' – south to the Dumghe Mountains, where they hid it in a cave. Intrigued, Parfitt decided to follow the trail, backed by a Channel 4 film crew from the UK. He followed the trail of the Ark from the temple mount to the Yemen, home of the Queen of Sheba. From the city of Sena in Yemen, Parfitt thinks it was ferried across to East Africa, and possibly to Great Zimbabwe, and wrote up his findings in a book, *The Lost Ark of the Covenant*.

Of course the Ark has become popular in fiction since the release of *Raiders of the Lost Ark*. It has made cameo appearances in two of the *Indiana Jones* sequels – *The Last Crusade* and *Kingdom Of the Crystal Skull* – as well as in series such as *The Librarians*, *Warehouse 13* and even *Da Vinci's Demons*, in which a replica prop is visible in the Vatican's Secret Archives.

The Danish film *Lost Treasure of the Knights Templar* in 2005 has the treasure be the Ark, powered by static electricity. This isn't as daft an idea as it sounds, as the presenters of *Mythbusters* found when they decided to see if the Ark, as described in the Bible, could give an electric shock if it was filled with a Bagdad Battery (a clay jug filled with acid, and an iron nail inside a copper cylinder as the terminals – a device found in the 1940s and suspected to have been used for electroplating in ancient times). They found that it could indeed give a nasty shock.

It's also associated with the Nazi Ahnenerbe organization in Daniel Easterman's 1985 novel, *The Seventh Sanctuary*, which places it in Saudi Arabia.

Over the past couple of decades, the Ark has also been the subject of various treasure and archaeology-themed documentary series, on both sides of the Atlantic, such as *Mystery Investigator*, *Raiders of the Lost Past*, and even *Ancient Aliens*, getting back to that *Manna Machine* April Fool theory.

# THE TRUTH IS OUT THERE

Despite what *Raiders of the Lost Ark* tells us, the stones bearing the Ten Commandments in the Ark were not actually the original ones written by the finger of God, but replacements – albeit also inscribed by God – after Moses got annoyed and broke the originals. Bear this in mind, because the whole story of the Ark is a story of copies and duplicates, basically.

Actually, the Hebrew word translated as 'Ark' in 'Ark of the Covenant' really means closet or cupboard, but somehow Cupboard of the Covenant, or *Raiders of the Lost Closet* just don't have the same ring.

More recent archaeological work in Israel has uncovered many smaller clay chests and boxes of varying style and size, but all designed to contain a stone piece with words of the Law of God on them, which could be accessed by a priest. In other words, every village at least, if not every house, would have one of these – several have been found in what were once gatehouses – and of course Jerusalem had the largest such closet, or Ark, in the kingdom, in the main temple.

There are two basic problems with the Ethiopian theory, both date-related. One problem is that the *Kebra Nagast* only dates from the 13th century, 1,800 years after the Ark was last mentioned by its original owners. The story is written so long after the events described that it's talking about what has already passed into legend and myth.

Now, it's true that the *Kebra Nagast* is inspired by earlier tales that existed before that, but only as far back as the 1st century AD, and that's still centuries after the events. Then there's the other date problem, which is that the version told in the *Kebra Nagast* is actually set around 950 BC – about 350 years before the Ark was threatened by the Babylonian destruction of Jerusalem.

The Ethiopian story gets round the problem of the Ark still being in the Temple of Solomon after Menelik I supposedly took it to Ethiopia by saying that it was swapped out for a replica. Apparently the Ark's owners didn't notice that their superpowered weapon filled with the actual power of God that could strike people dead had been replaced by a regular wooden box.

As for the Lemba story, linking the Ark to southern Africa, their folklore says that the Voice Of God was a box of the same dimensions as the Ark, and could only be carried by priests, who must carry it by means of poles. Like the Ark, it was forbidden to touch the ground. The Voice of God was also said in Lemba folklore to be a weapon that could sweep aside enemy armies and unwary Lemba with heavenly fire – just like the Ark. The idea that the Ark was taken to Yemen does agree with some texts written by Arab converts to the then-new religion of Islam in the 8th century.

Interestingly, the Buba clan of the Lemba have a DNA marker which links them to the population of the Levant, which suggests some of their descendants did come from there. According to the Lemba, however, the Ark fell apart after its arrival in Zimbabwe and was replaced by a replica.

The replica, at least, really exists, and is stored in the Harare Museum of Human Science, having been discovered in the 1940s. It's definitely not the original Ark, according to both Lemba tradition and radiocarbon dating, which dated it to 1350.

There is also the issue, which must be addressed at some point, of whether the Ark ever existed at all. There's no real reason either to doubt or believe the Old Testament story – and there's certainly archaeological evidence for a lot of other physical objects that are mentioned in there – such as the Solomon's Temple, the great Menorah, the Shewbread table, etc. What there isn't, where the Ark of the Covenant is concerned, is corroborating tales from other contemporary cultures.

You'd think that if the Israelites were carrying around a box that could deliver food, kill people with bolts of light, and knock down city walls, somebody else would have mentioned it. In particular, you'd think that the Philistines would have mentioned capturing it and hanging onto it for seven months. Nobody does mention it, however; not even in the context of being glad to get rid of it after it brought those plagues of hemorrhoids.

Scientifically, it has been proved that the Ark could have held and delivered an electrical charge, albeit of barely one volt. This is a far cry from being able to demolish cities, bring down plagues, and knock dozens of people dead at a stroke. It's more than enough, however, to really impress worshippers and make them think they've been stung by the power of God. That said, the Bible doesn't actually specify that it's the power in the Ark that knocked down the walls of Jericho – it could have been the trumpets, or a group of sappers working at the back while all the defenders were watching the daily processions.

Of course, just because the technology makes this possible, doesn't mean the original Ark was ever used as anything more than simply a ritual altar and to hold the Word of God in, inscribed on stone, just like all the other, smaller, arks. After all, the Romans had all the pieces of technology to make a gramophone, but simply never put them together that way.

Experimental archaeology has also proved that, yes, artisans and craftsmen were certainly up to the job of creating the Ark, even in campsites during 40 years of nomadic wandering.

That said, nobody's actually even sure exactly what sort of wood the Biblical 'gopher wood' was – other than that the name has to be a transliteration, and certainly is no relation to the North American animal. The most likely options are that it is either cedar (qapros in Hebrew) or cypress (gopher in Greek). Both woods are native to the area where the Ark would have been built.

## WHERE IS IT NOW?

The mystery of the Ark's location isn't actually that much of a mystery if you regard the Biblical accounts of it as accurate. It actually simply tells us outright what happened to the original Ark: Jeremiah hid it in a cave so that it would not be taken by the Babylonians.

There's no mention in either the Bible or Babylonian records, or any other tale from the period of it being taken by the invaders; it simply disappears from that point on. It is, therefore, presumably still there, barring interference from weather, seismic activity, or lucky goatherds chasing wandering goats.

Where's the cave? On Mount Nebo, according to *Second Maccabees*, the mountain which Moses had climbed in order to view the Promised Land (or 'God's Inheritance', as *Second Maccabees* calls it). There, Jeremiah set up the Ark with a tent over it, and a few other ritual bits and pieces, in a cave, and then blocked up the entrance. According to this text, Jeremiah's own followers, who had, well, followed him, found him but could not see the concealed cave entrance even when they were standing pretty much right next to it. Jeremiah suggested this was due to some power of God, hiding the entrance from those not meant to find it. The text intimates that it will, at some point, be found when the time is right, by God's chosen finder.

Specifically, Jeremiah said, 'The place is to remain unknown until God gathers his people together again and shows them mercy. Then the Lord will disclose these things, and the glory of the Lord will be seen in the cloud, just as it appeared in the time of Moses and when Solomon prayed that the Temple might be gloriously sanctified.'

So, if we believe this version (and to be fair, it's from one of those sections that's more historical, about who ruled which land) the Ark was removed from the temple at the time of Nebuchadnezzar, and so far has not been returned. Mount Nebo itself is a rather flat-topped hill in Jordan. In the Biblical book of *Deuteronomy*, Moses is shown the Promised Land from the summit, and indeed the summit does give a panoramic view of the Holy Land. The Jordan Valley is visible from it, as is Jericho, and if you squint on a very clear day you can just about make out Jerusalem from there too.

Moses was supposedly buried there too, though the only tombs so far discovered are part of a basilica dating from the 4th century AD. Although there have been archaeological digs at Nebo since at least the 1930s, so far nobody has dug up the Ark.

The Lemba Ark in Zimbabwe definitely exists, but is a 14th-century construction. If the original preceded it, it was acknowledged as destroyed sometime around AD 1300. Either way, there's no point looking there.

Otherwise, the best option is still Ethiopia. What the Ethiopian angle has going for it is that that the church themselves outright say, 'Yep, we've got it, had it for centuries; we can't show you it, but it's in this little adobe church guarded by one monk, honest, straight-up guv, would we lie to you?'

It must be said that it's unlikely that Ethiopian church is simply lying to get more tourists. They have a long history of Ark-worship, going back centuries, and it's very clear that there is a strong belief at the core of their church that they do have the genuine Ark of the Covenant. They have festivals devoted to it, and to the story of it coming to Ethiopia, and pretty much every church in the country has their own replica ark. These replicas are paraded in towns and villages across Ethiopia on holy days.

More empirically, there are three different routes by which it's claimed to have got there, and there are a long list of texts that agree on many elements of Ark lore.

There's actually little doubt that the Church of Our Lady Mary Of Zion at Aksum does hold an ancient ark, or tabot, as the Ethiopian Orthodox Church calls it, but it's unlikely to be the original one; rather it's more likely to simply be the oldest ark still in existence. Remember that this branch of the religion values the Ark as a symbol of their covenant with God, hence the name. This is why all their churches have arks too, symbolizing their keeping faith with that covenant.

The thing about Ethiopia and arks is that it is a country of copies of the Ark, with an Orthodox Church based around copies of the Ark. This is quite literal: every church in Ethiopia has an inner 'Holy of Holies' room containing a draped ark. Some of them are bigger than others, and all of them tend to be paraded on special feast days.

They can't all be clones of the same ark, given the size differences between different local churches, but they don't have to be. What we call an ark was just a word for a box containing written stones representing the Law of God. It's now thought entirely likely by historians that pretty much every family in Israel at the time would have an ark of sorts for their ritual and worship – ranging in size from the full 3ft-long chest to pottery ones the size of a large coffee jar, in which stones with the words of the law could be kept.

Even with the original Ark long gone, the prime temple of the kingdom would also have had to have had an ark, and this would presumably have been the flashiest and most accurate to the original, regardless of the period. If any ark was smuggled south to Ethiopia, it would have been this; the Second Temple's ark.

It wouldn't be the *real*, original Ark of the Covenant in literal physical terms, but in the hierarchy of the religion, and in accuracy of replication, and in both spiritual and physical value, it would have filled that role. Today, of course, it would be almost as valuable a treasure to find, both in terms of historical value, and being a golden work of art.

What's actually in that church? Almost certainly the oldest currently surviving ark. Perhaps the wrong question is being asked. Perhaps the right question is: 'is the oldest replica of the Ark of the Covenant a valid historical treasure in its own right?'

## THE OPPOSITION IN YOUR WAY

There's no guarantee that there was actually a single original Ark of the Covenant, so you may have to settle simply for the oldest one extant.

If you're poking around Mount Nebo, you won't have to worry about large mammalian predators, but will want to look out for rattlesnakes – which love to hide in caves – the Palestine viper, a yellowish 4ft snake with a zigzag camouflage pattern; the Israeli mole viper, a black 3-footer, and the common viper. Also be careful of the deathstalker and southern mankiller scorpions, as well as the black widow and Mediterranean recluse spiders. They will all be well camouflaged and blend in with their surroundings.

Take the usual precautions for a desert environment: stout boots and thin trousers are advised. Hats, plenty of water.

Health-wise, rabies-shots are advised.

Ethiopia is a different matter. Before we get on to the actual hazards, you need to understand one thing about the Church of Our Lady Mary Of Zion at Aksum.

You're probably wondering how come nobody has ever just walked in, overpowered the solitary elderly guard, and walked out with the Ark, replica or otherwise. The answer is very simple and has nothing to do with the supernatural powers ascribed to the Ark. The big problem is that the chapel was built around the Ark, and it is basically a very strong bomb-and-quake-proof bunker. From the door, the entrance turns immediately left, then makes a tight right angle to the right at the first corner, then another right angle, and basically approaches the Ark's room from the opposite side. The corridor is too narrow, and the corners too tight, to allow the Ark out.

You'd have to use so much explosive to make a big enough hole that you'd probably flatten half a city block around the church, and definitely destroy the contents – which would kind of defeat the purpose of the exercise.

You'd then have to deal with the Ethiopian military. The Ethiopian National Defence Force is relatively small, not greatly funded and largely comprises Cold War-era Soviet tanks and fighters. Despite this, it's one of the best trained forces in Africa and works within a good economy, making not just its own small arms, but those for many African countries. They've handed the notorious terrorist group Al-Shabaab their asses several times, but have also been responsible for atrocities in Somalia. Either way, you don't want to mess with them.

Aksum is in the north of Ethiopia, and generally pretty safe – certainly safer than the southern parts, which the Foreign Office advises UK travellers to stay clear of. Although there is armed banditry in the Ogaden Desert of the south-east, and Da'esh is starting to operate in the country, petty crime is highest in the capital itself, Addis Ababa.

There used to be a problem with local children mobbing Western visitors, whom they called Faranji (from the old Venetian word for foreigner – this is also the source of the name Ferengi in *Star Trek*), but this is rare now.

Pickpocketing is the biggest human problem you're likely to find, along with people insisting on being (fake) guides and bag-snatchers.

Endemic diseases include HIV/AIDS, tuberculosis, malaria and onchocerciasis and dracunculiasis.

Crocodiles, leopards and lynxes are all potential threats as are hyenas. Lions are no longer an issue in the northern part of the country. Snakes are relatively uncommon, but you'd be wise to watch out for cobras – both the Egyptian cobra and the red spitting cobra, which has a red hood and spits venom, hence the name.

# TREASURES OF THE COPPER SCROLL

✖ TREASURES OF THE COPPER SCROLL

## WHAT IS IT?

Well, not the Copper Scroll itself, of course – that's a treasure, but not lost, as it's safely ensconced in the Archaeological National Museum of Jordan, in Amman. When it was found, the site of Qumran was in Jordanian territory, which is why it's in Amman rather than Jerusalem.

The treasures of the scroll are caches of gold and silver coinage, plus assorted gems and priestly ritual vessels and vestments, clues to the locations of which are given in the Copper Scroll. There are 63 caches of treasure, while a 64th item listed on the scroll is an expanded copy of the document, with additional clues and details to help find the 63 actual treasures.

Although the scroll describes the nature of the cached loot spread across the various locations, few scholars, archaeologists, or treasure hunters seem to agree on the actual source of the treasures inventoried. Some believe that it is the contents of Solomon's Temple – or the First Temple, as it's sometimes called – rescued from its destruction at the hands of King Nebuchadnezzar in the 6th century BC. Others think it is the treasure contents of the Second Temple – sometimes called Herod's Temple, because he refurbished it around 25 BC – built on the same site and robbed by the Romans in AD 70. Alternatively, perhaps it belonged to the Essenes, who lived at the site where the scroll was found, or maybe it was the savings and valuables of the rich nobles of 1st-century Jerusalem.

In any case, they are treasures listed as being hidden somewhere between Jerusalem and Jericho, in the desert around the northern end of the Dead Sea, in the 1st century AD.

## HOW MUCH IS IT WORTH TO YOU?

Anywhere between about $9 million (based upon an estimate of $1 million in 1960) and billions, in any currency you care to name. In fact, some of the 1950s translators of the scroll assumed, given the amounts mentioned, that the scroll must simply be reporting folklore or old tales of vast riches.

For example, the first entry in the scroll reads: 'In the fortress of the valley of Achor, under the steps with the entrance at the east go forty cubits: A strongbox of silver and its vessels, 17 talents by weight.' A talent in the 1st century was meant to be as much as a man could carry, and is generally considered by archaeologists to be around 70lb. So, that's 1,190lb of silver, which would be worth about £200,500 ($340,000) today.

In fact, the amount of gold – 40 tons in total – listed in the inventory is a full quarter of all the gold known to have existed in the world at the time. The amount of silver listed – 65 tons in total – is an equal amount to *all* the silver known to have existed in the 1st century. That's over £9.6 billion ($16 billion) worth of gold, and over £25 million ($41 million) of silver.

## THE STORY

In 1947, a Bedouin goatherd had lost one of his goats, which, being good at climbing, had traipsed off along some scree-covered rocky cliffs in the desert around Qumran, at the north end of the Dead Sea. Tracking his goat, he found himself exploring a network of caves, and inside these caves, the goatherd found ancient bits of wood and pottery, and, more importantly, scrolls. Lots of scrolls.

Most of the scrolls were what we would think of as ancient scrolls today – made of papyrus, and preserved by how amazingly hot and dry it is in the area – there's simply no humidity to promote the growth of bacteria that cause rot.

Word of the discovery soon got out, and the original group of scrolls themselves sold at auction for a quarter of a million dollars. Archaeologists and bedouin were soon racing each other to find more scrolls – and the Bedouins had the advantage of local knowledge. In total, 47,000 fragments of over 900 scrolls in Hebrew, Aramaic, Greek, etc., and including such treasures as early drafts of parts of the Bible, as well as other ancient documents, were found. Everything seemed to have been cached by an ascetic Jewish sect called the Essenes, who had lived in the area in the 1st century.

The Copper Scroll itself was found in cave no. 3 in 1952 – and in fact was the only Dead Sea scroll found by archaeologists, in this case on an expedition sponsored by the Jordanian Department of Antiquities. The Bedouin had found all the others, and discovered a good trade in selling them to the archaeologists. This also worked for the archaeologists, who didn't have to risk life and limb in oven-like cliff-side caves.

The scroll is a sheet of copper, thin enough to have been rolled up. Unrolling it was trickier, because nobody wanted it to split. In 1955, Jordan sent the scroll to England to be carefully cut open. It turned out to be about a foot wide, 8ft long and written in a long-dead patois of Hebrew.

As metal was valuable in ancient times, the fact that this scroll was made of copper was an immediate sign that it was special; there must have been a reason for wanting to be really sure it lasted in perpetuity. And the lettering on the outside had the words for 'gold' and 'silver' on it.

When this was translated, it turned out to consist of a list of 64 locations at which treasure could be found hidden – most of it gold and silver – divided into 12 columns. Different translations have slight variations, although the basics and amounts are the same. Differences include whether a feature of a location is in a particular direction, faces that direction, or should be approached from that direction. For example, Milik's translation of the first cache mentions steps heading eastwards, while Allegro's version has it as steps that simply are to the east – these are not necessarily the same set of steps!

For no readily apparent reason, some of the entries in the scroll are followed by two or three Greek letters. No-one has ever figured out why.

The 'official' version of the text reads (with the Greek letters also transliterated):

## Column 01
*In the ruin of Horebbah which is in the valley of Achor, under the steps heading eastward about forty feet: lies a chest of silver that weighs seventeen talents. KEN. In the tomb of the third section of stones there is one hundred gold bars. Nine hundred talents are concealed by sediment towards the upper opening, at the bottom of the big cistern in the courtyard of the peristyle. Priests garments and flasks that were given as vows are buried in the hill of Kohlit. This is all of the votive offerings of the seventh treasure. The second tenth is impure. The opening is at the edge of the canal on its northern side six cubits toward the immersed pool. CAG. Enter into the hole of the waterproofed Reservoir of Manos, descend to the left, forty talents of silver lie three cubits from the bottom.*

## Column 02
*Forty-two talents lie under the stairs in the salt pit. HN. Sixty-five bars of gold lie on the third terrace in the cave of the old Washers House. QE. Seventy talents of silver are enclosed in wooden vessel that are in the cistern of a burial chamber in Matia's courtyard. Fifteen cubits from the front of the eastern gates, lies a cistern. The ten talents lie in the canal of the cistern. D.I Six silver bars are located at the sharp edge of the rock which is under the eastern wall in the cistern. The cistern's entrance is under the large paving stone threshold. Dig down four cubits in the northern corner of the pool that is east of Kohlit. There will be twenty-two talents of silver coins.*

## Column 03

*Dig down nine cubits into the southern corner of the courtyard. There will be silver and gold vessels given as offerings, bowls, cups, sprinkling basins, libation tubes and pitchers. All together they will total six hundred nine pieces. Dig down sixteen cubits under the eastern corner to find forty talents of silver. TR. Votive vessels and priestly garments are at the northern end of the dry well located in Milham. The entrance is underneath the western corner. Thirteen talents of silver coins are located three cubits beneath a trap door in the tomb in the north-east end of Milham.*

## Column 04

*Fourteen talents of silver can be found in the pillar on the northern side of the big cistern in Kohlit. SK. When you go forty-one cubits into the canal that comes from* [there's a blank space here] *you will find fifty-five talents of silver. Dig down three cubits in the middle of the two boulders in the Valley of Achor, and you will find two pots full of silver coins. At the mouth of the underground cavity in Aslah sit two hundred talents of silver. Seventy talents of silver are located in the eastern tunnel which is to the north of Kohlit. Dig for only one cubit into the memorial mound of stones in the valley of Sekaka to find twelve talents of silver.*

## Column 05

*A water conduit is located on the northern side of Sekaka. Dig down three cubits under the large stone at the head of this water conduit to discover seven talents of silver. Vessels of offering can be found in the fissure of Sekaka, which is on the eastern side of the reservoir of Solomon. Twenty-three talents of silver are buried quite nearby above Solomon's Canal. To locate the exact spot, go sixty cubits toward the great stone, and dig down for three cubits. Thirty-two talents of silver can be located by digging seven cubits under the tomb in the dried up riverbed of Kepah, which is between Jericho and Sekaka.*

## Column 06

*Forty-two talents of silver lie underneath a scroll in an urn. To locate the urn, dig down three cubits into the northern opening of the cave of the pillar that has two entrances and faces east. Twenty-one talents of silver can be found by digging nine cubits beneath the entrance of the eastward-looking cave at the base of the large stone. Twenty-seven talents of silver can be found by digging twelve cubits into the western side of the Queen's Mausoleum. Dig nine cubits into the burial mound of stones located at the Ford of the High Priest to find twenty-two talents of silver.*

## Column 07
*To find four hundred talents of silver measure out twenty-four cubits from the water conduit of Q[this bit's damaged] of the northern reservoir with four sides. Dig six cubits into the cave that is nearby Bet Ha-Qos to locate six bars of silver. Dig seven cubits down under the eastern corner of the citadel of Doq to find twenty-two talents of silver. Dig three cubits by the row of stones at the mouth of the Kozibah river to obtain sixty talents of silver, and two talents of gold.*

## Column 08
*A bar of silver, ten vessels of offering, and ten books are in the aqueduct on the road that is to the east of Bet Ahsor, which is east of Ahzor. Dig down seventeen cubits beneath the stone that lies in the middle of the sheep pen located in the outer valley to find seventeen talents of silver and gold. Dig three cubits under the burial mound of stones located at the mouth of the Potter ravine to find four talents of silver. Dig twenty-four cubits below the northward burial chamber that is located on the south-west side of the fallow field of the valley of ha-Shov to reveal sixty-six talents. Dig eleven cubits at the landmark in the irrigated land of ha-Shov and you will find seventy talents of silver.*

## Column 09
*Measure out thirteen cubits from the small opening at the edge of Nataf, and then dig down seven cubits there. Seven talents of silver and four stater coins lie there. Dig down eight cubits into the eastern-looking cellar of the second estate of Chasa to obtain twenty-three and a half talents of silver. Dig sixteen cubits into the narrow, seaward-facing part of the underground chambers of Horon to discover twenty-two talents of silver. A sacred offering worth one mina of silver is located at the pass. Dig down seven cubits at the edge of the conduit on the eastern side inside the waterfall to locate nine talents of silver.*

## Column 10

*When going down to the second floor, look to the small opening to find nine talents of silver coins. Twelve talents lie at the foot of the water wheel of the dried up irrigation ditches which would be fed by the great canal. Sixty-two talents of silver can be found by going to the left for ten paces at the reservoir which is in Beth Hakerem. Three-hundred talents of gold and twenty penalty fees can be found at the entrance to the pond of the valley Zok. The entrance is on the western side by the black stone that is held in place by two supports. Eight talents of silver can be found by digging under the western side of Absalom's Memorial. Seventeen talents are located beneath the water outlet in the base of the latrines. Gold and vessels of offering are in this pool at its four angles.*

### Column 11

*Very near there, under the southern corner of the portico in Zadok's tomb, beneath the pillars of the covered hall are ten vessels of offering of pine resin, and an offering of senna. Gold coins and consecrated offerings are located under the great closing stone that is by the edge, next to the pillars that are near by the throne, and toward the tip of the rock to the west of the garden of Zadok. Forty talents of silver are buried in the grave that is under the colonnades. Fourteen votive vessels possibly of pine and resin are in the tomb of the common people and Jericho. Vessels of offering of aloes and tithe of white pine are located at Beth Esdatain, in the reservoir at the entrance of the small pool. Over nine-hundred talents of silver are next to the reservoir at the brook that runs near the western entrance of the sepulchre room.*

### Column 12

*Five talents of gold and sixty more talent are under the black stone at the Western entrance. Forty-two talents of silver coin are in the proximity of the black stone at the threshold at the sepulchral chamber. Sixty talents of silver and vessels are in a chest that is under the stairs of the upper tunnel on Mount Garizim. Six-hundred talents of silver and gold lie in the spring of Beth-Sham. Treasure weighing seventy-one talents and twenty minas are in the big underground pipe of the burial chamber at the point where it joins the house of the burial chamber. A copy of this inventory list, its explanation and the measurements and details of every hidden item are in the dry underground cavity that is in the smooth rock north of Kohlit. Its opening is towards the north with the tombs at its mouth.*

So, for over 70 years, people have been scouring the Israeli and Jordanian desert for these treasures.

## PREVIOUS SEARCHES IN FACT AND FICTION

The leading figure of exploratory searching for the treasure was John Allegro, who had been involved in getting the thing unrolled and translated in the first place. Long story short, the copper had oxidized, and could not be simply unrolled, as it would disintegrate if attempted. Ideas for opening it included reducing the copper with hydrogen – which would have disintegrated it – or using electrolysis to restore the copper back to a pre-oxidization state, which would defy all the laws of physics and metallurgy.

John Allegro, however, decided to try having it gently cut apart and reassembled flat. At first he wanted this to be done at Manchester University, who refused to take the risk, so he turned to Manchester's College of Technology, where Professor H. Wright Baker had the idea of coating the scroll with transparent epoxy to hold it together, before cutting it away one millimetre at a time. In the end, it was cut into 23 strips, which could then be reassembled and read.

Allegro wanted to hold a press conference and announce the finding of the translation being a treasure guide. This didn't go down too well with the French scholar in charge, Father Roland de Vaux of the École Biblique et Archéologique Française de Jerusalem. With the scrolls being important religious artefacts, a team of clergymen had been assembled to take charge. De Vaux assigned Father Joseph T. Milik to edit the text for publication. They told him to keep quiet, partly to hold off amateur fortune hunters, but mainly because Milik and de Vaux didn't believe a word of the scroll. They thought the amounts mentioned were just too outrageous – with things like 65 tons of silver in one place, and 25 tons of gold in another – to be possibly true. (These amounts were more than anyone believed had existed in one place in the 1st century.)

De Vaux and Milik thought that the scroll being in a different medium from the others was a sign that its content was just a legend, while Allegro thought it proved the story, because why else use such a fancy medium? Allegro also felt that after all his work he was being side-lined by Vaux and Milik. And he might have been right, because they stopped responding to his translation and letters. They refused to let him publish anything about it. They banned him from the lab and lectures and threatened him with loss of tenure.

In 1959, Milik published the Hebrew text of the scroll, with a commentary which essentially said it was a fake, at least in the sense of being a lie on the part of its 1st-century creators. Allegro then published his unofficial translation in 1960, which was hugely popular, because it said there was plenty of treasure out there to find. The French published Milik's translation in 1962.

Allegro, however, wasn't just a translator. He decided to prove the truth of the scroll by finding some of the treasure himself. First, however, he needed some financial backers – But the École Biblique, Manchester University and Jordanian University had all been put off him. So the *Daily Mail* put up the money and sent a reporter along. King Hussein of Jordan decided to join in with funding and army support – after all, anything found would belong to him.

Allegro first went to Khirbet Mird, site of the Judean fortress of Hyrcania, on the West Bank of the Jordan, about 4 miles from Qumran. He believed the fortress belonged to Herod and fit the first location in the scroll. And he found the narrow stairs, going 300ft down, and a vault at the bottom – but it had been trashed in the past. Marble columns knocked down, mosaic floors hacked up. Needless to say there was no treasure remaining. Allegro's camp was then hit by a sandstorm and destroyed.

Next, he looked at Khirbet Qumran itself, linking it with a location referred to in the scroll as Sakata. A small hoard of silver shekels – three pottery jugs full – had been found there years earlier, before the scroll was found, so this suggested that it might be a location. Metal detectors were used now, but they were triggered by natural magnetic ore, and journalists were crowding the site every day. Allegro did find a cave concealed in a cliff face, with bones and pottery dating to 400 BC – but this predated the Essenes and there was no treasure.

So he went to Jerusalem and found what was referred to as the Tomb of Zadok – which was empty. Finally, he went to the Temple Mount itself. There's a honeycomb of tunnels under there, and some two dozen of the scroll's locations are around the Temple Mount – but no permission was given to dig there. Even King Hussein wouldn't put any pressure on the Israeli authorities to let him mess with the Dome of the Rock.

A different Bedouin had found other caves on the opposite side of the valley from Qumran, accessible only by mountain goat or helicopter, and this was another location Allegro wanted to match up with the treasure list. Allegro raised enough funds to explore this second set of locations: Christmas cave, Mazin (a 1st-century Jewish rebel base) and Ein Feshkha.

King Hussein of Jordan lent support again and came to visit the camp on Christmas day 1962, but all Allegro could show him were Roman coins and gear from AD 70. Christmas cave contained a long tunnel leading to lots of bats, Roman lamps, wool and jugs of Byzantine coins from around the 6th century, but none of the treasures listed in the scroll. Nor were any treasures found at Mazin or Ein Feshkha.

Allegro's searches came to nothing, and the French team, who had done their best to get him out of the way, were sure that his translations were no more than a fairy tale. He died in 1988, almost alone in still believing the scroll was true and the treasure existed. But … in the 1990s and noughties his translations were independently confirmed as accurate. To this day, however, supporters of each side still cast aspersions upon the other as being unreliable.

Others think because the Essenes wrote the scroll at Qumran, they were describing bits of Qumran itself as hiding places. There is some logic to this, as some of the descriptions do fit – for example, Khirbet Qumran is technically within the valley of Achor, mentioned in the first column. Retired fire marshal and arson investigator turned private Copper Scroll researcher Jim Barfield applied the directions to Qumran, finding that the only stairs 40 cubits long did have an entrance at the east, as per a version of the first entry in the scroll. He also found points matching various other caches from the scroll, within the ruins of Qumran. However, 'stairs heading east' is not the same as 'steps with the entrance at the east', so there is still no real certainty. There may simply be a variation in idiom between translations, or it could simply be that the stairs at Qumran and the stairs listed in the scroll are not the same place. Either way, no treasure was found there.

Barfield's theory is that having the ascetic Essenes guarding a lot of treasure was like having eunuchs guarding the vestal virgins: they're the last people anyone would expect to have the loot, and since they had no interest in material wealth, they could be trusted to keep it safe and not spend it themselves. He also believes the treasure is from Old Testament times, belonged to Moses and came from the same Tabernacle that held the Ark of the Covenant.

Barfield came to believe that the various hiding spots he believes he has found at Qumran – even though none contained the treasures mentioned – line up to point to the last location on the list. In 2009 he persuaded the Israeli Antiquities Authority to allow a dig, which found nothing. Barfield thinks he simply hasn't dug deep enough yet, and that $3 billion of gold and silver – plus gems – is buried in a squat pyramid-like building, which still exists at Qumran. As if that wasn't enough, he also claims that this is where Jeremiah hid the Tabernacle and the Ark of the Covenant, according to his interpretation of *Second Maccabees* (see the chapter on the Ark of the Covenant).

In 1964, a Texan Baptist minister (now retired), Vendyl Jones, got bitten by the scroll bug and began a life-long search for the treasure. He wasn't immediately rewarded, but his persistence paid off in 1988, when his team found something of interest in a Qumran cave: an earthen vessel filled with what had originally been oil used in the temple to cover sacrifices – one of the libation vessels mentioned in Column 3 of the scroll.

## THE TRUTH IS OUT THERE

Nobody is actually certain who wrote the Dead Sea Scrolls in general, or whether the Copper Scroll was written with them or separately. Its script is a little different than those of the other scrolls, partly because it has been hammered into the metal with a die-punch, rather than written by hand. It was also not the work of one person – it's in at least three or four hands – which means probably no single scribe knew the whole piece of any treasure location description given in it. This may also explain why there is no particular order to the inventory – locations seem to be jumbled up at random.

It's also written in a later form of Hebrew than the Biblical sort that is more commonly seen by archaeologists. This language is more similar to the Mishnaic Hebrew in use in the 1st century AD. This has led some scholars to think it must have been written by a priest from the Temple of Herod (built in 20 BC), and also because it refers to vessels of a kind that would have been used by the priesthood. Herod's Temple, also known as the Second Temple, was definitely big enough and flashy enough to have been the source of such a large treasure hoard.

The Romans trashed the temple around AD 70 after an uprising, so perhaps a priest wrote it as a memo to describe hiding the treasures of a temple to prevent losing its contents to the Romans. So the directions in it refer to stuff that only local priests at the time would have understood (e.g. direction to 'look under the grave' – only a local priest would have known which grave in which cemetery).

As for the locations in the inventory...

Nobody has identified Horebbah, and most scholars seem to think it's either fictional or at least too vague a name to tell whether it was town, an area or a building. The same goes for Milham, was it a village, a region, a geographical feature, a building, or even a person? Nobody knows.

Achor, however, did exist, and is just into the desert north-west of the Dead Sea. There is a fortress built into a cliff there on Mount Hyrcania, called Khirbet el-Mird. This was used in the 1st century, and there is a set of steps that match the description – you can also see the valley where the scroll was found from there. The steps were discovered in the 1950s, but were filled in with dirt from 2,000 years of flash floods. In 2000, the Israeli Antiquities Authority allowed a dig to begin. Over four years, archaeologists excavated a narrow (only two people can squeeze in at a time – and that's if they're stick-thin) tunnel of steps down from an eastern entrance. At the bottom, 300ft down, the tunnel splits in two, leading to two ... walls of bedrock.

It's possible that it was used as a safe to stash loot, but if so, it has obviously been removed at some point in antiquity. Or maybe the vault was never finished.

Matia's Courtyard is also a mystery, though a number of scholars think that the reference to a cistern in it means it was at the First Wall of Jerusalem, as there is a big cistern under there. However, there are cisterns of one kind or another all over ancient Israel, so there's no real evidence to identify this one with Matia's Courtyard.

The Wadi Atsla is north-west of the Dead Sea, and is only about about 2km from the site of Qumran. Speaking of which, most researchers now agree with Allegro's theory that the town listed in the scroll as Sekaka was in fact Qumran itself.

The Queen's Mausoleum must have been in a pretty high-class area, which has led to the theory that it might be in the vicinity of Jericho, as the Hasmonean dynasty of kings and queens had built apartments and lived there some of the time, and so had also presumably built tombs. What's more interesting is the reference to Beth Haqoz – there was a dynasty of priests near Jericho called Hakkoz (considering the varying translations this probably is the same name), who had been treasurers of the Second Temple. This also makes them possible candidates for having been involved in creating the scroll and hiding the treasure.

Dok is a real place, a couple of kilometres north of Jericho. Kozibah was also real, and part of the Wadi Qelt – specifically the stretch between Ein Qelt and Jericho. Wadi Qelt is a little valley north-west of the Dead Sea, in which the monastery of St George was built into caves in the cliff wall in the 5th century. The Copper Scroll mentions this place as having 70 talents of silver, and two of gold. There are hundreds of caves at Wadi Qelt, as well as a monastery built into the cliff. The monastery has been there for 1,500 years and there have been no reports of anyone finding the treasure.

A Nataf wasn't a specific place, but a structure like a large bird-house, with lots of holes for birds to come and go from. Either it must have been one at an unnamed place, or else somewhere had this as a nickname, probably because of looking like one.

Horon was a small city about 10 miles north-west of Jerusalem, while on the south side of Jerusalem, the modern Kibbutz Ramat Rachel is on the site of what used to be Beth Hakerem.

Absolom's Tomb/Memorial/Monument is one of those that depends whose translation you like best. Near the Temple Mount in Jerusalem there is a 1st-century structure called Absolom's Tomb, which is the name John Allegro gave to the Absolom entry in his translation. This is the Kidron Valley. It's known that there's a cistern at that spot – an underground water tank/reservoir, already dug before the scroll was written, and therefore handy for stashing loot in – but excavation on the Temple Mount is forbidden, so nobody has dug it up. There was, however, also an Absalom's Monument, as per the Milik and Official translations, and this was in the Ancient Royal Valley, the Rephaim Valley. This site, however, runs a mile or so south-west from the southern end of Jerusalem. Take your pick as to which site is more likely.

Mount Garizim was the site of a Samaritan temple to the Hebrew God. Beth Shem is perhaps an abbreviation or error for Beth-shemesh, a city that lay about 19 miles west of Jerusalem (and was associated with Samson in legend).

The École Biblique were also digging around the neighbouring site of Ein Feshkha at the time they were dealing the Copper Scroll translation, and so, unsurprisingly, this site has also become associated with the scroll locations. This was an oasis closer to the Dead Sea, not far from Wadi Qelt, and once was a farming town, though only low remnants of walls remain. The oasis had a spring flowing into the Dead Sea. In the scroll, there's mention of a place called Beth-Tamar, 'house of the date palm' – which is what Ein Feshkha was, back in the day. They grew date palms to make wine from, you see. Likewise, there were underground cisterns there to collect the juice from the harvested and pressed dates, into which loot could easily be stashed, and there are a lot of such cisterns mentioned in the scroll. According to ground-penetrating radar, there are some anomalies underground which could be some of these cisterns, or geological features. Or treasure, who knows?

The search would be a lot easier, of course, if the *other* copper scroll had been found. Oh yeah, there are two, and the one we know about is just the edited highlights version. It includes an 'also available' in the form of 'A copy of this inventory, its explanation and details of every item is in the dry underground cavity that is in the smooth rock north of Kohlit.'

The problem is nobody quite knows where this Kohlit – mentioned in several columns of the scroll's text – was or is. There was a region called Kohlit on the east side of the River Jordan, but this wasn't a single place; it was a wide area, big enough to encompass 60-odd towns and villages (which were conquered by Alexander Jannaeus in the 1st century BC). There's nothing in the scroll to narrow the location down, and so none of the specific descriptions match a single place.

Interestingly, there *is* a single city called K'eley Kohlit in Ethiopia. Given the legends linking the Ark of the Covenant with Ethiopia, and the fewer legends linking the Ark with the scrolls, it's perhaps surprising that nobody has yet produced a gold-embossed paperback expose claiming that the Ethiopian Kohlit is the one where the Copper Scroll treasure is hidden.

Other potential sites, especially obscure ones, are most likely between Jerusalem (where the treasures presumably came from) and the Dead Sea, where the scroll was hidden. It's logical to assume the Essenes or the priesthood stashed the loot on the way. Also, the same road was an ancient road between Jerusalem and Jericho, so the route may have had treasure cached all the way along it.

The Essenes aren't quite the only suspects in having hidden the treasure, though. Some other scholars think the treasure belonged not to the Second Temple but to the elite citizenry of Jerusalem – a rich city in the 1st century – living on Mount Zion. Jerusalem was a rabbit warren of tunnels and cisterns, so there were plenty of underground hiding places.

According to this theory, the treasure is made up of the possessions of many families, all gathered together to be hidden out of reach of the Romans. This does, however, fly in the face of the scroll itself listing several of the caches as being comprised of priestly garb and equipment, and items that would be more Temple-related than just flush-with-cash citizen-related.

## WHERE IS IT NOW?

Well, there's good news and there's bad news. The good news is that Milik and de Vaux's theory that it was all fictional is pretty much now accepted as wrong, and that treasure really was hidden around the region and inventoried in the scroll.

The bad news is that it has probably all been found and spent in the nearly two millennia since then. Several locations, as described above, have been identified, but with no treasure remaining to be found in them. There is, however, that vessel of sacred oil found in 1988. Likewise, the deposit listed as being in the 'Cave of columns' – the 25th item on the scroll – is also thought to have been found.

In 1960, a number of ritual implements made of bronze were found buried 4½ft under a cave now called the 'Cave of Letters'. Its description, however, matches the description of the Cave of Columns with two openings, which was listed in the Scroll as the site for a cache of priestly tools bured three cubits down. And three cubits is 4½ft. There was also a broken stoneware jar and fragments of another scroll. The finders thought these were Roman items stolen by revolutionaries in AD 132, but this makes little sense. Why would revolutionaries carefully bury captured enemy gear? And, of course, the fact that it was buried right where the Copper Scroll says ritual items would be found also mitigates against them being Roman items.

That said, the pieces of pottery do have representations of the Roman goddess Thetis on them – but Herod, whose temple the stuff probably came from, was a pro-Roman king, who presided over a Romanization of the culture.

Where are they now? On display at Israel Museum's Shrine of the Book.

As for the rest of the hoard, there has been almost 2,000 years for the Bedouin, Crusaders, Persians and others to have found the stashes – always assuming that Roman soldiers didn't just torture the priests to find the locations and grab them in AD 70.

Since most of the caches in the list are described as having been hidden within constructed settlements, it's hard to imagine that they all remained undiscovered under those circumstances. On the other hand, the fact that two items – albeit not actually treasure – have been found makes it equally easy to imagine that there is more stuff still out there. It's always worth looking anyway, as the area has been a busy one throughout history, so there are treasures from many periods around – just at the beginning of 2015, 20lb of gold coins were found in a dried up harbour at Caesarea, though these are from around the 10th century AD and so unrelated to the Scroll.

The most likely locations, therefore, would be the more remote ones in caves and hills, rather than in settlements. The problem being that the names and geography have changed over time. Nevertheless, it all seems to centre on the north and east of the Dead Sea – and if someone could definitively identify the Scroll's choice of Kohlit, that would probably be the most useful option.

## THE OPPOSITION IN YOUR WAY

The biggest problem with getting anywhere near any of the known locations is that they're all in territory frequently fought over by both standing armies and terrorists, and the first entry –Achor – is in a live-firing range for Israeli artillery and tanks. Which is inconvenient to say the least.

Aside from such physical hazards, the region is also a bureaucratic minefield for archaeologists and treasure-hunters, with bits of sites being administrated by different authorities, which makes getting all the right permissions more of a slog. Because the region is home to sites sacred to three major religions, permission is denied to excavate at certain places – the Temple Mount is an obvious one. That said, archaeologists have found that it is possible to get permissions to search the spoil heaps produced by necessary building and maintenance work around this part of Jerusalem.

Of course, the fact that it is a centre point for three huge religions means that there are also constant expeditions from companies, religious organizations and universities around the world, all competing for the same permissions and licences to dig – and that will be your biggest obstacle.

Although there's obviously a lot of unrest, terrorism and organized crime in the region, 'normal' crime and street-crime are actually pretty rare in comparison to other first-world countries.

Israel has no remaining large mammalian predators, though there are endangered numbers of lynxes, Arabian leopards and sand cats still remaining, as well as the hyena.

There are several venomous snakes in the area – including rattlesnakes – which love to hide in caves and shaded holes during the day, exactly where you'd be digging. The most dangerous is the Palestine viper, a yellowish 4ft snake with a zigzag camouflage pattern, common throughout the Middle East. There are also the Israeli mole viper, a black 3-footer, and the common viper, known locally as a black adder.

You should also watch out for the deathstalker and southern mankiller (the clue's in the name) scorpions, as well as the black widow and Mediterranean recluse spiders.

# DRAGONS AND TREASURE

In all this talk of lost treasures waiting to be found by adventurous searchers, we mustn't overlook the hoards of those most famous treasure collectors: the dragons. The image of the magnificent dragon slumbering atop a surprisingly comfortable pile of jewels and gold coins is something of a familiar cliché – but it is both of those things for a reason. Clichés become clichés because they work.

Obviously you won't need to worry about encountering or having to engage in combat with any dragons during your treasure-hunting exploits; they're well-known to have been extinct since at least the 14th century.

The difficulty, then, would be in locating dragons' hoards. However, you'd be wasting your time, as, by definition, the post-slaying part of every dragonslayer's adventures involved a lot of accounting of the fortune amassed by the late reptile. This leaves us simply with the historical mystery of why dragons and treasure went so well together in the first place.

All joking aside, the basic reason why Western culture has ended up associating dragons with treasure is psychological: a treasure to be won gives a number of dragonslayers a motive for taking the beast on in combat and, conversely, if there was to be a treasure that a story's hero or heroes must win, then what more terrifying and dangerous guardian could stand in the way?

It's all the fault of the Greeks, of course.

In Greek mythology, the legendary heroes such as the Argonauts often stumbled across treasure left by either the gods, titans, or previous kings. Unfortunately for these heroes, the treasures tended to be guarded by assorted monsters, which were called Drakon – the Greek word for guardian or 'watcher'.

In Scandinavia and the rest of Europe, the monsters who often had hoards of treasure waiting to be a reward for the men who slew them were called wyrms. Fafnir is one of the most famous examples, having been turned into a giant serpent by Loki as a punishment for having hoarded gold – which would then be stolen by Sigurd.

In the Middle Ages, tales from different parts of the world were translated into various different languages, and somewhere in the mix the word Drakon got applied to these non-Greek guardians or watchers, and so it became commonly viewed that dragons loved nothing better than to sit on treasure hoards.

In more modern times, from Tolkien's villainous Smaug onwards, stories about dragons have given them a more prosaic reason for hoarding precious metals and stones: to encrust their vulnerable bellies with glittering armour.

Today, however, there are no dragons, and the guardians of lost treasure are far more likely to be equally deadly drug gangs or terrorists.

All of these venomous creatures tend to be well camouflaged for a desert environment, and so stout boots and thick trousers are advised. Don't even think of wandering any of these sites in flip-flops.

Health-wise, rabies-shots are advised, as it is present in Israel, along with a high population density of stray dogs. Leishmaniasis is also endemic to the region, carried by sandflies – this is usually relatively harmless, but painful and inconvenient, and it can cause life-threatening fever in rare cases. If you're visiting the Jordanian side of the border, be aware that the respiratory illness MERS has been reported there, though it hasn't made it to Israel yet.

Thankfully, medical care in both Israel and Jordan is among the best in the world (except in the Palestinian Territories), so if you do come a cropper you should be very well looked after.

# ALL AT SEA

Although we tend to think nowadays – thanks to the movies, TV and videogames – of treasure hunters as roguish individuals, be they explorer, archaeologist, tomb robber, or enthusiastic amateur, most treasure hunting is actually done by licensed international companies. Furthermore, it tends to be done at sea.

There are some good reasons for this. For one thing, there's strength in numbers – not combat strength, but the physical ability to lift more stuff. All that gold is pretty damn heavy, after all. It also makes good use of technologies and engineering that had been developed through the two world wars, and brought something good out of them. Most practically of all, the simple fact is that the

vast majority of lost treasure was lost at sea. The ocean floor around the world is littered with shipwrecks, and most of them carried something that was or is now of some value to somebody.

Ships have been sinking for as long as shipping has existed, whether due to piracy, storms, warfare, icebergs, or shallow rocks coming out of nowhere. Most recoveries of historic treasure – especially historic bullion and ingots – is a product of the maritime salvage industry. Partly this is because of post-World War II equipment – sonar, diving gear and so on became available to maritime industry and archaeology. Ships full of mini submarines, however, do not come cheap, and cost thousands of dollars a day to run.

Probably the most famous such organization is actually semi-fictional; Clive Cussler's NUMA. It's semi-fictional because Cussler also created it as a real-world non-profit archaeological organization, as well as having it be a fictional government department. The fictional NUMA has saved the world multiple times, while recovering some of the most famous historical treasures and artefacts, but the real NUMA hasn't been too shabby either – it found and raised the Confederate submarine *Hunley* (one of the earliest submarines ever made), and was also instrumental in discovering the extant location of the legendary *Mary Celeste* after nearly 200 years.

A more representative example of marine salvage would be Odyssey Marine Exploration, a US-owned and British-crewed deep-water salvage company who are the subject of the TV reality series, *Treasure Quest*. There are bigger companies who've made more spectacular finds, but the TV show will give you a good idea of how such firms operate, and the various bureaucratic hoops they have to jump through to get commissions, salvage contracts and permissions to explore wrecks – which may involve several countries all needing to give the right documentation.

# OTHER TYPES OF TREASURE

Although most people think of treasure as being coins, jewels, bullion, precious metals, historically significant objects, or artworks, there are other kinds of valuables for which people search and which have different kinds of value.

There are many types of film and TV prints which are now missing, either through loss or the decay of the actual celluloid. In some cases, film prints were deliberately destroyed for one reason or another. For example, the first ever LGBT-themed movie, *Anders Als Die Andern (Different from the Others)*, starring Conrad Veidt, and made in 1919, was the victim of attempted erasure by the Nazis, and now only half of it remains. The other half would, therefore, be a treasure of sorts.

Many TV shows around the world were originally destroyed because of lack of storage space, or because it was never expected that anyone would want to see them again, or because the contracts with the performers didn't allow reuse or repeats. Now that the cultural and historical value of these archives have been recognized, individuals and companies are searching for them. Most famously, the search for such lost episodes of *Doctor Who* regularly makes the news in the UK.

The biggest problem with searching for such archive film is the nature of the celluloid, which is both highly flammable and decomposes into a lump over time, especially if not stored under proper conditions. This isn't just a problem with old and fragile film stock, or footage that is slated for deliberate erasure, however – the rise of digital non-physical media – cloud storage and so forth – has led to another type of loss.

Films and other forms of artwork which exist only in digital form are vulnerable to magnetic damage and server outages – in 2014 digital works by Andy Warhol, and NASA footage from the moon, were recovered from degraded floppy disks just in the nick of time – and it's known that other works have been lost in similar ways.

Cryptids are another example of a priceless treasure sought by people, which could be of inestimable value to science. Cryptids are unknown animals, some more plausible than others, which have yet to be properly discovered.

At the less-likely end of the scale, the person who brings in a live Bigfoot or Yeti, or a living dinosaur, would make their fortune – and, strange as it sounds, there are people who look for exactly these creatures, and not just on silly reality TV shows. Several scientific expeditions have been made to the Congo in

search of what the locals call mokele-mbembe, which is reputed to be a type of sauropod dinosaur. (This overlooks the fact that the descendants of dinosaurs which didn't go extinct are what we now call birds.)

On the more believable end, it's certainly possible that some animals believed to be extinct may still exist. The coelacanth was rediscovered in 1936 after having been thought extinct for 65 million years, after all. Today in Tasmania there are still sightings of the thylacine, or Tasmanian Tiger, which was declared extinct in 1936, and it's currently thought, based on DNA evidence, that the legendary Yeti might actually be a species of bear thought to be extinct since the last ice age.

Almost anything, if it's of value to science, a culture, or even a person, can be treasure, especially if it's lost. Even languages have been lost and found over the centuries, and a last native speaker of a language could be an invaluable treasure, as could the patient zero of a disease outbreak, or people with immunity factors that can be replicated for the fight against disease.

Documents and books, lost Shakespeare folios and suchlike can also be fantastically valuable finds. Treasure has never just been gold and silver and precious stones; it always has been, and always will be, something more than that.

# TEN BOOKS WORTH HUNTING

Ten books about or featuring treasure hunting worth reading – e.g. *Treasure Island*, *King Solomon's Mines*, maybe a non-fiction or two as well.

## TREASURE ISLAND BY ROBERT LOUIS STEVENSON

As with many Victorian (and early 20th century) novels, this classic tale of buried pirate treasure was originally published as a serial, in the children's magazine *Young Folks*, in 1881 and 1882, before being published as a book in 1883.

Although the magazine was in what publishing would now call the YA market, the novel doesn't read as being aimed at children. Rather it's a crisp adventure with a literal boatload of memorable classic characters, based on a mix of nautical folklore, pirate history and Stevenson's own imagination, inspired by childhood walks around islands.

It's a vital story in the history of treasure hunting, because it introduces so many elements that we find familiar, such as pirates burying their loot, peg-legged villains, parrots and so on. It's also very good; there's a reason why it hasn't been out of print in 200 years, and has had so many screen adaptations, as well as being so influential in later years. If you haven't read it, you're missing a treat.

## KING SOLOMON'S MINES BY H. RIDER HAGGARD

Another hugely influential Victorian adventure – this one published as a hardback book from the outset (in 1885), rather than being serialized first. It works as a wildlife travelogue, adventure tale and treasure-hunt story all in one.

Written as British exploration peaked, it's a memorable adventure flushed with the sensations of Africa, and features the memorable big-game hunter Allan Quatermain, who is a prototype for the sort of knight-errant adventurer that action and adventure stories so depend on. It's also somewhat racist and, unfortunately, its attempts to be fair in this regard really throw the failures more into relief, but this is perhaps inevitable given the era in which it was written.

Like *Treasure Island*, it introduces many tropes of the genre, such as the long travel sections and dangers en route. It also shares another very important connection with Stevenson's book: Haggard's brother had bet him five shillings that he couldn't write and publish a book that would capture the audience and attention of *Treasure Island*. Henry won the bet, though he did so by being inspired by a travel memoir, *Through Maasai Land* by Scottish explorer Joseph Thomson, which had come out in January. This led some to accuse him of plagiarism, but since Haggard was writing fiction, it'd perhaps be well enough to call it research.

## TREASURE BY CLIVE CUSSLER

Actually, most of Cussler's action-adventure novels have a pretty similar formula, involving a historical shipwreck or disappearance, some sort of modern supervillain with a global (and usually environmentally themed) threat, and a lost ancient treasure, which is somehow connected to both of those elements.

This particular novel is a good standalone example of the format and rollicking good fun too. Treasure-wise, it includes the contents of the Library of Alexandria and Aztecs.

## THE SIGN AND THE SEAL BY GRAHAM HANCOCK

This was one of the first books to make the connection between Axum in Ethiopia and the Ark of the Covenant. It also – along with *The Holy Blood and the Holy Grail* – kick-started the genre of gold-embossed paperbacks telling tales of ancient historical conspiracies and lost religious secrets/artefacts.

Unlike *The Holy Blood and the Holy Grail*, this book is mainly about a single artefact, and it actually works well in terms of being a travelogue through Egypt, Sudan and Ethiopia. Whatever you think of the likelihood of the Ark being in Ethiopia, or any of the pseudohistory that the author later got into, this is one of the most readable tales of someone travelling through distant parts of the world in search of a piece of history.

## CAPTAIN KIDD AND HIS SKELETON ISLAND BY H. T. WILKINS

Harold Thomas Wilkins wrote quite a few books about adventuring and treasure-hunting throughout the 1930s and 1940s, but this is the one that proved both most popular and most influential in the treasure-hunting community.

As the title implies, it's a tale of the notorious Captain Kidd and his buried treasure, first published in 1935, and it inspired many a reader to go hunting for pirate treasure simply by virtue of telling an exciting story of pirates and treasure, and including maps purporting to show where Kidd buried still-undiscovered loot. People have been searching for the true location of 'Skeleton Island' ever since, and it has inspired quite a few fictional epics (such as the Isla de los Muertos in the *Pirates of the Caribbean* films).

Of course, Wilkins was quite open about these island maps being fictional, to add to the excitement of the story, but this hasn't stopped people from believing that they're tweaked versions of a real place – and that they were based upon treasure maps found hidden in a piece of furniture at Palmer's Pirate Museum in Eastbourne. The island is actually a composite of several places around the world, arranged to make a suitably exciting location, but the book is worth tracking down as a prime example of pirate treasure lore. And, who knows, perhaps it *is* really intended as a disguised visual code to a real location...

## THE SEA HUNTERS BY CLIVE CUSSLER

Speaking of Cussler, it's also worth checking out both this book and its sequel, *The Sea Hunters II*, which are collections of non-fiction tales of his nonprofit company's exploits in searching for historical shipwrecks.

Among their discoveries are the Confederate submarine CSS *Hunley,* and the last resting place of the legendary *Mary Celeste.* Few of the expeditions dealt with actual treasure in the gold, silver and jewels sense, but they are all interesting and readable accounts of the searches for historically valuable vessels, and make an interesting crossover between fictional and real treasure hunting. Thankfully Cussler and his team didn't have to deal with would-be dictators, terrorists with WMDs, or any of those obstacles that his fictional hero, Dirk Pitt, has to deal with when treasure hunting. They do encounter natural and environmental obstacles, however, similar to those faced by the characters in his novels, and so it's interesting to see a comparison of those.

The books also spawned a National Geographic TV series that ran from 2002–06.

## THE QUEST FOR THE GOLDEN HARE BY BAMBER GASGCOINE

Published in 1983, this is actually the behind the scenes story of an intentional modern treasure hunt, which spawned a whole genre. Basically, Gasgcoine, famous in the UK as host of the TV quiz *University Challenge*, was the independent witness and referee of the hunt for a golden pendant in the shape of a hare, which was buried in the UK in 1979 by Kit Williams, the author and illustrator of a book called *Masquerade*. The book contained a series of paintings that could be interpreted to provide clues to the location of the hare.

This book, however, is the tale of how the project came about, how it was run, and all the fun that ensued afterwards, including accusations of cheating and insider knowledge by the person who claimed the prize, and how some completely different people reached the correct solution.

As well as being a good background on the creation of the book, it's also a fascinating look at how the treasure bug grabs people, as some readers continued to search for the prize even after it had been awarded, and the original book had been reprinted with the solution and the name of the prizewinner!

## THE SECRET BY BYRON PREISS

This is one of those armchair treasure-hunt books, the genre of which was sparked by *Masquerade*. The difference is that this American version, published in 1982, is still looking for solutions.

Inspired by the success of *Masquerade*, Preiss hid 12 ceramic keys in cities around the US, and each key found could be handed in and exchanged for jewellery to the value of $1,000. He created a book of poems illustrated by John Jude Palencar, and each illustrated poem would lead to the location of one of the keys. This was published in 1982, and the first key was found in Chicago in 1984. The second key was found in Cleveland 20 years later, in 2004. Preiss died in a car crash the following year, without ever having told anyone else the locations of the remaining ten keys.

Those keys are still out there, so if you fancy trying your luck at hunting the oldest armchair treasure…

## THE MONUMENTS MEN BY ROBERT EDSEL

This book – which is a lot more accurate than the film of the same name – tells the story of the Monuments, Fine Arts and Archives programme run by the US military in World War II. Although not intended as a treasure-hunting group – their remit was closer to a police unit, in that they were sent to preserve cultural treasures in war zones, and try to recover stolen objects – the book is well worth a read from a treasure-hunting viewpoint, simply because this group ended up being the main people who discovered Nazi hoards dotted around Germany.

## TRUE TALES OF BURIED TREASURE BY EDWARD ROWE SNOW

Originally written at the end of the 1940s, this covers 17 treasure subjects, concentrating on those based along the US East Coast. It introduced Oak Island to the general populace, and also has fun pieces on various pirates (having followed on from Snow's earlier book, *True Tales of Pirates and Their Gold*), Blackbeard and Henry Morgan being particularly charged with burying piles of loot.

Much of it has subsequently proved out of date, and some of the treasures in it have been found since, but it's still a lovely nostalgic piece that inspired many treasure hunters of the past few decades. The highlight is the final chapter in which Snow gives his own experience in recovering buried treasure from Strong Island off Massachusetts.

# Ten Movies Worth Hunting

## RAIDERS OF THE LOST ARK

The definitive treasure-hunting movie. Well, really you could take this to mean the *Indiana Jones* movies as a series. Of course this movie, and later its spinoffs and sequels, really launched a new era of public love for exploits involved in digging up lost historic treasures.

Famously, the tone and style were meant to pay homage to adventure serials of the 1930s and 1940s, which often dealt with two-fisted tough guys in search of stolen gold, either looted by gangsters, or held in distant cities ruled by ancient cults. Those original vintage flicks tended to feature heroes who were pretty much cowboys or frontier explorers with the serial numbers filed off, and a different jacket and hat. *Raiders* manages to marry that tone up with a more modern viewpoint, in that the hero is a professor of archaeology, which in theory would entail him having spent years doing really boring excavations somewhere off-screen.

Indy's adventures, however, somehow just hit that right mix of period pulp, modern storytelling, myth, archaeology and adventure, which makes everybody able to imagine themselves going off on their own and beating the bad guys to a famous priceless treasure, in a world that was a little simpler and more clear-cut.

## NATIONAL TREASURE

This movie and its sequel, *Book of Secrets*, both involve their characters in place-to-place treasure hunts and puzzle-solving. In this sense, the films echo the sort of tone that the creators of *The Beale Papers* were aiming for, blending a mix of historical tease, brain-bending and straightforward running and dodging.

In many ways the first film prefigures the sort of historical conspiracy treasure hunting movies that Dan Brown and his imitators have subsequently turned into a global brand, and which has given the US something of a historical treasure mythos to play with.

It's also – the first film in particular – good fun, with all the elements you could want from a light-hearted adventure, including witty banter, chases and Sean Bean (spoiler) not dying.

## PIRATES OF THE CARIBBEAN: CURSE OF THE BLACK PEARL

The original movie and pretty definitely not the sequels, may be the definitive pirate treasure movie for the modern age. On the one hand it's a swashbuckling seaborne action romance in the mould of the classic Hollywood swashbucklers (especially *The Crimson Pirate*, from which it borrows a number of scenes outright, but which isn't a treasure-related movie), on the other hand it's a ghost story/zombie adventure, and, on the gripping hand, it's a treasure movie in the vein of Stevenson's *Treasure Island*, with a search and race for a cache of (cursed) Aztec gold in a vault in a lost island.

What could be more piratey or treasurey than that? Not a lot, and both of those tropes still have huge power to hold the attention of audiences, as the massive success of the film and its sequels has shown.

## THE GOONIES

Another movie about about pirate treasure, but in a different way. This is one of those 1980s coming-of-age kids' adventure movies that is probably ingrained into the psyche of a whole generation.

It's a modern-day tale of a group of kids searching for old pirate treasure, with the aid of puzzles and treasure maps, and, to be honest, it's a bit saccharine in that post-ET Spielbergian Hollywood way, but it does also catch the mood of childhood excitement for tales of pirates and buried treasure.

## AGUIRRE, THE WRATH OF GOD

A film about the Spanish search for El Dorado, it's not really a treasure movie, or even really a treasure-hunting movie, but a historical epic about the Conquistadores in South America.

It's also a good exploration of obsession and single-mindedness under duress. Which isn't really that surprising when you consider that this is a collaboration between director Werner Herzog and actor Klaus Kinski, both of whom are legendary for being obsessive, and occasionally getting mad enough with each other on set that they tried to kill each other.

It's definitely more a drama about endurance than an action adventure, but it really carries the tone and atmosphere of how things were for the European explorers who came to plunder the New World. It very much gets into the heads of these people and gives a good understanding of what drove this invasion and occupation.

It's also gorgeously filmed too, which is another good reason for checking it out.

# KING SOLOMON'S MINES

This book has been filmed plenty of times, and some of these movies are better than others. The 1937 version starring Cedric Hardwicke and Paul Robeson is usually referred to as the most faithful to Haggard's book, though the musical interludes with Robeson say otherwise. Allan Quatermain himself, however, is played much more faithfully by Hardwicke than by anyone who followed (even though he's called 'Quartermain' here). This version also introduces the idea of a missing man's daughter requiring a guide for an expedition, rather than his brother; this change persisting in basically all the screen versions of the story.

Most critics rate Stewart Granger's 1950 version – filmed in three African countries, rather than a British backlot – as the best version, even though it drifts further from the source material, especially in its portrayal of Quatermain. It certainly has spectacle, and some quality actors, but is perhaps rather slow for a modern audience. Fast cutting isn't everything, however, and while the 1950 version departs from the book's details, it does have the right atmosphere and feel to live up to Haggard's novel.

None of these departures from the book are anything like as extreme as the changes in the cheesy 1980s version with Richard Chamberlain. It's actually an updating of the story, albeit staying with a period setting, bringing the tale up from the 1880s to 1913, with the kaiser's army in East Africa as the bad guys. Despite a critical mauling this does have some positive points to being a bargain *Indiana Jones* knockoff. The slight update in time works well, still being far enough back to have that almost Victorian setting. Chamberlain's Quatermain is Indy's poorer relation, but likeable enough to lead a chase for the treasure and, overall it is a cheerful and tongue-in-cheek piece of 1980s fun. It also has a lovely jaunty musical score from Jerry Goldsmith, and plenty of actual treasure to be found in the mines themselves.

Stay well away from the sequel, though.

# TREASURE ISLAND

Another classic book that has been repeatedly filmed, starting with a silent version in 1918, acted by children (it was part of a series of

Fox productions acted by children, called the Sunset Kiddies series), and is itself – like a second silent version, starring Lon Chaney – now a lost film, which is a sort of treasure in its own right.

The most famous, and critically acclaimed version is Disney's 1950 film, starring Robert Newton as Long John Silver. This is a good adaptation, capturing the feel of Stevenson's novel, and is also worth taking a look at from a perspective of cinema history, as it was the first entirely live-action Disney feature film. In fact Robert Newton made such an impression as Long John Silver in this film that not only did he get a sequel movie, *Long John Silver*, but also the first TV series based on the franchise, *Long John Silver*, shot in colour in Australia in 1958. Actors in pirate movies ever since have emulated his accent (most notably Geoffrey Rush as Hector Barbossa in the *Pirates of the Caribbean* series.

Even the Muppets have had a go at this one, with *The Muppet Treasure Island*, which is a surprisingly good musical comedy version, mixing human and muppet casts, with Tim Curry hamming it up as Long John Silver.

## KUMIKO, THE TREASURE HUNTER

This a new darling of the awards and festival circuit. In this Japanese coming-of-age drama, the titular character sees a movie about a Wild West outlaw who buries his loot and decides to travel to America to look for it.

This isn't an action or adventure film but rather an exploration of how the mystique of buried treasure gets a hold of young minds and leads some people off on that treasure-hunting path in life. If you're looking for heroes dodging traps and rivals to get rich and donate stuff to museums before the world is destroyed, then this is not a film for you. If you want to be reminded of how it was to hear about lost treasure for the first time and how cool it seemed, then this may well be a good find.

## RACE FOR THE YANKEE ZEPHYR

This was a pretty low-budget treasure-chase movie shot in New Zealand in 1980, in which the owner of a helicopter tour business finds himself in a race with a gangster (*The A* Team's George Peppard) to find and recover a cargo of gold aboard a plane that crashed in World War II.

The part with the crashed plane carrying loot is actually true – a Douglas DC-3 Dakota carrying payroll for US sailors of the Pacific Fleet did crash off Cape York, at the very tip of Queensland, Australia, in 1944, but this was quickly recovered in reality.

Nobody will ever pretend that this is a classic film, but it works on a more local, grittier kind of level than most treasure-hunt adventures, by not being a globe-trotting chase for a world-famous legend, but simply a rivalry between people for a local find. Call it another guilty pleasure, if you will.

## IT'S A MAD, MAD, MAD, MAD WORLD

This is a legendary 1963 comedy about a group of motorists who find themselves in a treasure hunt for a gangster's stolen loot, after they stop to assist him when his car crashes. In essence it's a chase movie, with everybody racing each other to the hidden loot, so it's not about archaeological derring-do. It is hugely influential, however, having spawned a sort of mini-genre of such films, which is still going strong today. The Rowan Atkinson movie *Rat Race* is a more recent example.

Oddly enough, the film itself is also an example of that other type of cultural treasure, the lost film – at least in part. Director Stanley Kramer – better known epic social dramas such as *Judgment At Nuremberg* – had originally envisioned a film with a more than three-and-a-quarter-hours runtime, but the studio, MGM, hacked it down by almost an hour. Over the years, some scenes were added back in for TV and video releases, but a good half hour or so was thought to be permanently lost, the footage destroyed.

Then, in 2013, this other form of lost treasure was discovered, and the most recent DVD and Blu-ray version is returned to the director's planned length. In this respect, it is itself partially a treasure trove which you can now view.

# RAID SOME TOMBS

A collection of the best treasure-hunting video games:

## TOMB RAIDER

Probably the most famous of all videogames based around treasure-hunting archaeologist/adventurers, the original *Tomb Raider* came out for PC, Sega Saturn and Sony Playstation – or PS One, if you prefer – nearly 20 years ago, and launched a franchise that's still going pretty well today. In fact, it also is one of the games that really made console gaming – and Sony's Playstation series in particular – a worldwide success.

Though the original game's graphics don't hold up today, the character of Lara Croft, and the mix of action, platforming and puzzle-solving were a recipe for success, and a whole series of games, plus spinoffs in the form of novels, comics and movies have all followed. Lara herself is something of a modern icon, and that isn't just because of her carefully designed looks, or the use of supermodels to portray her in advertising: people love what she does. They love the independent Lady Croft, who travels the world exploring dangerous ruins and recovering ancient treasures – which, in this franchise, often have mystical powers, rather than just being valuable gold or silver artefacts. Lara also visits a number of fantastical locations during the series, including the Mayan underworld, Xibalba, a lost world full of dinosaurs, Atlantis, and an Egyptian city occupied by jackal-headed mummies. Unlike real treasure hunters, she often has to face off against monsters and supernatural powers.

Not bad going for a character who was originally only made female so that Core Design (the company who made the first six games) wouldn't get sued over the leather-jacketed bloke they originally intended to have as the lead character.

There have been many games in the series, of varying quality, including sequels, remakes and even a recent prequel reboot. Not all of them are as good as they could be – *The Angel of Darkness* in particular is pretty rubbish – but the first three games still hold up well in gameplay, if you can accept the graphics of the era. If not, then the original game was also remade for HD a few years ago, and fits neatly into a fun trilogy with *Legacy* and *Underworld*. The 2013 reboot is also pretty good.

For what it's worth, the second movie of the pair, *Cradle of Life*, is the better one, though it did worse business because audiences remembered not liking the first...

## THE SECRET OF MONKEY ISLAND

Back in 1990, Lucasarts – the gaming division of Lucasfilm – released this point-and-click adventure. For those of you too young to remember such things, you'd move the cursor over an object or character and click it with the mouse to interact with it in whatever way the game intended.

This game was basically a *Treasure Island* kind of idea, set in the golden age of piracy, and had your character explore and solve puzzles to find the elements needed to go up against a ghostly pirate. If this sounds potentially familiar, it may be because the creators of the game admitted to being inspired by a certain theme park attraction named Pirates of the Caribbean. The game was successful enough to spawn several sequels, and was remade for HD in 2009. It had a memorable blend of exploration and puzzle-solving, as well as a fine mix of humour and thrills, though the names of the characters could have used some work (you play one Guybrush Threepwood) and the bad guy character is called LeChuck). Nevertheless, this was one of the most successful PC games ever, and still holds up well today.

## INDIANA JONES AND THE

It should come as no surprise that Indy has had a long history of videogame spinoffs, starting with a text adventure called *Revenge of the Ancients* back in 1987. His greatest gaming acclaim, however, is probably for *The Fate of Atlantis*, a point-and-click PC adventure from 1992, which is still fondly remembered today (and if you have a Wii, the Wii version of *The Staff of Kings* also includes the full *Fate of Atlantis* game as an unlockable extra – its only console appearance.

The series went into proper third-person 3D with *The Infernal Machine* in 1999, and both this and 2003's *The Emperor's Tomb* are quite good for their day, though the latter should be played on PC or an original Xbox, as the PS2 port is hopeless.

The most recent Indy videogames, of course, have been the Lego ones, which are surprisingly good fun.

# UNCHARTED

In a lot of ways, the *Uncharted* series is what *Tomb Raider* was originally conceived of as being. There's a leather-jacketed heroic treasure hunter in the Indiana Jones mould, and the gameplay is a mix of third-person action and platforming, very like in *Tomb Raider*.

Nathan Drake's exploits are more grounded in the real world, however, with his enemies being mercenaries, smugglers, looters and so on, rather than supernatural demigods, or monsters. Likewise, the locations he visits are more typically realistic locations, though he does still drop in on Shambhala in the second game.

There's more of an ensemble cast to the *Uncharted* series than in *Tomb Raider*, and the visual style is quite distinctive also, but in a lot of ways the two series complement each other quite well. As with the other franchise, *Uncharted* has spawned assorted spinoffs, especially in the form of comics and graphic novels, and a movie is planned.

Sadly the series is PS3 exclusive – or PS4 in the case of the upcoming fourth game, *Thief's End*, but if you have a PS3, the series is worth a look, with the second game, *Among Thieves*, being probably the best of the three so far.

# ASSASSIN'S CREED IV: BLACK FLAG

Technically the *Assassin's Creed* series has had a certain amount of treasure hunting since *Assassin's Creed II*, in the form of sparkling chests to be found and unlocked for cash, as well as there being occasional artefacts to be found, such as the Pieces of Eden which are a central part of the series' story arc. *Assassin's Creed III* also features missions related to Captain Kidd's legendary treasure and involves a trip to Oak Island.

*Black Flag*, however, is worth seeking out less as an *Assassin's Creed* game, and more as the best golden age pirate game you're likely to find. There are treasure chests to locate and dig up, rum to drink and Blackbeard (and several other real-life pirates) to interact with. If the word treasure makes you think of pirates with chests full of loot, digging holes on sandy beaches, this is the game for you, even if you don't normally like the series.

It also does a good job of reinforcing the fact that, historically, most of what pirates took from ships wasn't actually chests of gold…

# SELECTED BIBLIOGRAPHY

*Raiders of the Lost Past* – TV series
*Arthur C. Clarke's Mysterious World* – TV series
*The Sign and the Seal* – Graham Hancock (Crown, 1992)
*Life Among the Pirates* – David Cordingly (Little, Brown & Co, 1995)
*In Search of King Solomon's Mines* – Tahir Shah (John Murray, 2002)
*The Holy Grail* – Richard Barber (Penguin, 2005)
*Before the Flood* – Ian Wilson (Orion, 2001)
*The Oxford History of Ancient Egypt* (Oxford University Press, 2000)
*Search In the Desert* – John M. Allegro (Doubleday, 1964)